THE BRIARMARSH CLOSE KILLINGS

A gripping murder mystery

GAYNOR TORRANCE

Jemima Huxley Crime Thrillers Book 2

Originally published as *Sole Survivor*

JOFFE BOOKS

Revised edition 2022
Joffe Books, London
www.joffebooks.com

First published by Sapere Books in Great Britain in 2020
as *Sole Survivor*

This paperback edition was first published
in Great Britain in 2022

Cover art by Nebojsa Zorić

ISBN: 978-1-80405-249-5

PROLOGUE

Bradley Rathbone was about to die.

This was not how he had imagined his life would end — alone and in agony. His breath rattled and rasped like sandpaper scouring splintered wood. Each subsequent inhalation became shallower and more painful than the last. His jaw, usually firm, had slackened, allowing blood and saliva to dribble from his lips, pooling in a filthy puddle where he lay.

Bradley had been far too slow on the uptake. He'd sensed something was wrong, but hadn't appreciated just how deadly the situation was.

Returning from the supermarket, his wife Sally had gone into their home ahead of him. When he walked through the front door the house had been oppressively quiet. It was never like that. Not with the vibrancy and chaos that came from living with three teenagers. There was always a background pulse coming from one or more of the rooms. Everyday normal sounds. Music. Footsteps. Voices.

Then Bradley heard something. It wasn't a shout, or even a scream. It wasn't anything he could easily identify. But whatever it was, it put the fear of God into him.

He raced up the stairs two at a time, calling Sally's name. The door nearest the top of the stairs was the entrance to the master suite. It was open, and he'd rushed inside, skidding to a halt.

Everything was as he had left it. It all appeared to be so very ordinary. Bed made. Curtains open. He could smell Sally's perfume.

But then Bradley sensed a movement behind him and before he had a chance to turn around someone pushed him hard. It caught him by surprise and he staggered forward.

Bradley hadn't felt the initial plunge of the knife, but the withdrawal of the blade was a different matter. It twisted slowly and deliberately in a corkscrew motion. He'd never experienced pain like it.

He made every effort to turn around, determined to look his attacker in the eye, but it proved to be too much for him and his legs crumpled. Once on the ground he was easy prey, and the frenzied attack really got underway.

Somehow, through the terror and pain, Bradley had the sense to play dead. He'd encountered enough psychopaths to know not to show fear. Remarkably, his strategy worked, and the rage soon subsided.

When he heard his attacker leave the room, Bradley allowed himself to take a shallow breath. Moments later, he lost consciousness.

Now he was awake, he had no idea of how long it had been, or whether his assailant was still inside the house. But he did know that he'd lost a lot of blood.

He forced himself to move. It took what little remaining strength he had to drag his body from the bedroom. Using his fingernails as makeshift crampons, he clawed his way across the floorboards to reach the landing.

He eventually became aware of a noise, and his eyes shifted to reveal a sight that shocked him to the core.

Suddenly everything made sense, but it was too late to make a difference.

For the first time in his life, Bradley Rathbone acknowledged that he had been an arrogant, stupid man. People had placed their trust in him, and it had cost them their lives.

Bradley finally accepted that he had been a fool.

CHAPTER 1

The call came through on Detective Inspector Jemima Huxley's day off. Jemima had only recently been allowed back to work after weeks of enforced sick leave. During that time, life in the Huxley household had been strained. At one point, courtesy of her husband, Nick, a few people were made aware of Jemima's deepest, darkest secret — her self-harming. A doctor had sedated her, and there were a few days of her life that she would never be able to recall.

Later, when Jemima realized what her husband had done, she wished the ground would open up and swallow her. As far as she was concerned, his actions were nothing short of a humiliating betrayal. She had spent years concealing her pain. Now people knew that she cut herself.

Nick understood that being a serving police officer meant the world to Jemima. It was one thing him insisting she get medical help, but it was quite another outing her to her boss — a move that could have cost Jemima her career.

Luckily for Jemima, Detective Chief Inspector Ray Kennedy had kept her secret. Instead of kicking her off the squad, he'd insisted that she attend mandatory counselling sessions. She'd reluctantly agreed to this course of action as it was the only way she would be allowed to return to work. It focused her mind, and Jemima had worked hard to confront her demons and rebuild her life.

At first, Jemima had been sceptical of the value of talking things through with a counsellor, believing that her problems stemmed entirely from her inability to become pregnant. But as she relaxed into the sessions, she came to realize that her issues were more complex and deep-rooted.

Jemima understood that there would be no quick fix. Instead, she had embarked on an emotionally draining and occasionally brutal process, forcing her to confront and re-evaluate aspects of her life that she had taken for granted.

To a certain extent, Jemima was grateful that Nick's actions had railroaded her down that particular path. In retrospect, she acknowledged that she couldn't have carried on with things the way they had been. Yet no matter how hard she tried, she couldn't let go of the belief that Nick had been disloyal by forcing her hand. And to a large extent that underlying sense of betrayal tainted their relationship. She still loved Nick, but she would never be able to trust her husband fully again.

The biggest shift in their domestic situation came a few weeks before Jemima returned to work. Nick's first wife, the mother of his son, was killed in a traffic collision. Thankfully, young James had not been in the car at the time, but Wendy's death hit him hard, and weeks later, he was still noticeably withdrawn.

Jemima welcomed James with open arms. It helped that he adored her. She had always had a close relationship with him, having spent years secretly wishing that he were her own son. Wendy's unexpected demise had made that desire a realistic proposition. Suddenly Jemima found herself with a ready-made family. James needed her, and she was deter-mined to be there for him. He was her priority.

With the funeral out of the way, paperwork had been submitted to allow Jemima to legally adopt him. James seemed as keen for this to go ahead as Jemima was. They had always been really close, and once, after a fight with Wendy,

James had even told Jemima he wished she was his 'real' mother.

By the time Jemima returned to work, the desire to have a child of her own no longer consumed her thoughts. She and Nick were awaiting test results in an attempt to establish the cause, if any, of Jemima's inability to conceive — though, given the recent stormy nature of their relationship, Jemima felt that it would be wise to hold off on expanding their family until they got their marriage back on track.

Jemima's thoughts flicked back to the voice on the phone. It was from the switchboard operator at the police station. As usual, his voice seemed far too calm and matter-of-fact for the information he was imparting. But after years of doing that job, it was probably nothing he hadn't heard before. The details were sketchy. There had been a murder in a domestic setting, and Jemima was warned that it was particularly bad.

Jemima made a note of the location — Lisvane. It was an area of Cardiff where a few months earlier mutilated corpses had been discovered buried in shallow graves in an area of private woodland. The address they were heading for was less than a mile from that particular location.

She called her partner, Detective Sergeant Broadbent, and told him to meet her at the house on Briarmarsh Close.

* * *

Jemima spotted Broadbent's car in the rear-view mirror as she neared the property. When they had both parked up, they saw that they were not the first on the scene. Two ambulances, a police car, and a Forensics vehicle were parked on the sweeping driveway.

As they got out of the car, a young uniformed officer walked towards them. He appeared punch-drunk. Over the years, Jemima had seen that look on many people's faces and wondered if it was his first encounter with a dead body.

'Were you the first on the scene?' asked Jemima, choosing to ignore the officer's obvious distress.

'Yeah, it was called in by a Mariella Derbyshire.' He read the name from a notebook held in trembling hands. 'She's very shaken up. I've got her in the back of my car if you want to have a word with her.'

'Keep her there for the moment. I want to take a look at the crime scene. I hope they haven't touched the body yet.' Jemima nodded towards the ambulance crew.

'One of the kids is still alive, but she's in a bad way,' the officer told her.

'Kids?' said Broadbent, the colour draining from his cheeks.

'Hasn't anyone told you?' asked the officer.

'Told us what?' replied Jemima.

'It's a massacre in there. There's blood everywhere. The whole family were butchered. Two adults, two kids dead. The girl's the sole survivor.'

CHAPTER 2

'What do you know about the family?' Jemima asked the officer. She swallowed hard, determined not to let her emotions get the better of her. In her book, it was acceptable for male officers to display vulnerability — at least that proved they were human. But there was no way she was going to allow anyone to see that she was fazed by any distressing situations the job threw at her. She needed everyone to respect her, especially since she'd had to take time off.

'Very little,' he replied, 'just that the family name is Rathbone, and the survivor is the fourteen-year-old daughter. Her name's Millie.'

A black BMW X5 and a red Mercedes-Benz CLA were parked on the driveway — evidence, if any was needed, that the family had been people for whom money was no object. The Mercedes was locked, but the door to the boot of the BMW was open and three bags of groceries were inside.

'Looks as though at least one of them had just got back from the supermarket,' said Broadbent. 'They're Waitrose bags. The nearest store is in Pontprennau. I'll ring Ashton and give him the vehicle's registration mark. The store will have CCTV coverage of the car park, so he can head over there, get the security tapes and ascertain the time of arrival and departure. That should focus the timeline, and we can see who actually went shopping.'

'Good idea,' Jemima replied. 'While you're at it, take a look through the bags and see if you can find a till receipt. With a bit of luck, they may be the sort of people who keep their receipts and not throw them in the nearest bin. The time of payment will be printed on it and should speed up Ashton's search. Whatever happened inside that house was still going on when they arrived home. Whoever was carrying the bags must have heard something to make them drop them like that.' Jemima pointed through the front door at the spilt contents and smashed glass from a shopping bag in the hallway.

'Or the killer could have been waiting out here,' Broadbent suggested, 'possibly hiding behind the other car to overpower the driver once they stepped inside the house.'

'Possibly, but if that happened, surely someone inside the house would have heard a commotion? These days, virtually everyone has a mobile phone, so one of them would have called the police. But there were no reports of that happening. The other flaw in that scenario is that this was a family of five. They wouldn't all have been submissive. Someone would have put up a fight or made a run for it. It would have been virtually impossible for an attacker to maintain control of the situation.

'I'd put money on it that the killer was already inside. As there are kids involved, are you OK with coming in there with me?' asked Jemima, as she headed for the front door. Broadbent had recently become a father and Jemima now wished that she had brought one of her childless officers with her instead.

'I'm fine. I'll finish up out here and catch up with you,' replied Broadbent.

Jemima approached the house. The door opened wider as a couple of paramedics manoeuvred a gurney. Jemima went over to take a closer look. She had seen some awful things throughout her years of service, but no matter how hardened she'd become, it still made her feel queasy.

The surviving victim was slight, with long hair the colour of golden corn. As it neared the scalp the hair was matted with congealed blood. It was impossible to say what the girl really looked like as her face was bruised and swollen. A brace fixed her head in position and the paramedics had already begun the process of administering blood and other fluids.

'How's she doing?' asked Jemima.

'Not good,' replied the lead paramedic. 'We haven't got time to answer questions now. The girl needs immediate surgery.'

'Sure. Sorry,' apologized Jemima. She stepped back and watched them load their patient into the ambulance. The girl was young, barely into her teens. If she made it through the next few hours, she could be the only witness to the murders of the rest of her family, but right now, she looked so frail and broken that it was difficult to imagine her making it through the day.

Jemima reached for her phone and called the station. The desk sergeant answered on the second ring.

'I need you to get someone over to the University Hospital right away,' she said. 'A teenage girl is heading there in an ambulance. Her family's been murdered and she has life-threatening injuries. They'll be taking her into theatre immediately. If she survives, I want a round-the-clock guard at her bedside. Her name's Millie Rathbone, and as far as I know, she's our only witness to the killings of her family.'

Jemima ended the call, got herself some protective overalls and took a deep breath as she stepped over the threshold of the house. The door opened on to a wide hallway with a staircase to the left. At the foot of the stairs, a section of otherwise polished wooden flooring was stained with blood. A radiator fixed to the side wall had traces of blood too. There were droplets visible on the stair treads, and small amounts of blood spatter low down on the wall adjacent to the other stains. Four bags of groceries were strewn across the hallway.

With the scene-of-crime officers already at work, Jemima ventured upstairs. She kept to the metal stepping plates, knowing from past experience to avoid treading on the blood stains. She had only ascended a few steps when she could see an outstretched arm with its fingers extended as though reaching for something.

'We have to stop meeting like this, Jemima,' said Jeanne Ennersley, the lead SOCO. 'You'll need to take care up here. There's trace evidence spread around a wide area.'

'What have you established so far?' asked Jemima.

'I'll walk you through, but make sure not to contaminate the scene. It's a five-bedroomed property. As far as I can see, the attack was confined to three of the bedrooms, but we're also collecting evidence from the landing area, the stairs and the hallway. We've got two dead teenagers — a girl and a boy. They're in separate rooms. It looks as though they were both suffocated in their beds and stabbed afterwards. There was a lot of rage in these attacks. I'd say the kids were killed first.

'Then we have an adult female, multiple stab wounds to the back and her throat was cut. She was found in the girl's room. Finally, there's an adult male with multiple stab wounds to the back, but he didn't die straight away. It looks as though he was attacked in the main bedroom then dragged himself across the floor to reach the landing.

'Another teenage girl was found unconscious at the bottom of the stairs. From the blood spatter I'd say she was trying to get away from the attacker and must have tripped and fallen down the stairs. The attacker most likely thought she was dead.'

'I wonder if she hid while the others were attacked?' asked Jemima, thinking aloud.

'That's for you to determine. All I can say is that killing the others wouldn't have been quick. She might have had time to get inside a cupboard or hide under the bed, and most likely made a run for it when she thought it was safe. It's a hell of a thing for her to have witnessed.'

Ennersley walked Jemima through the rooms and showed her the bodies.

'Should I come up?' called Broadbent from the bottom of the stairs.

'Don't bother. I've seen everything I need to,' said Jemima, as she headed down the stairs. 'It's a bad one,' she continued when she reached him. 'This wasn't a random burglary gone wrong. This was vicious, personal and planned. Whoever's responsible set out to annihilate that family, and they almost succeeded. We need that girl to pull through. She's probably going to be our only witness.'

CHAPTER 3

Jemima and Broadbent left the house and walked back over to the officer standing by the patrol car.

'This is Mariella Derbyshire, one of the next-door neighbours,' said the officer, nodding towards the woman sitting in the back of the car. His composure had returned, he was looking more confident than he had a few minutes earlier.

Mariella stepped out of the vehicle and extended a shaky hand. Her face was pale and blotchy, her eyes bloodshot.

'I'm Detective Inspector Huxley, and this is Detective Sergeant Broadbent,' said Jemima as she shook hands with the woman. 'What can you tell me about the family?'

'They're my friends and neighbours. The adults are Sally and Bradley Rathbone. The kids are Millie, Lauren and Jonathan. Sally and I work together. We're GPs at a local practice. Bradley's a psychiatrist at the University Hospital of Wales. How are they? No one's telling me anything.'

'When did you first notice something was wrong?' asked Jemima, ignoring the woman's question.

'About four o'clock. Sally invited me over for a barbeque. As I walked up the drive, everything looked normal. Their cars were in the usual places. I noticed that the boot of the BMW was open and that there was still shopping inside, so I presumed they had just returned from the supermarket. But when I rang the doorbell there was no answer. I opened the letterbox and peered through. That's when I saw Millie at the foot of the stairs. I have a front-door key in case they lock themselves out, so I rushed back to get it and I called the emergency services.

'I was struggling to get the key in the lock when this officer arrived. I'm usually good in an emergency. I've been taught to put my emotions aside. It's part of my training. But this was too personal. I was all fingers and thumbs. You see, they're like family to me. Anyway, I explained to this officer that I was a GP, and when I finally managed to open the door, he allowed me to go in and check on Millie.'

'You said that the Rathbones' cars were on the drive. So the BMW and Mercedes are theirs?' asked Broadbent.

'Yes,' said Mariella. 'Are Sally and Bradley in there?' she pressed.

'There's no easy way to say this, but I'm afraid that the rest of the family are dead,' said Jemima.

'No! They can't be,' wailed Mariella, bereft at the news of losing her friends.

'Is there someone we can call for you?' asked Jemima.

'My husband and sons have gone fishing. They went last night and won't be back until tomorrow evening.'

'Well, Sergeant Broadbent will take you home and sit with you for a while. Once you are feeling stronger, he will take your statement. I know it's hard, but anything you can think of may prove useful.'

While Broadbent guided Mariella back into her home, Jemima paced the narrow pavement bordering the road directly outside Briarmarsh Close. It was a small entrance with insufficient room for two vehicles to pass. The three houses were sheltered from view by a large copper-beech hedge, and the deliberate planting of a variety of trees and shrubs meant that each house had an entirely private aspect from the neighbouring properties.

There was a possibility that one of the residents could have spotted the perpetrator entering the close if they happened to look out of a front window at that exact moment in time. But the chances of that happening were not great.

Having convinced herself that the killer could have entered the property unseen by others, Jemima headed back to the Rathbone house and checked the doors and windows for signs of forced entry. There were none, but a set of French doors at the rear of the property were unlocked.

'Jeanne, I need someone to dust these doors for prints!' she ordered.

While this was being done, Jemima walked through the other downstairs rooms. She noticed lights flashing on both the washing machine and the dishwasher, indicating that they had completed their cycles. She asked for prints to be taken from the visible surfaces and the contents of the machines to be bagged as potential evidence.

Jemima headed outside into the garden. It was an extensive open space with a natural hedge separating it from the neighbouring properties and the field beyond. The garden was well maintained and clearly an area used for entertaining. There was a hot tub, an elaborate barbeque, and a purpose-built bar area with a set of high stools. To the left-hand side of the garden was a substantial building that housed a heated swimming pool and a gymnasium.

Until today this would have been a desirable property with a price tag to match. It was situated on a plot of land at least half an acre in size and was far enough away from each of the neighbouring properties not to be easily overlooked. But for the foreseeable future prospective buyers would probably avoid the area like the plague.

A rotary line was filled with washing, gently lifting in the breeze. It was a typical domestic scene, so at odds with the horror inside the house. The Rathbones had been going about their normal Saturday routine, oblivious to the awful fate that awaited them.

The stark reality was that although it was rare for an entire family to be murdered inside their home, it was something that could potentially happen to anyone. And this attack hadn't been carried out under cover of darkness. It had occurred during the day.

The thought sent a shiver down Jemima's spine.

CHAPTER 4

Once she had finished inside the property, Jemima headed over to Mariella Derbyshire's house, where Broadbent let her in.

'How's she doing?' asked Jemima.

'Not too bad. She managed to get in touch with her husband and he said he'll come straight home.'

'Did you get a signed statement?'

'Yes, but it doesn't give us anything to go on.'

'I want to have a word with her to get some initial background information on the victims,' said Jemima. 'Do me a favour and arrange for a female PC to come and sit with her until her husband gets back. Then go and have a word with the other set of neighbours. Find out whether they saw or heard anything unusual.'

Jemima found Mariella sitting at her kitchen table. Her hands gripped a brandy glass so forcefully that her knuckles were white.

'Don't worry, I've only had a couple of sips,' she said with a weak smile. 'It's medicinal. I just need something to take the edge off things. I can't believe what's happened. Sally and I have been friends for almost twenty years. We're like sisters.'

'Tell me about the family,' said Jemima, as she pulled out a seat and sat down.

'Sal and Brad are . . . were . . . the nicest people. We've been Sal's neighbours for the best part of eleven years. Brad and Millie moved in about five years ago when Sally and Bradley got married. Then Lauren and Jonathan joined them early last year.

'Sally couldn't have children, you see. Millie is Brad's daughter from a previous marriage. Lauren and Jonathan were Brad's brother's children. His brother and sister-in-law died in a freak powerboat accident. Brad and Sal took the kids in. They treated them like their own. Jonathan was quite withdrawn at first, but Brad worked wonders with him, and Jonathan was starting to come out of his shell. Lauren could be a bit moody at times, but then who wouldn't be if you'd had your world turned upside down.'

'And what about Millie?' asked Jemima. 'How did she adapt to the new family dynamic — having her cousins come to live with her?'

'Well, it wasn't as if they were strangers. But you could never tell with Millie. She's a quiet girl. Always has her head in a book. Very polite. By all accounts she's brilliant, but I've never known her to have many friends over, and I think there may have been some issues between her and Lauren.'

'Issues?' enquired Jemima.

'Oh, you know, the usual petty teenage girl squabbles, but nothing too serious. I think they just weren't the closest of friends.'

'And did your kids spend much time with the three of them?'

'Not with the girls. Seth's a few years older and has his own circle of friends. But Thomas and Jonathan were always hanging out together. They were in the same class at school and had similar interests. This is going to hit Tom hard.' Mariella stifled a sob.

'Did you and Sally spend much time together out of work?' Jemima asked, once Mariella had recovered.

17

'My husband, Mark, played golf with Brad. Sal and I used to joke about being golfing widows. But we had our Monday night Pilates class and our yoga class on a Thursday. Most Saturday nights we'd meet up for drinks, either here or around at theirs. We were best friends.'

'What was the Rathbones' marriage like?' asked Jemima.

'They were happy. In the last year, they'd had their ups and downs with the arrival of Lauren and Jonathan. But their relationship was rock solid.'

'No affairs?'

'Absolutely not. It's unthinkable. They were in it for the long haul. Sally was single until she got together with Bradley. She always said he was the love of her life.'

'And what about Bradley? Did he feel the same way?' pressed Jemima.

'Absolutely. He was devoted to Sal,' said Mariella.

'Were either of them experiencing problems at work?'

'I couldn't answer for Bradley. He's a psychiatrist at the University Hospital, so it's possible there could have been some issues there. He's more likely to have confided in my husband than me. As for Sally, there was an incident a few years back when a male patient became fixated on her. He'd been making regular appointments with Sal about trivial things and wouldn't agree to see any other GP at the practice. It went on for a couple of months, and Sally started to feel uncomfortable with the situation.

'She spoke to me about it and reported it to the practice manager, who telephoned the guy and explained that Sally's patient list was being reduced and he would be allocated to one of the male partners. As you can imagine, that conversation didn't go too well. Less than an hour later he turned up at reception shouting and demanding to see Sally. He didn't hurt anyone, but he was verbally abusive and refused to leave. The police were called and arrested him for threatening behaviour.'

'Did Sally have any problems with him after that?' asked Jemima.

'Not that she could directly attribute to him. He was removed from her patient list, but a couple of weeks later she went out in the morning to find the word BITCH scratched across the bonnet of her car. She called the police, but there were no witnesses and nothing to tie the guy to the incident.'

'Do you recall his name?' asked Jemima.

'It was Jason. Jason Venter.'

'That's helpful,' said Jemima, making a note of it. 'You mentioned that Millie was Bradley's daughter from a previous marriage, but you didn't seem to suggest that there was a shared custody arrangement. Did his first wife die?'

'No. Bradley never mentioned her, but Sally told me that she was serving a prison sentence. Their youngest child died as a baby and she was convicted of killing her. Sally said that Bradley felt so guilty about it, what with him being a psychiatrist. Apparently, he hadn't picked up on warning signs that anything was wrong. From what I've been told, he was completely devastated, as you'd expect.'

'So what happened?' asked Jemima.

'I don't know the details. Sally only mentioned it once. This was before Bradley moved in. She didn't elaborate, and it didn't feel right to push her for details.'

'Do you happen to know the woman's name, and where they lived back then?'

'She's called Isobel. And I think they may have lived somewhere in the Vale of Glamorgan, but I can't be more specific than that.'

'And do you know how long ago this happened?'

'It must have been about seven years ago,' said Mariella.

CHAPTER 5

Broadbent was leaning against his car when Jemima returned. He was talking to someone on his mobile phone and quickly ended the call. Jemima could tell by the look on his face that he had been speaking to his wife.

'No answer from the neighbours. Blinds are down so looks like they're away. I've asked the uniforms to keep an eye out for them, so we'll know as soon as they return. I was just speaking to Caro. With everything that's happened here I just needed to know that she and Harry are OK. I know it's stupid, but there you go,' he said sheepishly.

Caroline Broadbent and Jemima had been close friends until recently, but their relationship had broken down following the christening of baby Harry. The Broadbents had asked Jemima to be their son's godmother, and she had reluctantly agreed to it. It had been a hard thing for her to do as Jemima was desperate for a child of her own. Things had got so bad for her that she regularly self-harmed, cutting herself with a razor blade to feel in control. Even Jemima's husband Nick hadn't appreciated just how bad things had got.

On the day of the christening, everyone had headed back to Broadbent's house and had taken the celebrations out into the garden. As time went on, some of the guests had gathered around Nick, who was busy regaling them with intimate details of a drunken amorous encounter he had witnessed between a prominent sportsperson and a TV presenter. His detailed descriptions were vivid, salacious, and particularly inappropriate given the setting. It made the story more shocking and compelling, and encouraged the others to press for more gossip.

Jemima was aware that Nick was drinking far too much. He was an accomplished raconteur and enjoyed being the centre of attention, but sometimes took things too far. The more alcohol he consumed the louder he became. She wished she could have a quiet word him and ask him to ease up on the beers but knew that any intervention would be unwelcome.

When Jemima returned to the kitchen to get a piece of cake, she heard Harry crying. It crossed her mind to call either Dan or Caroline, but she decided against it when she saw them laughing and joking with Nick and some of the other guests. She was aware that the couple had had a tough time since the baby's arrival, and it was good to see them enjoying themselves. Instead of disturbing them unnecessarily, she checked every apparent cause of Harry's distress and concluded he didn't need changing or feeding, but he did seem to enjoy the motion of her jiggling the pushchair up and down.

Jemima had glanced out of the window again, but Dan and Caroline had seemed so happy and relaxed that she didn't want to disturb them. Instead, she tore a sheet of paper from a pad and wrote a quick note explaining that Harry was unsettled and that she was taking him out for a walk until he dropped off again. She had placed the note on the kitchen work surface and headed off with Harry.

Jemima had acted with the best of intentions, but in retrospect, she acknowledged it was a bad decision. As the sensible thing would have been to clear it with Caroline and Dan first.

Of course, she had no way of knowing that when the next person entered the room, the breeze would blow the note to the floor. And she had been mortified to realize that when Caroline noticed that Harry was missing, Nick had joked that since Jemima appeared to be missing too, she had most likely kidnapped him as she was so desperate to have a baby.

Almost an hour later, Jemima had returned to a chaotic scene. Caroline Broadbent was screaming hysterically about her son having been abducted. Dan was busy trying to calm her down, saying that Jemima would never do anything like that and insisting that Nick was just winding her up. Meanwhile Nick sat there surveying his handiwork, grinning inanely as he swigged another beer and watched the scene play out in front of him.

It had caused a rift between Jemima and Nick. Awful things had been said and done — things that had a negative impact on their marriage. Her husband's drunken malicious accusation had taken everyone by surprise. It had shocked and upset Jemima so much that it severely weakened what up until that point she had considered to be an unbreakable bond. He'd intentionally distressed her friends and had humiliated her. It felt as though her own husband had stabbed her in the back.

That was when everything had fallen apart for Jemima. The need to cut herself was so overwhelming that nothing else mattered, and the result had been worse than usual. When Nick sobered up, he had found her bleeding in their bathroom. He'd called a doctor, who had sedated her, and she'd been forced to take some time off work.

Things with Nick were still rocky, but Jemima's relationship with Broadbent was back on track. Jemima had apologized profusely for her lapse of judgement and Nick's drunken behaviour. They agreed to put the misunderstanding behind them, but Caroline was not the sort of person to forgive and forget so easily, and at the moment their days of socializing were well and truly over.

'Did you find the receipt for the groceries?' Jemima asked Broadbent.

'No. It's either been tossed, or it's on one of the victims. Since we haven't had access to the bodies, we've got no way of knowing. But Ashton's got hold of the security tapes. He's going through them now.'

* * *

Back at the incident room, Detective Constable Finlay Ashton was busy studying CCTV footage from the supermarket's car park. Having been drafted in as part of the team investigating the bodies found at Llys Faen Hall, Ashton had been transferred to them as a permanent member of the squad. He had a degree in computer forensics, which made him an expert in all things technical. It often speeded up inquires but how much longer he would remain as part of the team was up in the air, as in a few weeks' time he was due to sit his sergeant's exam. If he passed that and the subsequent interview, he would have his pick of jobs, as his technical skills were in demand throughout the force.

'Any luck so far?' Jemima asked him.

'Not yet,' replied Ashton, glancing up from the screen. 'I had to start from just before the store opened, as I've got no way of knowing what time they might have arrived. And just because they had Waitrose bags doesn't mean that they actually shopped there, as most people re-use their bags now.'

'That's true. But the Rathbones may have been creatures of habit, loyal to a particular supermarket. If you draw a blank with Waitrose, you'll have to extend the search to other supermarkets. Keep going on those tapes for now. Have you got the CCTV footage from inside the store?'

'It's here,' he said.

'Broadbent, you start trawling through that. We need to establish who went shopping and get ourselves some sort of time frame for when they were likely to have returned home. These are photographs of each member of the family, so you should be able to spot them.' Jemima handed the prints over. 'I'm going to make some enquiries about a man called Jason Venter. He's currently a person of interest as he had an unhealthy obsession with Sally Rathbone.'

'Jason Venter?' asked Ashton, his eyebrows arching in surprise.

'You know him?' asked Jemima.

'Know *of* him — if it's the same person,' corrected Ashton. 'I'm surprised you haven't heard the name. There's a Jason Venter who is quite a celebrity in the art world. He's very much in vogue at the moment. One of the young royals attended an exhibition of his up in London and ended up purchasing some of his work. Since then, he's had work commissioned by a couple of Hollywood A-listers. He's a money-making machine at the moment. Everyone who's anyone is jumping on his bandwagon.'

'How do you know all this?' asked Jemima.

'I've always been into art. It's a passion of mine. The *Sunday Times* did a feature on him a few months ago. Come to think of it, he mentioned there that he'd had a bit of a rocky start in life. I seem to recall that he's set up a bursary for local kids from low-income families to enable them to study art. But, if it's the same Jason Venter, I think you can cross him off the list of suspects. He's hardly ever in Cardiff. He spends most of his time in London.

'If I remember correctly, he's busy putting the finishing touches to his latest collection, and then he's off to New York. One of their top galleries is displaying some of his work. He's due there later next week. Take a look. It's right here on his Facebook page.' Ashton tapped his phone and held it out for Jemima to look at.

'I hope your admiration for him isn't going to get in the way of your professionalism, because right now Venter is a suspect,' Jemima said abruptly. 'Get one of the PCs to find Venter's Cardiff and London addresses. I need to speak to him before he leaves the country. In the meantime, I'm going to do some research on Bradley Rathbone's first wife. According to Mariella Derbyshire, she was sent down for killing their baby daughter. Chances are she's still tucked up in that cell of hers and won't have had anything to do with these deaths, but we'd better check it out.'

CHAPTER 6

Jemima sat at her desk, switched on the computer and set about finding out everything she could about Bradley Rathbone's first wife. It wasn't that difficult as there was plenty of information about her court case online. She soon confirmed that seven years earlier, a Mrs Isobel Rathbone had been found guilty of murdering ten-month-old Lydia Rathbone at the family home in Cowbridge.

Within seconds, Jemima burned with an incandescent rage that radiated throughout her entire body. She knew without any shadow of doubt that if Isobel Rathbone appeared at that moment, she would have happily beaten the woman to a pulp.

Jemima recognized that she was experiencing an inappropriately extreme reaction. She and Nick had been trying for a baby for so long but it still hadn't happened. And whenever Jemima heard of crimes against children, the injustice of it made her blood boil. It seemed so unfair that women who were so unsuited to motherhood were able to have children in the first place, when she was not.

It was clear from documented information that Isobel Rathbone had not done herself any favours. She had taken no responsibility for her actions throughout the trial, where she consistently asserted her innocence. A recording had been played of a distraught, almost incoherent Isobel, begging the emergency services to attend. She claimed that she had found her baby unresponsive in the cot.

When paramedics arrived at the scene, they had discovered Isobel clutching the dead child and crying hysterically. A post-mortem revealed petechial haemorrhaging, bruising to the face, especially the mouth and nose, and a small number of cotton fibres lodged in the nasal cavity, consistent with a cushion found on a chair in the nursery.

Evidence from health professionals suggested that there had been no cause for concern about the baby's wellbeing. Isobel had been regarded as a good parent, always taking Lydia for routine appointments, during which nothing untoward had been found.

Lydia was Isobel's second child. The first, Millie, aged seven, had been playing downstairs when Lydia's lifeless body was discovered. The defence offered evidence that Isobel was suffering from postnatal depression, though the prosecution played this down. Isobel's GP stated that there had not been any suggestion that she posed a danger to herself or to anyone else. Indeed, her husband, Bradley, who was a psychiatrist, asserted that his wife's mental state had never given him cause for concern.

Isobel was sentenced to twelve years in prison, and from the time of her arrest she had no contact with either Bradley or Millie. Bradley wasted no time in filing for divorce, which was granted shortly after the trial ended.

The information on the screen was an emotional trigger for Jemima. Fortunately, she had the presence of mind to take a step back, breathe out and slowly count to ten. That baby's murder was none of her concern. It had been dealt with.

Over the years Jemima had learned to keep her emotions in check, but that only applied in her professional life. It was a self-preservation technique to prevent herself from becoming depressed, going insane or, worse still, dishing out her own style of vigilante justice on those occasions when she felt the system had let vulnerable people down.

Serving officers frequently had it drummed into them that they shouldn't become personally involved. It was sound advice in an ideal world, and an easy mantra to spout, but it was damn near impossible to remain impartial when you had the first-hand experience of the devastation wreaked by some of society's detritus.

Throughout her career, Jemima had been required to deal with the very worst instances of human behaviour, but despite recognizing her own prejudice towards Isobel Rathbone, Jemima could not shake the thought that the woman must be a cold-hearted bitch.

CHAPTER 7

'Back of the net!' yelled Ashton, performing a drumroll on the desk. 'I've just spotted the Rathbones. They arrived at the Waitrose car park at 10.42. There're two of them getting out,' he said, pointing at their images on the screen.

'It's definitely Bradley and Sally Rathbone?' said Jemima, as she headed towards his screen.

'Absolutely. Take a look for yourself.' He smiled broadly.

'Any kids with them?' asked Broadbent.

'No,' replied Ashton. 'He's pointing the key fob to lock the doors, and they're walking away from the vehicle.'

'Look at that. They're holding hands. Hey, nice watch. Top of the range Rolex, if I'm not mistaken,' said Broadbent, pointing at Bradley's wrist.

'Yeah? How can you possibly know that?' demanded Ashton.

'Well, a guy like that would be loaded. Fancy house. Fancy car. Fancy watch. Stands to reason,' said Broadbent, bristling at Ashton's suggestion that he could be mistaken. 'Oh, and he's just leaned in to kiss his wife's cheek. Backs up what the neighbour said about them being happily married.' He was keen to move the narrative on before Ashton had a chance to call him out again.

'This footage should help you target the search of the internal CCTV footage,' said Jemima, turning to Broadbent. 'We need to know what time they left that shop. And facts only, Dan. No surmising. It's not helpful.'

Broadbent reddened and muttered that he was positive it was a Rolex. Ashton suppressed a smile but said nothing.

Jemima knew that she had not done herself any favours by spending time delving into Isobel's background. She was sickened at the thought of the woman killing her own child, but it was in the past.

Back in the here and now there were four murder victims and a teenage girl whose life was hanging in the balance. They were the priority and required Jemima's undivided attention.

'I've got various calls to make,' she said. 'I need to know how the SOCOs are progressing, do some background checks on Jason Venter then contact the Psychiatric Department at the UHW and find out more about Bradley Rathbone. Did he have a problem with any of his patients? Did he have any known enemies? Make a list of people he was close to, as we'll need to speak to them.'

* * *

First on Jemima's list was Jeanne Ennersley, who informed her that all the bodies had been removed from the house and that John Prothero had confirmed that he would be carrying out the post-mortems. So far there was no sign of the weapon. There was still a lot of work to be done at the murder scene, and she suggested that Jemima contact her again the next morning, as she'd be better placed to give her an update.

* * *

Ashton's earlier revelation about Jason had taken Jemima by surprise. She had verified that the Jason Venter registered at the surgery was the celebrated artist, and that complicated things — if she didn't do things by the book, it could bring a whole heap of trouble down on their heads.

Jemima soon established that Jason Venter had come to the attention of the police on a few occasions. He had spent his childhood in Splott, an area in the south of Cardiff. His first brush with the law was at the age of eight when he was caught, along with a few other lads, smashing the windows at Willows High School. He was taken home and given a talking-to by a local police officer, who noted that the parents seemed like decent people, and Jason appeared to be suitably sorry for his actions.

Two years later, Jason was caught spray-painting a wall of a local community centre. It was an unauthorized act but was not a run-of-the-mill tagging. It had actually been an attempt at painting a scene. Rather than punish him, he was allowed, under the supervision of a local artist, to continue with the transformation of the wall. After that, there had been no reports of Jason coming to the attention of the police until they were called to the incident at the medical centre, where he was arrested and subsequently let off with a warning.

Two months later he was questioned about an act of criminal damage to a vehicle owned by Sally Rathbone. He denied all knowledge of the incident, and there was no evidence linking him to the crime.

On the face of it, Jason Venter seemed an unlikely candidate for these brutal murders. Apart from his apparent obsession with Sally Rathbone, and her unfounded allegation that he had damaged her car, there were no other reported incidents to suggest that he had contacted her. There was also nothing in his file to indicate that Jason had a history of violence. But right now he was a person of interest and Jemima was determined to follow it up.

Broadbent looked up from his screen and spoke loudly, breaking Jemima's concentration. 'I've trawled through the CCTV footage. The Rathbones reached the till at 11.17. I've got them heading back to the car at 11.33. They went to the petrol station and left there at 11.45.'

'Well done, Dan,' said Jemima. 'Check that no traffic incidents were affecting the most direct route from the supermarket to their home. If there weren't any, I'd say it's safe to assume that they could have arrived back at about midday. They clearly had no idea of what was about to happen. Did anyone manage to get an address for Jason Venter?' she asked, turning her attention back to Ashton.

'Yes. I asked one of the PCs to find it. I've got it here.' Ashton held up a piece of paper.

The address was in the Whitchurch area of the city, on one of the more expensive roads, where the properties were old, large, and worth a lot of money.

'Do we know where Jason Venter is at the moment?' asked Jemima.

'No, his Facebook page said that he was supposed to be attending a charity event in London today. It's taken me a while to find a contact number there. I've only just finished speaking to their PR guy who confirmed that Jason was a no-show. They've been trying to get hold of him for much of the day. But he's not answering his phone.'

'Damn,' muttered Jemima. 'If Venter attended the event, we could have easily ruled him out of the investigation. Well, we've got no choice. We'll both go to Venter's house in Whitchurch. If he's there, we'll bring him in for questioning. If he's not, we'll speak to the neighbours. Find out if anyone knows his current whereabouts or have seen him today.'

'I've just had a call to say that Mark Derbyshire has arrived home,' said Broadbent.

'I can always take a PC with me if you want to head over to Lisvane?' Ashton suggested.

'Normally I'd agree. But I want to be there to witness Venter's reaction first-hand. Broadbent, give the Derbyshires a ring and tell them it'll be a few hours before I can get over to their house. Tell them to stay put as I need to get Mark Derbyshire's take on Bradley Rathbone.'

CHAPTER 8

It was already dark when Jemima and Ashton arrived in Whitchurch. Jason Venter's property was a large, detached, Victorian house, set back from the pavement. A boundary wall bulged noticeably in places, forced out of alignment by a dense hedge that had been planted far too close to the brickwork. To the side of the property was a wide driveway. Strands of multicoloured fairy lights lit up a mulberry bush planted in the front garden.

As Jemima stepped out of the vehicle, she could see that someone was at home. The ground floor windows were open, and the smell of cannabis was unmistakable. She could hear David Bowie's voice as one track faded and another began.

Jemima pressed the doorbell. They waited, but no one answered.

Jemima bent down, opened the letterbox and hollered, 'Police! Open up, Mr Venter!' After a few more seconds she turned to speak to Ashton. 'If we stand here any longer we'll end up getting high. Venter's probably too far gone to hear us above that racket.'

Ashton headed for the window. Jemima saw him open it further and then jump back in shock.

'Wake up!' he yelled. He turned to Jemima. 'Call the fire brigade! There're two of them in there and the place is about to go up!'

Ashton hoisted himself through the open window before Jemima had time to reach for her mobile phone.

'Ashton, don't be stupid! Get out of there!' yelled Jemima. As she spoke into the phone, Jemima rushed to the open window to get a look inside. A couple lay passed out on the sofa, and next to them an overturned candle had set a discarded cushion alight.

'Venter, wake up! The house is on fire. You've got to get out of here,' bellowed Ashton. His warning had no impact on either Jason Venter or his companion. Ashton shook them violently but failed to wake them up. 'Guv! Get in here now! I need help to get them out!'

'Use the rug to smother the flames!' yelled Jemima.

But it was too late. In the time it took Ashton to look down and notice the rug, the fire had ignited it as well. There was nothing else available. The oxygen from the open window was fuelling the blaze. Visibility decreased as the smoke became dense.

Jemima saw Ashton grab hold of Jason Venter and struggle towards the window, but the flames were blocking his way. There was no time to lose.

In desperation, Jemima tried the front door, and discovered that Venter had forgotten to lock it. It was a welcome stroke of luck. 'Head for the hallway!' she yelled. 'It's safer this way.'

Jemima ran inside, pushing past Ashton to get to the woman. 'Come on!' she shouted, as she hoisted the woman off the sofa. 'We need to get out now before the whole place goes up!'

CHAPTER 9

It had been a close call, but Jemima and Ashton got the couple out safely. As soon as Ashton and the other two had been taken off in ambulances, Jemima got back into the car and headed towards Lisvane. She was covered in soot, and smelled of smoke, but it was not the time to worry about her appearance. There was still a lot to do, and because of how much smoke Ashton had inhaled, they were now a man down. The roads were still quiet as she hit speed dial to let her Chief Inspector, Ray Kennedy, know what had happened.

A police officer stopped Jemima's vehicle at the entrance to Briarmarsh Close. She had not seen him before, and he apparently had no idea who she was. He looked like an old-school bobby, and Jemima's immediate thought was to wonder how effective he would be if the killer returned to massacre another set of neighbours. As she opened her window, he crouched down to peer inside the vehicle, getting far too close to the side of her face.

'What's your business here, miss?' he asked, in an officious manner. She could smell a concoction of rotting food and tobacco on his breath. It made her want to gag.

'I'm Detective Inspector Huxley.' She hurriedly rummaged through her bag to locate her warrant card, in the hope that she'd find it before he had a chance to breathe on her again.

'Right you are, ma'am,' he said, when he had satisfied himself of her credentials. 'On you go.' It was irritating, but at least he was doing his job correctly.

Jemima parked on the Derbyshire's driveway, noting that a Lexus GS F was now parked there too, alongside Mariella's Mazda CX-5.

She pressed the bell and the door was answered by a handsome man who seemed vaguely familiar to her. He was tall and athletic-looking. His physique was emphasized by a tight-fitting T-shirt that showed off his pecs.

'Detective Inspector Huxley,' she said. She went to shake his hand. His grip was double-handed and firm. The contact lasted longer than necessary, and as he released the pressure, his fingers splayed down her wrist and palm in an awkwardly suggestive manner.

'Mark Derbyshire,' he replied. As he spoke, he looked directly into her eyes in a manner that seemed far more intimate than appropriate. 'Have you been fighting fires, Inspector?' he asked, giving her a quizzical look.

'Something like that. I apologize for my appearance,'

'Come inside. You think you recognize me, don't you?'

'Yes, but I don't know where I've seen you before,' said Jemima. She was doing her best to quell an unexpected feeling of embarrassment. It was clear from the few seconds she had spent in his company that Mark Derbyshire was a confident alpha male. Given his close relationship with the victims, he didn't appear to be overly affected by the brutal nature of their deaths.

'Actually, we've seen each other on a couple of occasions, but never when I've been dressed like this. I'm a barrister with the Temple Court Chambers. Come through. We're in the kitchen.'

Jemima smiled to herself. How could she not have recognized Mark Derbyshire? That sense of self-entitled superiority was a prerequisite for success in his chosen career. He spent much of his working life in a public arena where he was expected to exude confidence and authority. A barrister needed to be a master manipulator, a raconteur who could charm, bully, convince and confuse, seamlessly changing tack to adapt to varying circumstances, or they let their clients down severely. And there was no place for the latter as word would quickly get around that they were not up to the job.

Mark Derbyshire was a member of the opposition, voraciously defending his clients against the charges they faced. But despite being part of the opposition, he was the one barrister most female officers hoped to see whenever they attended court. Everyone dreaded coming up against him, as Mark was a sharp operator, always on top of his game. But the flip side was that he was exceptionally easy on the eye and that somehow seemed to make him less annoying.

Mark stood aside and let Jemima walk ahead of him. With each step, she was uncomfortably aware of him behind her. It was as though she could feel his eyes undressing her, and she wished that she'd had the sense to insist that he lead the way. The thought was an unsettling, unwelcome distraction.

As she entered the kitchen, Jemima was surprised to find Mariella sitting in the same seat as earlier. She wondered if the woman had moved from there in the intervening hours.

'Any news on Millie?' asked Mariella. 'I've tried ringing the hospital, but they wouldn't tell me anything as I'm not family. You'd think I'd have known that would be their response.'

'The last I heard she was still in surgery,' said Jemima. 'Though that was a few hours ago.'

'Have you arrested anyone yet?' asked Mark.

'No,' said Jemima.

'I took the boys straight to my parents' house,' said Mark. 'We're off there too, once you've gone. I don't think it's safe for us to stay here until we know what we're dealing with. Mariella said you wanted to speak to me to get some background information on Bradley.'

'That's right. At the moment we've very little to go on, so we're looking into every aspect of the Rathbones' lives. Familicide is rare, and you'll know from cases reported in the media that it's often the father who is responsible.'

'Let me stop you there, Inspector,' said Mark. His tone was unexpectedly harsh and authoritative. 'I hope you're not suggesting that Bradley is responsible for what happened?'

'Not at all,' said Jemima. She suddenly felt as though she was defending her position in court. 'I can't go into details at the moment, but it's highly unlikely that this was a murder–suicide. We're not treating it as such. I just know that you and Bradley were close. Chances are he confided in you, and something he may have said could lead us to whoever did this.'

'I see,' sighed Mark.

Jemima noticed his shoulder muscles relax beneath his T-shirt and she found herself admiring them despite herself. 'Are you aware of any problems Bradley or other family members may have had? Did any of them feel threatened in any way?'

'Brad had his fair share of problems. I understand that Mariella's already told you about his first wife, Isobel?'

'She has.'

'Well, that affected Bradley deeply. He blamed himself for what happened that day. It made him question everything he had taken for granted. It was particularly hard for him as he was a psychiatrist. You see, Brad believed that he should have picked up on some warning signs, but he didn't. He knew that Isobel had been tired and out of sorts in the lead up to that day. But he had no idea that it would result in such a tragedy.

'He tortured himself for a long time afterwards. Brad told me he considered abandoning his career and starting over again. At one stage he even thought about emigrating. But he had to do what was best for Millie. She had already been through so much in her young life. So Brad decided to continue with his work, as it allowed him to provide her with some semblance of stability.'

'Did Bradley ever mention receiving any threats to his own or his family's safety?' pressed Jemima.

'Not from Isobel. They'd had no contact with each other for years. But there was one person you may want to take a look at. I can't give you a name. Brad wouldn't go into specifics as he was hot on patient confidentiality, but there was a guy who really shook him up. Ask the chap who heads up the Psychiatry Department at the UHW. I'm confident that Brad would have reported the incident.'

'I didn't know about that,' said Mariella. Her tone was suddenly confrontational. 'Why didn't you mention it before?'

'It wasn't my story to tell,' said Mark, shrugging off his wife's annoyance.

'Thank you. I'll look into it,' said Jemima. It seemed that her visit had not been a complete waste of time. 'Is there anything else either of you can think of which may have some bearing on the events next door?'

'I wish there was,' sighed Mariella. 'I've been playing everything over in my head, but there's absolutely nothing.'

'Same here,' said Mark. 'We're both rather shell-shocked at the moment. But if anything springs to mind, we'll let you know.'

Jemima sensed that Mark Derbyshire was far from being shell-shocked, and the subtle wink he gave confirmed her assessment of him. There was something off about the man. He had flirted with her from the moment she arrived. She couldn't decide whether or not his wife was oblivious to his inappropriate behaviour.

'I'll need to speak with your children at some stage soon,' said Jemima.

'I don't think that will be necessary,' said Mark. 'They were with me when this happened. They're already upset, and I don't believe they'll be able to tell you anything useful.'

'I need to build up a picture of what the Rathbone children were like. It's likely that your sons will know more about them than yourselves. Especially Thomas. Your wife's already told me he had a close friendship with Jonathan.'

'In that case, I insist that one of us be there when you speak with them,' said Mark.

'Of course,' said Jemima. 'You know that we would never interview a child without an appropriate adult being present.'

'Inspector, has anyone been in touch with Sally's parents?' asked Mariella. 'I forgot to mention them earlier, but someone should really let them know.'

'Do you have their names and contact details?' asked Jemima.

'Dominic and Alice Renshaw. They live in Blackwood, but I don't have an address. Their numbers should be stored in Sally's phone.'

* * *

Jemima was glad to return to the car. It was a relief to get away from Mark Derbyshire. Although she had gone there specifically to speak with him, she felt angry with herself for allowing him to make her feel this way. She never usually had a problem putting people in their place. Mark Derbyshire had a way of taking charge, steering people in the direction he wanted them to go. It was unsettling.

Exhaustion settled over Jemima, weighing her down. At that moment she would have loved nothing more than to head back home, strip off her smoke-soiled clothes and luxuriate in a hot bath. But that wasn't an option. The first few hours of a case like this were so important. She needed to push on and gather as much information as she could.

There was a slight niggle behind her left eye. She'd first noticed it when she was talking to the Derbyshires. The sensation wasn't harsh enough to be painful, but experience had taught her that a headache was imminent, which wasn't surprising given the day's events. Jemima rummaged in her bag until she found a strip of paracetamol, but she'd forgotten to leave a bottle of water in the car and was forced to swallow them dry. Her phone sounded. It was Broadbent.

'We've heard that they're keeping Ashton in overnight. I think it's just precautionary,' he said.

'Have you informed his girlfriend?'

'Yeah, Ingrid said she'd go straight to the hospital,' said Broadbent.

'Is Venter up to talking?'

'Not at the moment. Last I heard he was still pretty much out of it. They're treating him for smoke inhalation and superficial burns. Once the effects of the drugs he's taken wear off, they'll sedate him, then gradually bring him out of it. They reckon he'll be in pain for a while, and there's a possibility of some residual scarring, but they don't think he'll need skin grafts. How are you doing, though? I heard you ended up saving all of them.'

'Yeah, well, it wasn't out of choice,' Jemima told him. 'Ashton went in there acting all gung-ho. It's lucky we didn't both end up getting hospitalized.'

'What state is Venter's house in? Will we be able to get inside and take a look any time soon?'

'I very much doubt it. There were two fire crews in attendance trying to get it under control. It's an old, large, detached house, but they've evacuated the adjacent properties as a precaution. I'd guess if there was any evidence inside linking Venter to the murders, chances are the fire would have destroyed it, or at the very least tainted it.

'Do me a favour, Dan, and send a couple of officers over to question Venter's neighbours. Some of them may have seen him throughout the day. At least we can start to get an idea of his movements. And make sure that we have a police presence there to secure the scene once the fire is out. I don't want to risk potential evidence getting lost or compromised further.

'We may also have another lead. I've just heard that Bradley Rathbone had concerns about his personal safety. One of his patients threatened him. I'm heading over to the hospital now to find out who I need to speak to in the Psychiatry Department. I'll check in on Ashton and Millie

Rathbone while I'm there. Maybe even find out if John Prothero has started on the autopsies.

'Oh, and Sally Rathbone's parents live in Blackwood. Their names are Dominic and Alice Renshaw. Let the Gwent force know and ask if they can send someone out to break the news to them. Once you've sorted out all that, you may as well get yourself off home. There's nothing more we can do tonight, and it'll be a long day tomorrow.'

CHAPTER 10

Jemima arrived at the hospital and wrinkled her nose in disgust at the thought of all the germs the building harboured. She wanted to be in and out as quickly as possible but knew it would be an extended visit if the pathologist, John Prothero, was still on duty. But first she wanted to check on Ashton, so she made a beeline for the reception desk to find out which ward he was on.

As Jemima reached her, the young woman behind the desk stifled a yawn.

'Sorry about that,' the woman said. 'I'm coming to the end of my shift. It's been a long day. But I shouldn't moan. Looks as though your day's been a lot worse than mine.'

'That's probably a fair assessment,' said Jemima. She asked the receptionist to find out which ward Ashton was on, and also sought directions to the Psychiatry Unit. 'Who's heads up that department?' she asked.

'That'd be Giles Souter.'

There was no need for Jemima to ask where John Prothero would be. She'd been to see him so many times that she could walk the route blindfolded.

Jemima arrived on the ward to find Ashton asleep. His partner, Ingrid, was perched on the edge of a seat, looking

42

small, doll-like and beautiful — in marked contrast to Jemima, who was covered in soot. She decided to leave them in peace, and silently cursed herself for not enquiring about Millie's whereabouts while getting directions from the receptionist. It was the obvious thing to have done, yet it hadn't even entered her head. It suddenly occurred to her that the shock of having to enter a burning building and rescue its occupants must have had more of an effect on her than she had realized. It felt as though she was running on empty.

Having come so far along the maze of hospital corridors it made more sense for her to enquire about Millie in the Accident and Emergency Department, which was only one floor down. The staff probably wouldn't thank her for it, but it would ultimately save her some time.

The noise hit her as soon as she reached the lower corridor. There was a wall of sound as people cried, complained, shouted, and tried to hold conversations. Almost every seat in the waiting area was occupied, while children played on the floor. It was complete chaos. Nurses shouted out patients' names, raising their voices as they walked through the melee, in search of the person they were trying to find.

A woman steadied herself against a wall, and during the short while that Jemima's gaze focused upon her, she bent over and vomited on the floor. A porter pushing a wheelchair expertly changed course and continued on his way without a backward glance.

Jemima thanked her lucky stars. She knew it would drive her mad if she had to work in a place like this. It was bad enough at the station, but this took things to a whole new level. It was the epitome of hell on earth.

The receptionist's fingers raced over the keyboard as she typed out Millie's name. Seconds later, she informed Jemima that the girl was still in surgery. No one was available to give a progress report.

The next stop was the Psychiatry Department, but the outpatient clinic was closed and the wards were locked. Jemima noticed an intercom near one of the doors. She pressed the buzzer.

'You can't come in,' said a woman's disembodied voice. 'We don't allow visitors this late in the day.'

'I'm not a visitor. I'm a police officer, and I urgently need to speak with Giles Souter about an ongoing investigation,' said Jemima. As she spoke, she tried her utmost to keep the irritation from surfacing in her voice.

'He's not due in until the morning,' said the woman.

'That's not good enough. I need a contact number for him. Come to the door. I'll show you my warrant card so you can verify my credentials. Then you can give me his phone number.'

'I don't know about that,' said the woman.

'I'll make it easy for you,' said Jemima. Her resolve to stay calm had disappeared. 'Come to the door, look at my warrant card and give me Giles Souter's contact number, or I'll have you arrested for obstructing a police officer, and you'll spend the night in one of our cells. Have I made myself clear?'

'You don't need to be so rude,' snapped the woman. Before Jemima had a chance to respond, the intercom crackled and cut out.

Jemima's patience had worn thin. She hammered on the door and peered through the glass panel. There was no way any jobsworth was going to ignore her. Eventually, a woman in a nurse's uniform walked towards the door, and the intercom crackled into life once more.

'Sorry about Phyllis giving you a hard time. She's one of our patients. We've been rushed off our feet, and she took it upon herself to answer the intercom. She knows she's not supposed to, but that doesn't seem to stop her. How can I help you?'

* * *

After getting Giles Souter's number, Jemima left the ward to find John Prothero. Prothero had been a pathologist for almost thirty years, spending his entire working life at the

44

University Hospital of Wales. He was finishing up for the day when Jemima approached him.

'Ah, Jemima!' he said. He always sounded genuinely pleased to see her. 'I was wondering when you'd turn up. It's good to see you. What scrape have you managed to get yourself into this time?'

'Just rescued one of my team from a fire. All in a day's work, eh?' she replied, with a weak smile.

'There's no denying you get stuck in. And here you are bringing me multiple homicides. As if I don't have enough to keep me busy,' he laughed. 'And where's that sidekick of yours? Don't tell me he's no longer with you? It brightens my day when I get the chance to watch him turn green around the gills.'

'You're a bad man, John,' scolded Jemima. 'You know Broadbent's got a weak stomach.'

'Daniel's a big girl's blouse if you ask me,' chuckled Prothero. 'Though I have to say, this is a particularly nasty incident. Especially as there're children involved. I've got all four bodies tucked up for the night. I won't be looking at them until tomorrow. It was unfortunate timing as I was already in the middle of a post-mortem when they arrived, and my assistant was busy too. Call by tomorrow afternoon. I should have made some headway by then. And get yourself home, girl. You look as though you could do with a bath and a good night's sleep.'

CHAPTER 11

The journey home was almost a complete blank. Jemima remembered getting into the car in the hospital car park. The next thing she knew, she was pulling up on the drive at the front of her house. As for the time in between, she had no idea what had happened. For all she knew, she could have knocked down a string of pedestrians or run a series of red lights. It was a worrying thought.

As she opened the front door, she could hear the familiar sound of *The Pirates of the Caribbean* coming from the living room where James was stretched out on the sofa.

'Only me,' she called, as she dropped her bag on the floor and headed into the living room.

'Hi, Jem,' said James. His welcoming smile faded on his lips. 'What happened to you?'

'I had to rescue someone from a fire,' said Jemima.

'Wow! That's super cool,' said James. He looked mightily impressed.

'And how's my favourite boy?' Jemima bent down to kiss his forehead and ruffled his messy brown hair.

'Gerroff me,' he laughed.

'Did you and your dad have a good time today?'

'I s'pose, but it'd have been heaps better if you'd been there.'

Hearing the obvious disappointment in James's voice, Jemima felt a pang of guilt. It was usually one of James's favourite activities, a fun few hours when they bonded as a family unit. But given the recent tension between Nick and his son, Jemima had suggested they go without her, in the hope that they would resurrect some of their former closeness. She realized now that her intention had been nothing but a pipe dream.

'Where's your dad?' asked Jemima, conscious of the fact that Nick was nowhere to be seen.

'In the kitchen. I think he's in a mood, so I'm staying out of his way.'

'I'll go and see what's up with him.' There was no sound coming from the kitchen as she made her way along the hallway. A glimmer of light bled from the gaps between the closed door and its frame. When she opened the door, Nick looked up from where he sat at the kitchen table. She could clearly see the annoyance on his face, which he made no attempt to mask.

'Where the hell have you been?' he growled. 'This was your day off. The last thing you said before James and I went out was that you'd have dinner ready for us when we came home. But as usual, you did nothing. Is it too much to ask to expect you to buck your ideas up and start putting us first for a change?'

Jemima sighed. They'd been together long enough for Nick to know that even on a day off she could be called back to work if a serious incident warranted her presence. He was being moody because James preferred her company at the moment. It sickened her that Nick was too lazy to put in the effort to go the extra mile with his son, as James was clearly still struggling to come to terms with major changes in his life.

'Grow up, Nick. You can see from the way I look that I've had a tough time, but you don't care enough about me to want to know what happened.'

'You're right, Jemima, I don't care,' shouted Nick.

'Shhh, keep it down,' she hissed. 'I don't want James to know we're arguing. He's got enough on his plate at the moment without having to worry about us.'

'Don't tell me what to do. You're not at work now. And it's a joke, you pretending to care about him.'

'I'm not pretending. You know I love him.'

'Not enough, Jemima. The truth is, I hoped you'd give up work after Wendy died. You spent years bleating on about wanting a child. Now we've got James living here full-time, but there's no thought of you putting your career on hold to give him the attention he deserves.'

'Don't go there, Nick. You're out of order and I'm not letting you guilt-trip me. I love that boy like he was my own. James doesn't need me to put my career on hold in order for him to know how much I care about him. He's got a closer relationship with me than he ever had with his own mother, and he knows I love him unconditionally.

'If you were being honest with yourself, you'd admit that the problem is us. I'm starting to think that we shouldn't have gone ahead with those fertility tests. Let's face it, our relationship isn't exactly in a good place. The rot set in the day you convinced everyone that I'd snatched Harry. I know it was because you'd had too much to drink and for some inexplicable reason you thought it was funny. But it wasn't. No one was laughing apart from you. You upset Dan and terrified Caroline. It was an awful thing to do and a hell of a wake-up call for me to realize that you'd been so heartless.'

'We all make mistakes, Jemima.'

'Well, that was a pretty colossal one. You shouldn't have done it. Dan and I are partners. It says something that even when you suggested that I'd abducted their kid, Dan was the one who had my back. Whereas you were the one sticking the knife in.'

'Why does everything have to be about you?' Nick shouted. There was no mistaking the frustration in his voice, or the contempt he felt towards her.

'What do you mean by that?' asked Jemima.

'Well, look at it from my point of view. People must think I'm useless. I'm married to someone who's so fucked up that she cuts herself instead of talking to me. Am I that bad a husband?'

'You outed me to my boss, without a thought for my career! You told Kennedy my darkest secret — something I've battled against for as long as I can remember. I've lived with the shame for years, but at least it wasn't out there for everyone to know about. I was managing my pain. I was coping.'

'No, you weren't. Self-harming isn't normal. It's sick. You don't need to cut yourself, Jemima, you choose to do it!'

'That just shows how clueless you are. You've no idea what it's like. You betrayed me, Nick. How can I ever trust you again?'

'I did it because I was desperate, Jemima.'

'Yeah? Well, so am I!'

'You should be thanking me, not complaining about it.'

'Are you that deluded that you actually believe you did a good thing?'

'At least now you're getting the help you need. You've turned the corner. You don't need to cut yourself anymore.'

'You're clueless, Nick. Just because I'm forced to bare my soul to a psychologist on a regular basis doesn't mean that I don't want to cut myself. It's not some masochistic urge that I give—'

'I don't want to hear your excuses,' Nick interrupted, slamming his fists on the table. 'It's time you grew up and acted like a proper wife and mother. Your priorities need to change. You're always involved in some drama, instead of putting this family first.'

'I can't believe you just said that. You're acting like a Victorian patriarch. It's pathetic. I do my best by you and James. I don't hear him complaining. I'm not stepping back from my career, Nick. I've worked hard to get to where I am. So, if you don't like it, you know what you can do. I've always been upfront about not having the luxury of a nine-to-five job. You knew that when we got together and nothing's changed. It's not the first time I've been called in on my day off, and it won't be the last.'

'Yeah, well, perhaps it's time you packed it in,' he countered.

'Fuck you, Nick.'

They fell into an angry silence. In recent weeks their relationship had become a battlefield. Jemima knew they were both doing their best to act like a happy couple whenever James was around, but that was becoming increasingly difficult to achieve. Things were getting increasingly worse, and with each passing day it was harder for Jemima to remember the good times.

'I ordered pizza earlier,' muttered Nick, in an attempt to calm things down. He pointed to the box on the kitchen table. 'There're a couple of slices left over, but it's probably cold now.'

Jemima kicked off her shoes, knowing that there was nothing to be gained by continuing the argument. She was too exhausted to fight, and the last thing she wanted was for James to sense the animosity between them. 'Thanks. I'm starving. But first I need to get out of these clothes and take a shower.' Grabbing a drink from the refrigerator, she headed upstairs. 'And don't anyone dare eat those pizza slices!' she called, forcing herself to sound upbeat for James's sake.

CHAPTER 12

The next morning, Jemima's phone rang as she pulled into the police car park.

'Giles Souter here. Sorry I didn't return your call last night. I'd attended a conference in Vienna and switched my phone off to board the plane. How can I assist you?'

'I need some information about Bradley Rathbone,' said Jemima.

'Bradley? That sounds ominous.'

'I'm afraid it is. Bradley was murdered yesterday, along with most of his family.'

'Murdered . . . Bradley and his family are dead?'

'Yes. I'm heading up the investigation, and I've been made aware of a recent incident between Bradley and one of his patients. So you'll understand the urgency. I need to see you as soon as possible.'

'Of-of course,' stuttered Souter, unable to hide his shock. 'When can you get here? I'll do my best to juggle appointments to suit you.'

'I've a few things to take care of first, but I'll be there within the hour. In the meantime, I suggest you make a list of anyone who posed a threat to Bradley. I'll need names, background information, anything you can give me.'

* * *

Jemima arrived at her desk to find some messages waiting for her. The Chief Fire Officer had confirmed that the blaze at Jason Venter's house had been extinguished, but the structure had to be made safe before anyone would be allowed to enter what remained of the property.

There was also a message from the police officer charged with keeping an eye on Millie Rathbone to say that she had survived the surgery. The girl was now in the Intensive Care Unit and he was guarding her.

Gwent police had broken the news of their daughter's death to the Renshaws and had supplied Jemima with their address. There was a note to say that, as expected, the Renshaws hadn't taken it well, and their son had travelled back to join them.

The final message was from the hospital to say that Jason Venter's injuries were less severe than they initially thought and that he was fit to be questioned.

'Morning, guv,' called Broadbent, as he wandered into the room. He had barely had time to reach his desk when DCI Kennedy appeared.

'Great news!' Kennedy told them. 'I've just spoken to Ashton's missus. Things have gone well overnight. They're waiting for the consultant's say-so to discharge our boy later this morning. I've told Ingrid to make sure he doesn't come back to work today. I don't want him keeling over. I've also managed to second Gareth Peters. He fitted in well last time. Since Ashton's not going to be in today and will be under par for a while, I thought you could do with the help. He'll get started later this morning.'

'Great! Gareth's a top bloke,' said Broadbent.

'Yeah, excellent news, but please tell me you haven't asked Will Sanders to come back?' said Jemima. Will Sanders was like Marmite. You either loved him or hated him. And as far as Jemima was concerned, it was very much the latter. In her opinion, Sanders was cocky and crude.

'Relax, Huxley,' said Kennedy, as a knowing smile played across his lips. 'You obviously haven't had your ear to the ground. Sanders had a big Lotto win and walked away from the force. He's living it up on the Costa del Sol. I've heard that he's planning to write a raunchy novel about a police officer. Let's face it, he's carried out more than enough research.'

'You can say that again,' said Jemima.

'So, what's the order of play for today?' enquired Kennedy.

'Broadbent and I are heading off to the hospital to speak to Giles Souter,' Jemima told him. 'We'll check in on Jason Venter and Millie Rathbone while we're there. After that, we'll be heading back to the crime scene, then up to Blackwood to meet Sally Rathbone's family. And hopefully John Prothero will have something for us this afternoon.'

CHAPTER 13

Giles Souter turned out to be nothing like Jemima had imagined. For some reason she had expected him to be much older, but he appeared to be in his early forties and was a handsome man.

'I'm afraid the news has thrown me off-kilter, Inspector. I've known Bradley for many years. He was a decent chap. For something like this to happen to him and his family . . . well, it beggars belief. We see and hear all sorts in this profession. It goes with the territory for there to be the odd violent outburst. But we have protocols in place to contain and diffuse those situations. Where were Bradley and his family when they were attacked?'

'They were at home,' Jemima replied.

'Patients have no access to our personal details, Inspector,' Souter told her.

'That doesn't prevent them from following any of you home from work or coming across you by chance,' Jemima pointed out.

'That's true, but doubtful,' said Souter. 'Much of our work is community-based. There are teams of qualified staff dealing with the day-to-day minutiae. Only the more complex, less routine matters are referred back to this department.

It's a common misconception that anyone with a mental illness poses a danger to the general public. But that's simply not the case. There have been tremendous medical advances in the last few decades, and our understanding of specific conditions has changed considerably.

'These days, most of our patients live in family units and hold down jobs. As long as they keep taking their medication, they are able to live relatively healthy lives. Any psychiatric patient deemed to pose a danger to the public would be sectioned under the Mental Health Act and would be housed in a secure facility.'

'With all due respect, Mr Souter, it's not unheard of for patients to stop taking their meds and kill unsuspecting members of the public,' said Jemima. 'As I explained over the phone, we've been informed that Bradley had an unpleasant encounter with one of his patients. At the moment it's just one of some lines of inquiry that we have to follow up.'

'And how many victims were there?' Souter asked.

'Two adults, two teenagers dead,' Jemima replied. 'One teenage girl currently hospitalized. The attack was frenzied and brutal.'

'Well, taking an educated guess, if this is the work of one of Bradley's patients, it could be one of two possibilities. You could be looking for an individual who has suffered a psychotic break. Or it could be the act of an actual psychopath.'

'What's the difference?' asked Jemima.

'It's important not to confuse the term psychosis with psychopathic behaviour,' Souter explained. 'Psychosis is an acute, treatable condition, from which it's possible for someone to make a full recovery. Someone suffering from psychosis can commit acts of violence against others, but the majority of sufferers pose a greater danger to themselves.

'I can see you're looking puzzled, so let me try to explain. Anyone who develops psychosis has a unique set of experiences and symptoms. For instance, they can become delusional or experience hallucinations.'

'So they see or hear things that aren't there?' asked Broadbent.

'Sometimes, but hallucinations are not just confined to sound or sight. They can encompass all or just some of the senses. So someone could also believe they smell, taste or feel as though they are being touched, when in fact there is nothing there. If they're delusional, they're absolutely convinced that certain false things are true. For example, they could believe that you have been sent to kill them, or that they have acquired some sort of invincible superpower. Their thought processes are confused. It's often a very upsetting and frightening time for them.'

'But couldn't the killer simply just be off their head on drugs? Or possibly a paranoid schizophrenic?' asked Broadbent.

'It's certainly possible to trigger a psychotic episode by taking drugs such as cocaine, amphetamine, LSD or methamphetamine. But as I've just explained, these people will experience hallucinations or delusions. Except in rare cases, they pose more of a danger to themselves than to others. As for schizophrenia, it comes under the same umbrella as psychosis, with episodes of paranoia, hallucinations and delusions. You can't rule it out at this stage, but I'd say it was unlikely. I think you should be looking for a psychopath.

'The reasoning behind my hypothesis is that the level of violence inflicted upon Bradley and his family feels more like psychopathic behaviour. Psychopaths are rare and dangerous people. They are living with a severe anti-social personality disorder, which means that they lack empathy, are highly manipulative, and often have a total disregard for the consequences of their actions. It also means that they are prone to violent outbursts.'

'So, can you point us to any patients who may have posed a threat to Bradley Rathbone?' asked Jemima.

'I was just coming to that, Inspector. Throughout his career, Bradley would have encountered a few psychopaths. Thankfully, they're not that common — but I've pulled a few names from our files. By giving them to you I risk breaking patient confidentiality. Though given what has happened I believe that these are exceptional circumstances. But I hope you'll do your best to keep my name out of it.'

'I can't promise it won't come out at a later stage if we end up arresting one of them for the murders,' said Jemima.

'Very well, but I want to make it clear from the outset that I'm not saying that the people on this list are serial killers or even murderers. They are merely patients who Bradley treated for psychopathy. I have no direct knowledge about any criminal activity they may have been involved in. Indeed, it is entirely possible that some, if not all of these individuals have not been involved in any criminal activity. The people I've flagged up are Ophelia Charles, Richard Norbert and Aileen Whittle.'

'And which of those attacked Bradley at the hospital?' asked Jemima.

'None of them. That was Cameron Short, but he's not a psychopath. Cameron has paranoid schizophrenia. He suffered a psychotic break at the time of the incident you're referring to. Cameron had been living quite successfully in the community until he stopped taking his medication. His delusions became more powerful, and he believed that the medication Bradley had prescribed was actually an attempt to poison him.

'Cameron turned up unannounced at the hospital. He forced his way into Bradley's consulting room, and before Bradley had a chance to react, Cameron had him pinned against the wall. He'd picked up a pen from Bradley's desk, had one hand round his neck and was about to stab him in the eye when a couple of security guards appeared and saved the day. We were all pretty shaken up. Bradley escaped serious injury, possibly even death, by the narrowest of margins.'

'And what happened to Cameron Short?' asked Jemima.

'He was sectioned immediately and placed on a locked ward. I believe he is still there now.'

CHAPTER 14

Jemima and Broadbent left Souter's office and headed along the corridor until Jemima found a quiet spot to call the station. Gareth Peters had already arrived, and when he answered the phone, Jemima's heart lifted — Peters was a welcome addition to the team. She relayed the list of names and asked Peters to run them through the Police National Computer, to establish whether any of them had a criminal record.

When she hung up the phone, they made their way to the ICU. At the door, Broadbent pressed the buzzer.

'Hello, who are you here to see?' asked a male voice.

'It's Detective Inspector Huxley, Detective Sergeant Broadbent. We're here to check on Millie Rathbone.'

'I'll be right out,' the voice told them.

Moments later, through the glass panel they could see a middle-aged man walking towards them. His shoulders stooped slightly, as though he was weighed down with a heavy load. He opened the door, and they saw how pale and tired he looked.

'I'm Dr Philip Walters,' he said. 'May I see your identification?'

They both showed him their warrant cards, and he stood aside to allow them to enter.

'The girl's a fighter,' he said, as they headed towards one of the wards. 'She's hanging in there, but we have her in an induced coma as it's better for her at the moment, given the nature of her injuries. She was in theatre for over three hours. Lost a lot of blood, and there were other complications. The next few days will be crucial, but all being well I'm quietly optimistic she should make a full recovery.'

'Will she be able to talk to us when she wakes up?' asked Jemima.

'I've no idea,' he said, shaking his head. 'Amongst other things she suffered head trauma, so we can't be entirely sure how well, or how quickly she'll recover. There is a chance she'll have suffered memory loss. Or she could make a complete recovery. She's in there if you want to look in on her,' he said, pointing to an open door.

As they entered the room, Jemima was struck by the fact that there were only a handful of beds in such a large space. But what stood out the most was the amount of equipment surrounding each of the beds. Everywhere you looked there was machinery with flickering displays. Visibly moving parts whooshed and clicked as they monitored or performed life-preserving actions. It was terrifyingly technical. Especially so, when you considered the fact that these people were reliant upon the machines.

Jemima shuddered.

At the far end of the room, a uniformed officer sat at the side of one of the beds. Broadbent smiled and raised his hand in recognition. The officer returned the smile.

'How's it going, Patterson?' Broadbent asked in a hushed tone.

'It's been very quiet,' said Patterson. 'They come along every so often to check on her and fiddle about with the equipment. But apart from that nothing's happened.'

'Has anyone requested a visit?' asked Jemima.

'No, and even if they did, the staff are aware of the background. The poor kid's got enough on her plate. No one's going to want to put her or anyone else at risk.'

Jemima did her best to avoid standing too close to the girl. The last thing she wanted was to become emotionally entangled in the case. And she sensed that was precisely what would happen if she looked at the teenager. Jemima would get sucked in, and there'd be no turning back. Their best chance of solving the case was for her to remain detached. At least that way she could think logically, and not allow emotional responses to muddy the waters.

Broadbent clearly had a different approach to things. He instinctively reached out and tenderly touched the girl's cheek.

'She looks so vulnerable,' he said, doing his best to hide his emotions. 'She's such a mess. It's impossible to recognize her from the photographs we found at the house.'

Their only sense of what Millie really looked like had come from studying those photographs. Millie was of average build. Before the attack, she had been a photogenic girl who looked more aloof and enigmatic than her years. Mariella Derbyshire had told them that Millie was a serious child, who spent much of her time studying, and Jemima thought that if the girl was also an introvert, it could easily explain why she hadn't appeared entirely relaxed in front of the camera.

'I hope you get the bastard soon,' said Patterson.

'Me too,' said Broadbent. 'Don't worry, kiddo. We'll get him for you.'

'Stay alert and keep us informed,' said Jemima. 'Come on, Dan, it's time to go.'

The only thing they could do for Millie Rathbone was to find the person who had done this to her and her loved ones. Every second counted. Jemima wanted this animal caught and placed behind bars before he had a chance of hurting or killing anyone else.

* * *

Jemima and Broadbent headed off in search of Jason Venter and found him arguing with one of the nurses.

'As I've already explained, you need to wait for the consultant, Mr Venter.' The exasperation in the woman's voice was clear. 'You haven't long regained consciousness. Amongst other things, we need to perform tests to establish whether or not there's been any permanent damage to your lungs. You also have some nasty burns and run the risk of infection and permanent scarring if they're not treated properly. At the moment you probably don't appreciate how much pain you'll be in. We've administered a strong dose of pain relief to keep you comfortable. But as its effects wear off, you'll soon notice the change.'

'Yadda yadda yadda,' Venter countered in a strange voice. 'I'm not interested in anything you have to say. You can treat me as an outpatient.'

The man looked far from all right. The skin on his face and neck was bright, shiny and blistered, and Jemima realized that his voice sounded unnatural as his injuries prevented him from easily moving his facial muscles.

'Well, if you're feeling fine you'll have no problem answering some questions,' said Jemima, as she marched towards him and held out her warrant card.

'What are you talking about?' he snapped. 'My house went up in flames last night, and I have valuable works of art there. I need to get back and assess the damage. My livelihood's at stake. I haven't got the luxury of sitting around all day.'

'I know your house went up in flames. I was one of the officers who got you out. You and your companion owe your lives to Detective Constable Ashton and myself. If we hadn't called at your house to bring you in for questioning last night you'd most likely be lying in the morgue,' said Jemima, already disliking the whining, self-entitled man.

'Why were you going to bring me in for questioning?' asked Venter, looking surprised.

'You're a person of interest in an ongoing investigation, Mr Venter.'

'And which investigation is that? Am I supposed to have run a red light?' he demanded.

'Nothing so banal, I'm afraid. At the moment I'm investigating a quadruple murder, but that number could soon rise if the other victim doesn't make it. You see, she spent most of the night in surgery. At the moment her chances of survival don't look that great.' Jemima wasn't averse to exaggerating the truth if it got someone's attention. Better to have the man shocked and cooperative than complacent and belligerent.

'What the fuck are you talking about? I haven't killed anyone! I'm an artist, not a bloody psychopath.'

'In that case, you won't object to answering my questions, so that I can rule you out of the investigation,' said Jemima.

At the sound of people approaching, Jemima turned to find a tall man, wearing a garish pink-and-white striped shirt, tartan braces, a red dicky bow and black trousers, striding purposefully into the room. He was immediately followed by one of the ward nurses and half a dozen medical students.

'Mr Venter!' the tall man bellowed. 'I do not appreciate having to take time away from dealing with other patients to come and sort out a badly behaved man-child who is having a temper tantrum! Now, as I understand it, you are making life difficult for the nursing staff by insisting that you are fit to leave. That is very foolish.'

'I feel fine,' said Venter.

Jemima noted the change in Venter's voice. Its pitch had become slightly lower and more conciliatory, suggesting that he was intimidated by this man.

'You may very well feel fine, Mr Venter. But that's down to the effectiveness of the medication. I can assure you it does not mean that you are fit to leave. Of course, we cannot force you to stay here against your will. The final decision is entirely yours to make, but I suggest that you think about it very carefully.'

'All right, I'll stay,' muttered Venter, averting his eyes from the consultant's piercing gaze.

'You've made the right decision. I will continue with my rounds, and I will speak to you in a couple of hours. And in the meantime, Mr Venter, I do not expect to hear that you have misbehaved again. Every individual here, be they staff or patient, deserves respect.' He turned abruptly, and the students parted, shuffling outwards and backwards to allow him to pass.

The man was a force of nature. Jemima marvelled at how, in such a short space of time, the consultant had managed to transform Jason Venter from an obnoxious arsehole to a sulking, childlike figure.

'Now, about those questions,' said Jemima.

'Do we have to? I'm in a lot of pain,' whined Venter.

'The sooner you answer my questions, the sooner I'll leave you alone to recuperate.'

'Fine,' he hissed.

'You've got five minutes, as long as you don't upset him,' said one of the nurses. 'Mr Venter needs further treatment. While he's a patient here, his medical needs come first.'

'What is your relationship with Sally Rathbone?' Jemima asked.

'I don't know any Sally Rath— Wait a minute, do you mean Dr Rathbone?' he asked. His voice changed slightly as he realized who Jemima was referring to, and she noticed that his breathing had quickened.

'Yes,' she said.

'I don't have a relationship with Dr Rathbone. I haven't seen her since she had me removed from her list.'

'And why did she do that, Mr Venter?'

'Because I developed a stupid crush on her, but I got over it pretty quickly. You don't realize what my life is like. I could pretty much have any woman I want. Or at least, I could until I started looking like a fucking freak,' he said, gesturing to his injuries. 'The doc made it plain that she wanted nothing to do with me, and I'm not the sort of guy to have to beg for it.'

'It's my understanding that you made a scene at the surgery when you found out that you were no longer her patient.'

'Yeah, well, I'm not used to being humiliated. But that was it as far as I was concerned. I put Dr Rathbone out of my mind. It was her loss, not mine. Anyway, what's that got to do with these murders you're trying to pin on me?'

'I'll get to that in a moment, Mr Venter. But first, I want to know why, if you were so over her, you went to her home and scratched the word BITCH on her car?'

'I never did that. I don't even know where she lives. Your lot investigated it and realized that her allegations were a crock of shit. Is she saying that I've done it again? If she is, then when was I supposed to have done it? Because I've got alibis for the last couple of days, so you can't pin that on me.'

'I would be very interested in hearing more about those alibis. You see, yesterday, Dr Rathbone, her husband and step-children were murdered at their home.'

'You what? Are you for real? Get this through your thick skull — I'm not a fucking murderer! And as far as I'm concerned, this conversation is over until I have my lawyer present. No fucking way are you going to fit me up for this!'

The same nurse that had set out the ground rules came rushing into the room. 'I want you to leave now,' she ordered, pointing towards the door. 'I told you not to upset my patient. You can interview him when he's well enough to answer your questions. But I'll not allow you to distress him while he's on this ward.'

CHAPTER 15

It was far too soon to check on John Prothero's progress, so Jemima and Broadbent headed off to Lisvane. They arrived at Briarmarsh Close to find Jeanne Ennersley and her team packing up their equipment at the crime scene.

'Perfect timing — I was just about to call you,' said Jeanne. 'I think we may have found the murder weapon amongst the contents of the dishwasher. Of course, I can't say for certain until I've had a chance to examine it properly. My initial thought is that the blade looks the right size, but I'll have to compare it to the wounds. Don't get your hopes up too much, though. The machine had completed its washing cycle, so there aren't any complete or partial prints. It looks like the knife is part of a set from the kitchen.

'Another interesting nugget of information is that we noticed the smell of bleach in the bathroom. I'd lay money on it that the killer had the confidence to hang around and take a shower. We've taken swabs.'

'Any prints on the washing machine or dishwasher?' asked Jemima.

'Plenty of prints on the surfaces, but none on the buttons. The killer was clever enough to wipe those clean. We'll have to compare the prints we have with those of the family members and see if any don't match.'

'Ring me as soon as you get any results,' said Jemima.

* * *

After Jeanne and her team left, Jemima and Broadbent were alone in the house. The absence of other humans made the property seem far too quiet and eerie. The dried-on blood spatter made it easy to visualize the scene they had walked in on less than twenty-four hours earlier.

'So what are we looking for?' asked Broadbent, averting his gaze from the dried-up pool of blood at the foot of the stairs.

'I'm not sure,' said Jemima, shrugging her shoulders. 'It's a fact-finding exercise. We're starting from scratch. We need to go through everything to see if there's anything which doesn't seem right. We need bank account details to check if they had money troubles. Collect all the photographs as we need to identify people they were connected to. Find names, addresses and telephone numbers for anyone they were in touch with. Go through every room, cupboard, bag and pocket, and look for receipts, ticket stubs or anything else which will help us build up pictures of these five lives. The tech teams are already working on their mobiles, laptops and tablets, but I want to be certain we don't miss anything here. I know we're living in the electronic age, but sometimes people note important things down on paper.'

'I'll start downstairs if you want to take the bedrooms,' said Broadbent.

'Fine by me,' said Jemima. 'But you've got to get over your phobia of blood sometime. Otherwise, you should consider the fact that you may have made the wrong career choice.'

'It's not that,' replied Broadbent, in a hurt tone. 'You know what my stomach's like. Sometimes I can't even face changing Harry.'

'I bet Caroline loves that excuse,' laughed Jemima.

'Ha-bloody-ha,' said Broadbent, as he headed towards the study.

Jemima set off up the stairs, wrinkling her nose at the numerous stains all about her. In this part of the house it was relatively easy to avoid stepping on them, but she knew that that wouldn't be the case when she reached the top of the stairs.

Jemima took a deep breath, steeling herself for what she was about to see. Once at the top it was clear from the drag marks that Bradley Rathbone had not died instantly. The pattern of blood showed that he had fallen to the floor in the master bedroom after he had been stabbed. A rug was sodden where he had been left to bleed out, but the killer had underestimated him. Bradley had dragged himself towards the stairs, most likely in an attempt to save Millie.

The next bedroom she came to was Jonathan's. If it weren't for the large bloodstain that had soaked into the mattress, it would have been easy to think it was just an ordinary kid's bedroom. There was no blood spatter, which Jemima knew from experience meant that the boy had been stabbed post-mortem. This in itself told her that the killer had a lot of anger towards the teenager as it hadn't been enough to merely take Jonathan's life. The killer had needed to vent his rage by stabbing the boy repeatedly.

The room was reasonably neat, apart from a pile of crumpled clothing discarded in the corner of the room. Even the teenager's desk was free of clutter. As she searched through Jonathan's belongings, Jemima had a hunch that there would be nothing to find.

Lauren's was a typical teenage girl's bedroom. Like her brother, she had been attacked while in bed and had been stabbed post-mortem. An ugly brown stain had spread over much of the mattress.

The walls of her room were pink, though most of the space was covered with posters of boy bands and arterial spray from the attack on Sally Rathbone. A cork noticeboard was full of photographs of Lauren and a few other girls, presumably her friends. On the windowsill, in a fancy silver frame, stood a photograph of Lauren, her brother, and two adults who Jemima thought must have been her parents.

Lauren's desk was strewn with schoolbooks, a selection of teenage magazines, and an open cosmetic bag. A small jewellery box sat on top of a chest of drawers. Jemima lifted the lid and was immediately transported back to her own childhood. She couldn't help but smile as tinny music played and a little ballerina twirled around. It was just like one she'd had when she was young.

Turning her attention to the contents of the box, Jemima rummaged through the girl's trinkets. There was nothing of any value, only a selection of cheap earrings and other fashion accessories. She opened the wardrobe to see it was packed full of clothes and shoes, but nothing Jemima wouldn't have expected to find.

As she worked her way through the contents of a chest of drawers, she discovered a journal, hidden inside a neatly folded jumper. The book had obviously been important to the girl as she had stored it out of sight and secured it with a small padlock.

Jemima took out an evidence bag and carefully placed the book inside. It would most likely turn out to be a pointless exercise reading a teenager's thoughts, but there was always the chance that it might provide some useful insight into the Rathbone family dynamic.

'I've found a collection of photograph albums,' shouted Broadbent. 'I've had a look around the other rooms too, but there's nothing of interest. Do you want any help up there?'

'Yeah, come on up,' said Jemima.

'It's a bloodbath,' said Broadbent, once he reached the top of the stairs. He looked paler than he had earlier that morning. 'You had any luck?'

'Not really. I've found Lauren's journal, but that's it so far. Do you want to make a start in the master bedroom?'

'Yeah, fine,' he replied.

Jemima walked into Millie's room and saw that it was a stark contrast to Lauren's. It was evident that these girls had little in common with each other. Instead of pictures of a favoured boy band, there was an illustrated poster of the periodic table and another with the muscles of the human body. In the far corner of the room stood a life-size anatomical human skeleton, fixed to a stand.

A quick look through the wardrobe and cupboards showed that Millie wasn't the sort of girl to spend her pocket money on looking fashionable. There was plenty of spare hanging space, and the clothes she had were far dowdier and more conservative than Lauren's.

There was a large number of textbooks piled on the desk. Some were schoolbooks. Others, to do with anatomy and psychiatry, suggested that Millie, even at this young age, might already be contemplating a career in medicine. With two doctors in the household, the adults' career paths appeared to have inspired the girl. Even at a cursory glance, it was clear that each book was well-thumbed, and it occurred to Jemima that these books might be the perfect hiding place for something of interest.

She picked up the first book, turned it upside down and flicked the pages to see if there was anything inside. Nothing dropped out, so she set it down and tried the next book, continuing until she was satisfied that there was nothing to be found.

A library card caught Jemima's eye. Millie obviously loved reading, and she wondered if the girl had visited the library on the morning of the attack. If she had already left the house, it could explain why she hadn't been killed like the others. She could have been the last of the Rathbones to arrive home. The library card could help establish a timeline for Millie's movements, so Jemima placed it in an evidence bag.

'How's it going, Dan?' she called, as she headed towards the master bedroom.

'I've found some bank cards, so at least we can start looking at their finances. But there's nothing else of interest.'

'I think we've found everything we're going to,' said Jemima. 'Let's bag everything up and head out.'

CHAPTER 16

After leaving the Rathbones' house, Jemima and Broadbent noticed that their other next-door neighbours seemed to have returned. When they knocked on the door, a woman answered and introduced herself as Rashida Siddiqui. She ushered Jemima and Broadbent into the warm, slightly stuffy, living room where her husband, Amjad, was already sitting.

Jemima introduced herself and Broadbent before they both perched on the edge of large, comfortable chairs, while the Siddiquis huddled close together on an over-sized sofa.

'Can I get you any refreshments?' asked Rashida.

'No, thank you, Mrs Siddiqui,' said Jemima.

'What has happened next door?' asked Amjad.

'Sometime yesterday morning your neighbours were attacked in their house,' began Jemima.

'Oh, no!' shrieked Rashida. She blindly reached for her husband's hand and squeezed it hard. 'Are they all right?'

'I'm afraid not. Mr and Mrs Rathbone were killed, as were Jonathan and Lauren.'

'Oh, no, no, no, no!' wailed Rashida, rocking back and forth. Her husband let go of his wife's hand and put his arms around her.

'This is awful news,' said Amjad, shaking his head in disbelief. 'But there is another child. Was she hurt too?'

'Millie was seriously injured during the attack. She underwent surgery, but it's early days,' said Jemima.

'Who would do such a thing?' said Amjad.

'We have no idea at the moment. And that's why we're talking to you,' said Jemima. 'We're trying to build up a picture of the Rathbones' lives. How long have you lived here?'

'Sixteen years and three months,' said Amjad.

'So you must know the Rathbones quite well?' asked Jemima.

'We didn't socialize with them. But we'd always speak to them if we happened to see them,' said Amjad.

'And you've just returned from holiday?'

'Just now. We had a lovely week, and now we've come back to this. It's awful,' said Rashida.

'Tell me about the Rathbones. What were they like?' asked Jemima.

'They were decent, respectful people,' Amjad replied. 'Happy to talk and didn't cause problems. Sally was there by herself for a long time. Bradley and his daughter moved in much later. The other two children came to live there sometime within the last year.'

'In the weeks before you went away, did you notice anything unusual? Anything which made you feel uncomfortable?'

'Yes,' replied Rashida.

'No, no. That's not relevant,' said Amjad, squeezing his wife's shoulder.

'I'll decide whether or not anything is relevant,' said Jemima. She sensed Amjad's reluctance to let his wife speak. 'Go on, Mrs Siddiqui,' she urged.

'Well, it was probably nothing, but I looked out of the bedroom window shortly before we went away. Sally was in her garden with Mr Derbyshire. I don't know what made me do it, but I had my phone in my hand, and I started filming them. I couldn't hear what they were saying, but I think they were arguing. All of a sudden he did the strangest thing. He grabbed hold of her, pulled her towards him and kissed her.'

'What exactly do you mean by that? Did Mark Derbyshire kiss her on the cheek, like you would a friend? Or did he kiss her on the lips in a more intimate manner?' asked Jemima.

'He kissed her lips. It wasn't the way you'd kiss a friend. He held her far too close, and Sally was struggling. She stamped on his foot, and he let go. Then she slapped his face and shouted at him. They were arguing, but I couldn't hear what they were saying. He kept reaching out to her. She kept pushing him away. But then my phone rang. When I looked out of the window again, there was no sign of Sally or Mr Derbyshire. But I've still got the video on my phone if you'd like to see it?'

'Yes, we would,' said Jemima.

For the next few minutes they sat and watched a recording of the encounter between Sally Rathbone and Mark Derbyshire.

'I'd like to take your phone so that we can download that video,' said Jemima, once it had finished playing. 'You'll get it back tomorrow.'

'That's fine by me. Do you think Mr Derbyshire had anything to do with their deaths?' asked Rashida.

'It's too early to say, but we'll question him about this apparent altercation,' said Jemima. 'So apart from that occasion, have either of you ever seen Sally Rathbone and Mark Derbyshire alone together?'

'No,' said Rashida.

'Never,' agreed Amjad.

'Have you ever overheard any arguments coming from next door?' Broadbent asked.

'No, nothing. As Amjad said, they were nice people.'

'Thank you for your help, Mr and Mrs Siddiqui. There'll be a police presence while we continue with our investigations. If there's anything else that comes to mind, no matter how insignificant you think it may be, then give me a ring on this number. It could turn out to be a vital piece of information.' Jemima handed Rashida her card. 'Don't forget, you can call me at any time. And if you notice any suspicious activity, then let the officer on duty know about it immediately.'

* * *

'Do you think there's a reasonable explanation for what we just saw?' Broadbent asked Jemima as they left. 'After all, Mark Derbyshire's got a stunning wife. Why would he want to risk his marriage by trying it on with her best friend?'

'Why indeed?' replied Jemima. 'But I can't say I'm entirely surprised. And that video footage shows that Sally Rathbone wasn't happy with his advances. There's something about Mark Derbyshire that doesn't feel quite right.'

'Isn't he the defence barrister that a lot of women have a crush on?' asked Broadbent.

'He is. Look, I didn't mention it before, but when I went to talk to him last night, he made me feel uncomfortable.'

'Well, he's used to tying us lot up in knots,' said Broadbent.

'That's not what I'm getting at. Mark Derbyshire came across as predatory.'

'What do you mean?'

'You'll probably think I'm overreacting, but when he shook my hand he held on to it for too long. As I pulled away, he ran his fingers down my wrist and palm. It was way too familiar, and highly inappropriate given the circumstances. I mean, his best friends have just been murdered, and he's trying it on? I need to speak to him again. But this time I want you with me. We need to go and speak to Sally Rathbone's parents, but ring Peters on the way and ask him to arrange for Mark Derbyshire to come into the station at six o'clock this evening.'

CHAPTER 17

Dominic and Alice Renshaw lived in Blackwood, a large town to the north of Cardiff. Their house was located on a newish estate of detached properties, tightly crammed together.

Broadbent pressed the bell. When the door was eventually opened, it was evident that the man in front of them wasn't Sally's father, as he was far too young. He could have been no more than mid-twenties and was someone to whom appearance mattered. He was casually dressed in tight-fitting ripped jeans and a snug T-shirt and looked as though he'd just walked off a catalogue shoot.

'Detective Inspector Huxley and Detective Sergeant Broadbent. We're here to see Dominic and Alice Renshaw,' said Jemima. She and Broadbent offered their warrant cards for inspection.

'My parents are expecting you. I'm Ben, Sally's brother. Come in, but I should warn you, they're both still in shock.'

Alice and Dominic Renshaw sat at the kitchen table, their hands cupped around full mugs of tea that had long since gone cold. Alice's hair was unbrushed, and Dominic looked as though he hadn't slept all night.

'Mum, Dad, the police are here,' said Ben.

'Have you arrested whoever did this to my girl?' asked Alice, looking hopefully at them. Her voice sounded high and unnatural. As she lifted her mug with both hands, Jemima noticed how much the woman was trembling.

'As you can see, my wife's not in the best of health. It's Parkinson's,' said Dominic. He touched her arm in a show of supportive affection. 'We're desperate to see Millie at the hospital but we're not up to visiting at the moment. She's may not be our flesh and blood, but we've got to know her over the last few years, and we've always treated her as though she were Sally's.

'Millie's a good girl. Didn't cause Brad or Sal a moment's trouble. We used to see her school reports, always top of her class. She had a bright future ahead of her. I don't know what's going to happen to her now. It's not as though we can look after her. Not with Alice's health being the way it is. And Ben's got his own life to lead. He's recently graduated, got himself a job up in London.'

'I'm sorry to intrude upon your grief. I can't begin to imagine what you're going through,' said Jemima. She was all too aware of how trite the platitude must have sounded. 'As yet we haven't made an arrest, but we have some lines of inquiry that we're following, and we need to ask you some questions. We're trying to build up a picture of Sally and Bradley's lives to find out if there was anything they may have been worried about. Any possible threats made against them or the children. In fact, anything out of the ordinary that may have scared, or even just unsettled them.'

'There was nothing,' said Alice.

'Well, that's not quite true,' said Ben. 'I know Sally didn't mention it to my parents as she knew it would upset them, but she told me that someone had stolen a ring that had once been our grandmother's. She swore blind that she'd left it in her bedroom. Bradley and the kids said they hadn't touched it, which made Sally think that someone must have gone into the house and taken it. It happened quite recently.'

'Did she report it?' asked Jemima.

'I don't think so.'

'Have you spoken to Bradley's first wife?' Alice asked. 'Sally said she was released from prison. Did you know that she killed her baby? The woman's obviously not right in the head. If she could do that, she's more than capable of killing Sally and the others.'

'Isobel Rathbone was released from prison?' said Jemima. She was so shocked by what the woman had just told them that she was unable to hide the look of surprise on her face.

CHAPTER 18

'Ring Gareth and ask him to find Isobel Rathbone's address,' Jemima told Broadbent after they had left the Renshaw's property. 'Tell him it's a priority. I was under the impression that she was still in prison, but Alice Renshaw clearly thinks she'd been released. If Isobel's no longer locked up, that makes her our prime suspect. In the meantime, we'll drop in on John Prothero and see how he's progressing with the post-mortems.'

* * *

Thirty minutes later they walked along a corridor in a part of the hospital that most people didn't get to see.

'In all of the years you've been coming here, I believe this is the first time you've caught me at my desk. It's such a shame, as I know how much Daniel enjoys his visits. He's quite the inquisitive one, aren't you, lad?' chuckled Prothero.

'Have you made much progress?' asked Jemima.

'All done and dusted.'

'I'm impressed. I wasn't expecting you to finish the post-mortems so quickly,' said Jemima.

'Oh, much as I would like to, I'm afraid that I can't take all the credit. I had help. I've got myself an assistant. She's bloody good too. Her name's Adannaya Okoro. No doubt you'll get to meet her sometime soon. But a word to the wise, don't show yourself up in front of her, Daniel. She'll laugh you out of the building if she sees you looking queasy.'

'Leave Broadbent alone, John,' chuckled Jemima. 'You're making him feel inadequate. So, what have you got for us?'

'Well, as you know, time of death is always an awkward one, unless there's a witness present. But, Jeanne Ennersley, being the consummate professional, recorded the ambient room temperature to compare to the temperatures taken from the bodies, which in turn enables me to make a realistic estimate. Allowing for the fact that both children were teenagers and not much smaller than the adults, the bodies should cool at similar rates. As a rule of thumb, an adult human body will cool about 1.5 degrees in an hour. As a result, we both concluded that the kids were killed about an hour before the adults.

'I can also confirm that, as per my original thoughts, there are some factors which suggest that both teenagers died from asphyxiation and were subsequently stabbed. Firstly, Jeanne supplied me with a set of crime-scene photographs, and there was no arterial spray surrounding the bodies. This in itself is a tell-tale sign that the kids were already dead when they were stabbed. Secondly, on both teenagers, the skin around the nose and mouth is paler, with evidence of cyanosis.'

'What's cyanosis?' asked Jemima.

'In layman's terms, it's a bluish tint, caused by a lack of oxygen,' Prothero told her. 'I also found bruising to the lips, gums and nose of both teenagers, along with some fibres lodged in their nasal cavities, most likely from their pillows. There are also petechial haemorrhages in their eyes.

'The boy was stabbed eighteen times in the chest and abdomen, whereas the girl had thirty-seven separate entry wounds. Also, there was some bruising around her neck, though the hyoid bone remained intact. None of the other corpses displayed similar bruising, though I'm not sure those bruises were inflicted at the time of death.'

'And the adults?' pressed Jemima.

'They're different,' said Prothero. 'I'd say that the woman was attacked first. The cause of death was blood loss. According to the photographs she was found face down on the floor in the girl's room, with arterial spray relatively low down. There were fewer entry wounds — only two, in fact. Now, if I had to take an educated guess, I'd say that the killer was already in the room when Sally Rathbone entered.

'To maintain control of the situation, he would have needed to silence her pretty quickly. So I think he grabbed her from behind, pulled her towards him and quickly stabbed her in the right-hand side. That would have brought her to her knees. There's damage to her face, suggesting that she hit the floor pretty hard. Whether that's because she lost consciousness, or because the killer slammed her face into the floor, I'm unable to say.

'But what I can tell you is that there's also evidence of bruising to her buttocks, which suggests to me that the killer knelt on them as he went on to kill her. When I examined the back of her skull, I found a clump of hair had been pulled out, which suggests that while the killer was kneeling on her, he pulled her head backwards, and slashed her throat from left to right, severing the carotid artery. At that point, death was imminent.'

'So we're looking at a right-handed killer?' asked Broadbent.

'I'd say so,' confirmed Prothero. 'More importantly, you're looking for someone who knows what they're doing. The woman was killed efficiently, to minimize any threat she posed.'

'Could we be looking at two different killers?' asked Broadbent. 'The children's murders seem more emotional and rage-induced, whereas from what you've said, the attack on Sally was controlled.'

'I wouldn't rule it out. But we've managed to confirm that the same knife was used to kill each of the victims,' said Prothero.

'Are you able to gauge the height of the killer from the angle of the first entry wound?' asked Jemima.

'It's difficult to be sure. If I had to hazard a guess, I'd say possibly around the same height as the victim, as the angle of the blade was quite level. But then again that could have been an intentional act designed to make us think he's taller or shorter than he is.'

'What about Bradley Rathbone?' asked Jemima.

'Well, he would have suffered more than the others as he didn't die instantly,' said Prothero. 'Bradley was bigger and presumably stronger, so it wasn't so easy to overpower him. He was stabbed in the back five times. The crime scene photographs showed evidence of a blood trail, suggesting that Bradley dragged himself from where he fell to the landing area near the top of the stairs, where he eventually bled out.'

'In your opinion, do you think that when the killer attacked Bradley, he just got sloppy? Or was he exhausted by the effort it had taken to kill the others?' asked Jemima.

'That's for you to figure out, Jemima. As I've told you many times in the past, I only deal with the facts before me. My role is to present you with some of the pieces of the puzzle. It's up to you to put them all together. Now, if you don't mind, it's been a very long day. I've been working since silly o'clock this morning and would like to go home and put my feet up for a while,' said Prothero, as he stood up and ushered them towards the door.

'It's all right for some having an early finish,' grumbled Broadbent, as he and Jemima made their way back to the police station.

'Well, it's going to be a late one for us,' Jemima told him. 'I want you to sit in on the Mark Derbyshire interview. I'll be interested to find out what you think of him. And hopefully Peters would have made some progress tracking down some of the people on Giles Souter's list.'

CHAPTER 19

'Well, hello there,' said Detective Constable Gareth Peters, as Jemima and Broadbent walked into the room. 'It's great to be part of the dream team again, even though it's such an awful case.'

Peters was one of those people who was well liked by everyone. He had a soothing, almost hypnotic voice, which had the effect of calming everyone around him. Even Jemima swore that she could feel her heart rate slow, and the tension leave her body whenever he spoke. And despite his gentle demeanour, he didn't feel the need to adopt any macho bullshit to be accepted. People just appreciated and respected him for who he was — a decent bloke and a damned good detective.

'How're you doing, mate?' asked Broadbent, as they shook hands like old friends.

'It's good to have you back,' Jemima told Peters. 'Have you managed to find Isobel's address?'

'Not yet,' he replied. 'I've spoken to someone who's sure they'll be able to help. I'm just waiting for them to get back to me.'

'Did you explain that it was urgent?'

'Of course I did. It'll take a little time as he's got to go through the correct channels. But he'll give me the information as soon as he has it. It won't speed things up if I keep pestering him.'

It was disappointing that the information wasn't readily available, but there were other avenues for them to explore in the meantime. 'So, what have you got for us, Gareth?'

'Well, so far, I've only been able to track down one person off that list of names you gave me. The others are proving to be far more elusive as there's no record of them on HOLMES.'

The Home Office Large Major Enquiry System was a god-send to police forces across the country, as it allowed them to share information, collaborate with other agencies and establish links that might have otherwise been missed.

'Tell me more,' said Jemima, as she perched on the edge of the desk.

'Richard Norbert is on the system,' Peters told her. 'But don't get your hopes up because he's not our man. He's a nasty piece of work, with a record as long as your arm. He's been in and out of young offenders since his teens. There's a history of violence, but he hadn't killed anyone until a couple of months ago when he murdered his next-door neighbours — an elderly couple with a dog. Apparently, their dog had been barking all hours of the day and night. Norbert claimed he tried to be reasonable and had asked them to keep the noise down. The couple were apologetic, but in Richard's words, "did fuck all about it", so after having a disturbed night's sleep he called around the next morning and blew their brains out. He also shot the dog. That was two months ago, and they arrested him shortly afterwards. He's currently on remand, awaiting trial.'

'Well, thanks to you, we can rule him out,' said Jemima.

The phone rang, and Broadbent answered it. 'That was the front desk to say that Mark Derbyshire's arrived.'

'Go and collect him, Gareth,' Jemima instructed. 'Bring him up to Interview Room 1. After that, I need you to keep searching for information on the others.'

'Right you are, guv,' said Peters, heading downstairs.

* * *

Broadbent and Jemima were already seated in the interview room when Mark Derbyshire was shown in.

The barrister breezed into the room with an air of entitled superiority. Instead of immediately sitting on the only available seat, he picked it up and moved it further away from the desk to allow him more room to cross his legs. In a display of confidence, he rested his right ankle upon his left knee.

'Just what are you hoping to achieve with this little charade, Inspector? Summoning me here like one of your suspects,' he demanded.

The majority of people summoned to a police station were nervous when they arrived — but not Mark Derbyshire. The man acted as he did in court. He was supremely confident in his ability to control any situation he was faced with.

'Mr Derbyshire, as you're aware, we're at an early stage in the inquiry,' Jemima began. 'When I spoke to you yesterday, I asked if you knew of anyone who had argued with or posed a threat to the Rathbones. You mentioned that Bradley had been threatened by a former patient, and we are following up on that particular line of inquiry. What you failed to mention is that you recently had an altercation with Sally Rathbone.'

'I really have no idea what you're talking about,' said Mark. 'Sally and I were friends. Admittedly, she was more Mariella's friend than mine. But I've known her for years, and we've frequently socialized as friends and neighbours throughout that time. Tell me, where did you get this information from?'

'You were seen trying to kiss Sally Rathbone, and she subsequently rebuffed your advances,' said Jemima.

'That's a slanderous accusation,' said Mark. His voice had suddenly adopted a more serious tone.

'You can deny it all you like, Mr Derbyshire, but I have the evidence to back up what I'm saying. Not only were you seen, but there is a video of the event. Sally Rathbone did not appear at all comfortable with this kiss. She pushed you away, then slapped your face and shouted at you. Is there anything you'd like to tell us about that incident?'

The tightening of Mark Derbyshire's jaw was virtually imperceptible, but Jemima spotted it. She also witnessed the vein in his left temple begin to throb slightly. Though when he spoke, his voice was calm and measured.

'I take it that you are referring to an incident which occurred ten days ago in the Rathbones' rear garden? But there is a perfectly reasonable explanation for what happened that day. And I assure you that you are misinterpreting what you've seen.'

'Then enlighten us, Mr Derbyshire,' said Jemima.

'On the day in question, I'd popped home to collect some documents that I'd forgotten to take to Chambers. I knew that Sally was home alone. It was her day off. I'd ordered a surprise present for Mariella and Sally had taken it in. She'd sent me a text to tell me that I could pick up the parcel whenever it was convenient. I replied by text a few hours later, telling her that I was on my way around to collect it. She then responded saying that she was in the garden and would leave the side gate open.

'When I arrived, I found Sally in tears. Apparently, she'd lost a ring which her grandmother had given her. I believe it was a diamond and ruby cluster. She told me that it was quite expensive. But, that aside, it was the sentimental attachment which caused the most upset. She said it was the only thing she had of her grandmother's.

'Sally had virtually turned the place upside down trying to find it. She'd worn it a few days earlier when she'd gone to the New Theatre with Mariella. Sally was sure that she had put it back in her jewellery box for safekeeping. To cut a long story short, I could see how distressed she was. So I put my arms around her. And yes, I did kiss her, but not in a passionate way. We're friends. It was a gesture to show that I empathized with her.'

'That still doesn't explain why she pushed you away and shouted at you,' said Jemima.

'I was getting to that if you'll allow me to continue,' said Mark. 'I'm not good with all that emotional stuff. I'm sure Mariella will tell you that I'm not the most sympathetic of people. In fact, I'm sure she'll describe me as emotionally repressed. My wife frequently points out that I have a knack of being far too blunt. It comes from having a career where I have to deal only in facts, things which I can prove. Well, unfortunately, this was an occasion when Sally didn't want to be told that it was only a ring, and if it didn't turn up, she could always buy herself a replacement.

'In retrospect, I appreciate that it was a crass thing to say. I have to admit I was shocked when Sally slapped my face and started shouting at me. But that's all there was to the incident. I wasn't making a move on Sally. Mariella knows all about it. She even said that she'd have slapped me too if she'd have been in Sally's shoes. Why don't you ask her about it? She'll confirm what I've just said.'

* * *

'What did you make of Mark Derbyshire?' Jemima asked Broadbent, after the barrister had left the building.

'He's supremely confident. I don't think much would faze him. But I wouldn't expect anything less from someone who spends their life putting on a performance to defend their clients. If he couldn't blag his way out of trouble, then there'd be no hope for the scumbags he represents.'

'My thoughts exactly,' said Jemima as they entered the incident room.

'Great timing,' said Peters, as he waved a piece of paper in the air. 'My contact's come through with the address. It seems that Bradley Rathbone's ex-wife lives a few miles from Lisvane.'

'Well, that definitely puts her in the frame. I think it's time we brought her in for questioning. It's your turn to drive, Dan,' said Jemima, as she tossed him the car keys.

CHAPTER 20

According to their information, the former Mrs Rathbone had reverted to her maiden name and was now known as Isobel Jones. Upon release from prison, she had gone to live with her sister Zoe, in a house on a small residential development near to Caerphilly Castle.

The journey up Caerphilly Mountain was slow and tortuous on the Cardiff side until Jemima and Broadbent reached the sharp bend at the Traveller's Rest, where the road dipped for a short while before ascending again towards the summit. But once they'd turned off near the Mountain Snack Bar, the view across the Caerphilly basin was spectacular. It was easy to spot the castle, with its moat and leaning tower, located right at the heart of the town centre.

As they pulled up in front of Zoe Jones's house, Jemima decided she was keen to study Isobel's response when they turned up unannounced on the doorstep. If she were the killer, she would undoubtedly be expecting a police visit, but if she had nothing to do with the terrible events at the Rathbone home, she would be surprised at the very least, and Jemima was pretty sure she could tell a genuine response from a faked one, no matter how good a liar someone was.

They got out of the car and headed for the front door. As Jemima pressed the bell, she could hear the sound of Westminster chimes announcing their arrival.

No one answered, but Jemima could just about make out the outlines of at least two people through the glass panel. She pressed the bell again and hammered on the door with the flat of her hand. This time it got their attention, and she could see the outlines move as one of them approached.

Moments later, the door opened to reveal a short, stocky man. He had a thick monobrow, narrow eyes and a scowl. Every inch of him suggested he abused steroids. His jeans looked uncomfortably tight as the material strained over his quadriceps, and at least three of the buttons on his shirt looked as though they were about to pop. His shirt collar was open, and Jemima could see that his thick neck was covered in tattoos, as were the backs of his hands.

'You better have a damn good reason for interrupting us like that.' His voice was a growl as he stepped forward to fill the space directly in front of Jemima.

'I'm looking for Isobel Jones,' said Jemima. She held out her warrant card to let him know he should back off.

'Well, she's not here,' he said, glaring defiantly at her.

'Who's there?' called a woman coming forward from the rear of the property. She looked pale, anxious, and was clearly upset. Her eyes were bloodshot, and she quickly wiped them on the sleeve of her cardigan.

'Are you Isobel?' enquired Jemima.

'She's my sister,' the woman replied shakily.

'I haven't got time for this. I'm outta here,' announced the man, barging forward and forcing Jemima to step back. 'I'll catch up with you later, Zoe.'

'I'm Detective Inspector Huxley, from the South Wales Police,' Jemima told Zoe. 'This is Detective Sergeant Broadbent. We need to speak to Isobel.'

'She's not here right now.'

'Who was that man?' asked Jemima.

'No one important.'

'Really?' said Jemima, raising her eyebrows in disbelief. 'Only you seem quite upset.'

'If you must know, he's a neighbour. He just called round to tell me that his dog's died. He knew that I liked her. That's why I was crying.'

Jemima silently gave the woman credit for coming up with the excuse on the spot, but Zoe was definitely lying.

'Isobel lives with you, doesn't she?' pressed Jemima.

'That's right. It's part of her parole conditions, but you'd know that. Look, what's this about? Why do you want to speak to my sister?'

'It's in connection to a current investigation. When was the last time you saw her?' asked Jemima.

'This isn't right. You just told me that you're from the South Wales Police? Well, this is Gwent's area, not South Wales, so, come on, what's this about?' demanded Zoe. Her face hardened, and she crossed her arms in defiance. 'I'm not answering any questions about my sister until you tell me what's going on.'

Jemima was about to speak when she noticed Zoe looking over Broadbent's shoulder. Jemima turned to find a woman walking towards them, and as she stared, her eyes were drawn to an over-full hessian bag slung over the woman's shoulder. Crumpled clothes spilled out over the top and sides. Even from a few feet away, Jemima could see that they were bloodstained.

'Isobel Jones?' asked Jemima.

'Yes,' the woman replied.

'Give me the bag,' demanded Jemima, holding her hand out.

'What are you talking about? Who are you?' said Isobel.

Jemima was dumbfounded. There was far too much blood on the clothing for there to be an innocent explanation, yet Isobel appeared unconcerned.

'Isobel Jones, I am arresting you on suspicion of the murders of Bradley, Sally, Lauren and Jonathan Rathbone. And the attempted murder of Millie Rathbone. Anything you say may be given in evidence. Cuff her, Broadbent,' Jemima ordered.

'What are you talking about?' wailed Isobel. 'I haven't killed anyone! You have to believe me.'

'These items suggest otherwise,' said Broadbent as he struggled to get the handcuffs on her.

'I can explain,' she cried.

'You can explain down at the station,' said Jemima. She grabbed Isobel's shoulder and led her towards the car.

'Which station are you taking her to?' shouted Zoe.

'Cardiff,' said Broadbent.

'I haven't done anything,' Isobel screamed. 'Don't let them take me, Zo.'

'Don't worry, Izz. I'll get you a lawyer, and follow you down!'

* * *

It was a stressful journey back to the police station, with Isobel wailing inconsolably about how she had been wrongfully arrested. The woman was getting on their nerves, and both Jemima and Broadbent were glad to hand her over to the custody sergeant.

'This is Isobel Jones,' Jemima explained. 'I've arrested her on suspicion of murder. Broadbent will stay with her until you've booked her in. We need these articles of clothing sent off for testing. And get a doctor to assess her. I want everything done by the book. Arrange for a female officer to take over from Broadbent as I don't want the suspect left on her own. Oh, and her sister's organizing a brief, so let me know when they turn up.'

CHAPTER 21

As Jemima entered the interview room with Broadbent, she immediately picked up on the tension between Isobel Jones and her lawyer. It was clear neither woman had been inclined to speak to the other. Their silence and body language screamed mutual contempt.

Jemima was surprised to discover that Zoe had asked Sophie Llewellyn to represent her sister. Sophie had proved herself to be more than capable on many occasions, but it was a well-known fact that she had suffered the heartache of three miscarriages and a still-birth. And Jemima knew from personal experience how an unfulfilled maternal instinct messed with your head. It was a reasonable assumption that it could affect judgement and impartiality when having to deal with a woman who had murdered her own child.

'I do not wish to be represented by this woman,' said Isobel. She glared defiantly at Jemima and Broadbent before either of them had even had a chance to sit down.

'Your sister has instructed me to represent you,' said Sophie.

'Well, I don't want you here!' snapped Isobel.

'Ladies!' Jemima jumped in. 'This squabbling has to stop. As this interview is about to commence, I will give

Isobel a few moments to decide whether or not she wishes to have you as her legal representative. But should you not wish to avail yourself of Ms Llewellyn's expertise then, given the serious nature of the charges against you, I would strongly advise you to use the services of the duty solicitor.'

'I don't need any legal representation,' countered Isobel. 'I haven't done anything wrong.'

'So, to be clear, are you discharging Ms Llewellyn?'

'Yes,' said Isobel. 'I want her to leave.'

'What a waste of my time,' grumbled the lawyer, as she walked towards the door.

'Would you like me to call the duty solicitor?' asked Jemima.

'I've already said that there's no need,' Isobel replied. 'I'm happy to answer your questions. I would have spoken to you at my sister's house, but you didn't give me a chance. You saw the bloodstained clothes and jumped to the wrong conclusion.'

'OK, we'll start the interview,' said Jemima. She started with the usual formalities and then began her questions. 'Yesterday afternoon, Bradley, Sally, Lauren and Jonathan Rathbone were discovered at their home address, having been murdered. Your daughter Millie Rathbone was also found there. She was unconscious, having sustained severe injuries. She underwent surgery, and although she survived, her prognosis is uncertain.

'When you were arrested earlier this evening you were found in possession of clothing covered in a substantial amount of dried blood. Those items of clothing have subsequently been sent off to our laboratory to establish whether or not the blood is from any of the victims.'

'It's not,' Isobel interrupted, 'and you're wasting time interviewing me.'

'Are those items of clothing yours?'

'Yes.'

'How did they get covered in blood?'

'A woman from work — her name's Rhona Cambridge — called me shortly after eight o'clock yesterday morning.

91

She recently split up with her husband. His name's Tony Cambridge. He's a thug, who's made her life hell. He's dodgy through and through. Rhona's better than that. She'd laid it on the line for him and told him to clean up his act or she'd leave him. But he didn't take her seriously, so in the end, she packed up her things and walked out on him. That was about a week ago, and she's been staying at her sister's ever since. Her sister's away at the moment, so Rhona has the place all to herself.'

'Get to the point, Isobel,' said Jemima, sighing impatiently.

'Two days ago, I'd just finished my shift and was heading home when I came across Rhona having an argument with her ex. I didn't know much about her up until that point in time. I'd seen her on the tills but hadn't taken much notice of her. I don't like getting involved with people after what I've been through.

'Anyway, this guy had her pinned up against a wall with a hand around her throat. He towered over her and was shouting and jabbing his finger into her chest. I could see that she was scared. My initial reaction was to turn around and walk away. I was about to, but at that moment she glanced towards me, and I could see in her eyes that she was begging me to help her. I got out my phone and shouted across to say that I was filming it and calling the police. Luckily, it was enough to bring him to his senses. He told her that it wasn't over and she'd better watch her back. But then he turned, looked right through me and walked away as though nothing had happened.

'My legs were like jelly, and my heart was racing. Rhona was sobbing and shaking like a leaf. Against my better judgement, I told her that I'd walk her home. That was when she filled me in on her car crash of a life. It was the first time since my daughter was killed that I actually felt sorry for someone else. That probably sounds awful to you. But then again, you've no idea what it's like to be me, and have to live with what's happened.'

Jemima raised her eyebrows but said nothing.

'Anyway, I gave Rhona my number and told her to call me if she ever needed someone to talk to. I didn't expect to get a call from her yesterday morning. She said that her ex-husband was outside her sister's place. Rhona was convinced he was going to hurt her.'

'If that's the case, then why didn't she call the police?' asked Broadbent.

'Would it ever occur to you that she probably doesn't trust the police? You see, it's easy to view the police positively when you're part of a privileged demographic group. But it's an unfortunate fact of life that actual justice is very much linked to who you are. There's a correlation based upon your perceived worth to society.'

'No, there isn't,' countered Jemima. She was annoyed by the rubbish this woman was spouting.

'Oh, you're so misguided,' said Isobel. 'Funnily enough, there was a time when I would have said precisely the same thing as you. But that was before Lydia was murdered and I was sent to prison for a crime I didn't commit.

'Rhona Cambridge knew that the police wouldn't take the threats seriously. She's not a white, well-connected, middle-class woman. She's mixed-race, poorly educated and lives in one of the roughest housing estates in the area. Rhona knew her wellbeing wasn't a police priority. But she had to get to work. She couldn't afford to call in sick or turn up late. She was already on a warning. That's why she rang me.

'I told her to stay inside and wait until I got there. I was going to threaten her ex with the police again if he didn't leave her alone. But by the time I arrived, I could see that he'd forced the door. I was scared, but I had to go in. Luckily for me, he'd already gone, but I found Rhona in a heap on the floor. She was unconscious. He'd beaten her to a pulp. I wouldn't have recognized her if I hadn't known it was her.

'I phoned for an ambulance, followed the instructions the operator gave me to check that her airway was clear, and I placed her in the recovery position. That's why my clothes were covered in blood. It was Rhona's. While the paramedics were seeing to her, I quickly changed into some of Rhona's clothes, and left the bloodstained ones at her place. I went in the ambulance with her and gave a statement to the police. And I'd say that it gives me an iron-clad alibi. Wouldn't you?'

'And the incident was investigated by Gwent police?' asked Jemima.

'Yes,' said Isobel.

'So why did you leave it until today to collect your clothes?' asked Broadbent.

'Because they kept Rhona in hospital overnight,' Isobel replied. 'I couldn't just go into someone else's house without them being there. They discharged her this afternoon and she rang me up and asked me to call around.'

'I'll get someone to check out your story. Until then, you'll return to the holding cell,' said Jemima.

* * *

'She didn't do it,' said Broadbent, as he and Jemima headed back to their desks.

'Doesn't seem likely,' Jemima agreed. 'It's a hell of a story to concoct — verifiable by all sorts of people. Check it out though. Touch base with Gwent. Get the incident number and ask them to forward the details on to us. The quicker it's sorted, the faster we can rule her out of the investigation. But we should still have those clothes tested, just to be sure.'

'The front desk rang to say there's a Zoe Jones demanding to see you,' Peters told Jemima.

'Shit! I suppose I'd better go and eat some humble pie.'

'Do you want me to go and talk to her?' asked Broadbent.

'No, it's fine. I made the decision to arrest Isobel, so this is on me.'

CHAPTER 22

Zoe Jones spotted Jemima as she entered the reception area and strode out to meet her with all the bravado of a boxer coming out of their corner at the sound of the bell. It didn't take a genius to see that Zoe wasn't about to be fobbed off. The woman's eyes had a hard, flinty edge to them.

'What have you done with my sister?' she hissed, through lips so tight they barely moved.

'Take a breath. You need to calm down,' said Jemima, holding her hands down and splaying her fingers in a conciliatory gesture.

'Don't tell me what to do. I've every right to be angry. I can assure you that Isobel didn't kill Bradley and the others.'

'I'm beginning to think you're right. Come and take a seat over here. I want to discuss a few things with you.' Jemima turned and led the way to a small waiting room.

'Are you admitting that you made a mistake?' challenged Zoe. She dropped heavily on to the vacant chair.

'It's looking that way. But given Isobel's connection to the victims and the fact that she was in possession of bloodied clothing, I had no choice but to arrest her.'

'Even so, this will have had a detrimental effect on Isobel. It's another wrongful arrest. It will have caused all sorts of awful memories to resurface. Things she's fought hard to try to move on from. You have to appreciate just how fragile my sister is. She's worked hard to put her life back together. Each day's a struggle for her. This incident could easily set her back, and I'll be the one left to pick up the pieces. You said earlier that Millie survived. How's she doing?'

'She sustained significant injuries and underwent surgery. At the moment it's too early to know whether there'll be permanent damage.'

'And you thought Isobel was responsible?' said Zoe, shaking her head in disbelief.

'As I said, given the crime scene, her links with the victims, and the fact that Isobel had clothes that were covered in a significant amount of blood, I had no choice but to arrest her. Since then, your sister has given a compelling account of where she was yesterday and explained why the clothes were covered in blood. My sergeant is currently verifying her story. If it all checks out, she'll be free to leave. Hopefully, it shouldn't take too long.'

'I know my sister. She doesn't have a bad bone in her body. She would have been terrified when you brought her in. I accept that you had your reasons for doing it, but you've forced her to relive her biggest fear. When she's stressed she has panic attacks and night terrors.'

'You just said it was another wrongful arrest. You believe that your sister didn't kill her baby, even though she was found guilty?' asked Jemima. She knew that it had nothing to do with the current investigation but was unable to stop herself from asking.

'Excuse me?' exclaimed Zoe. Her voice had ratcheted up a notch, and she slammed her fists on the table in front of her. 'I don't have to explain myself to you, Inspector. I've always known that my sister was innocent. The guilty verdict was yet another miscarriage of justice. Aren't we the lucky ones, supposedly having one of the best legal systems in the world?' It was impossible not to notice the sarcasm dripping from each word.

'I believe that we get it right most of the time,' said Jemima, speaking in an even tone.

'You keep telling yourself that if it helps you sleep better at night. But as far as I'm concerned, you lot are more than capable of fitting people up.'

'What do you mean by that?' asked Jemima, bristling at the woman's put-down.

'Oh I haven't got the time or the inclination to have that particular conversation. Now, if you don't mind, I'll go back to the reception area and wait for my innocent sister to be released.'

* * *

Jemima headed back upstairs, puzzled and annoyed by Zoe Jones's outburst.

At the trial, independent medical evidence had been presented showing that Lydia Rathbone had not died of natural causes and claiming that Isobel had been suffering from post-natal depression. Throughout the police investigation there had never been any suggestion of anyone else's involvement in the child's murder.

But Lydia's murder had been dealt with. Justice had been served. If Gwent police were able to confirm Isobel Jones's story, and the timeframe ruled her out of committing the murders, then Jemima would never have to see the woman again. And that would suit her just fine.

Broadbent looked up as Jemima walked back towards her desk. He raised a hand to call her over.

'Any progress?' she asked.

'Gwent have confirmed the incident. The call came in shortly after eight o'clock yesterday morning. It's been verified as originating from Isobel's phone. The paramedics were in attendance when the police arrived. They all commented on the fact that Isobel's clothes were covered in blood. The paramedics praised her actions, said she'd stayed calm and followed telephone instructions to the letter, which helped

97

the victim. She travelled to the hospital in the ambulance, and while the victim was being treated, Isobel gave a statement to the police.'

'Was anyone able to confirm how long Isobel remained at the hospital?' asked Jemima.

'A couple of the nurses said that she was at the victim's bedside until at least six o'clock yesterday evening.'

'So she's in the clear,' said Jemima. 'OK then, ring the custody sergeant and tell him to release her without charge.'

CHAPTER 23

As she headed home for the night, Jemima's thoughts were many and muddled. So far, every potential lead had provided false hope. Despite working diligently, they were no closer to establishing a motive for the murders, or to identifying the killer. Every theory about the case was based on conjecture. As they pushed ahead to try to establish the facts, they kept finding that they had got it wrong.

It had been a day of gathering facts and testing the water to see if anything would bite. So far, the scattergun approach had thrown up more questions than answers. It was clear that there were a few people who held grudges against either Bradley or Sally. And it was possible that at least one of those grudges may have festered to the point where someone wanted to hurt them. Though, any possible motives only related to the adults.

What didn't make sense was that the killer had suffocated two of the children. And their deaths clearly hadn't satisfied him as he'd gone on to carry out frenzied attacks on their corpses. The question that had to be answered was whether or not the excessive level of violence inflicted upon the children was undertaken to intensify the emotional pain the adults would feel when they discovered the bodies? Or was Jemima looking at this in the wrong way, and the children were actually the primary focus of the attack?

It had been another tough day and Jemima was exhausted. There had been no time to think about anything other than the case. And with everything that was going on at home at the moment, she wished she had taken time out to check in on Nick and James.

Nick had been resentful of her having to go to work. Jemima sensed that his resentment would have intensified throughout the day. She should have called him. At least it would have demonstrated that she cared. As it was, her lack of thought meant that he was sure to bang on about her job being the most important thing in her life.

Jemima was also worried about how James was coping with the death of his mother. Her heart went out to him. It was impossible not to love him. She'd felt that way about him from the moment he came into her life. He was adorable, loving, open and accepting of her relationship with his father. Jemima had spent many years wishing that the boy could have been her own child. And now, with Wendy's untimely death, her wish had been granted. He was not of her bloodline, but that didn't matter. She was determined to look after him as if he was her own.

As much as she loved James, she was under no illusion that they would face problems along the way. James hadn't had a close relationship with his mother, as Wendy Huxley hadn't been the most loving parent towards her son. Wendy's top priority had always been her own self-interest. Her next had been making life awkward for Nick. In the past, James had told Jemima he wished that she was his mother instead, but Jemima knew that it was one thing for a child to say that and quite another having the reality foisted upon them.

Then there was Nick. Things hadn't been great between them since the incident at Harry Broadbent's christening party. And after their argument last night . . . Well, they'd just have to put their personal problems aside and do what was right for James. The boy needed them to be strong for him. And Jemima was determined that that was what would happen.

As Jemima opened the front door, the first thing she noticed was the silence. It was immediately disconcerting. She knew that Nick and James were at home as she'd seen Nick's car on the drive. He never went anywhere without it. There was always music blaring from some part of the house whenever Nick was home. And James spent much of his time watching the TV or playing some noisy game on his console.

'Hello?' she called.

There was no answer. The door to the lounge was closed. Jemima opened it and tiptoed into the room to find James on the sofa. He was curled up in the foetal position, sucking his thumb. It was a habit he'd grown out of almost four years earlier.

Jemima knelt down in front of him and stroked his hair. His eyes flickered as he focused on her, noticing her for the first time.

'Do you want a *cwtch*?' she asked.

James didn't need to be asked twice. He always loved having cuddles. He nodded his head and scooted over so that Jemima could lean back and wrap her arms around him. She held him tight, wanting the boy to know that he was safe and loved.

James clung to her as though his life depended upon it, and his small body radiated heat. Jemima kissed his head and felt him relax against her. It wasn't long before James's tears began to flow. His body heaved as he let go of a well of pent-up emotions. He sobbed loudly and unashamedly. It broke Jemima's heart that this amazing boy, who she would willingly lay down her life for, was forced to cope with something an adult would have difficulty coming to terms with.

It took a while for James to quieten down. Jemima didn't know how long they'd sat there, but her arms ached from holding him so close. Eventually, his breathing slowed to a regular rhythm and she noticed that his eyes had closed. He was finally asleep.

Jemima needed to move. She struggled to change her position, doing her best not to disturb James more than necessary. The last thing she wanted was for him to wake up. She cradled his head and gently placed it on a cushion. She draped a throw over his body to ensure he stayed warm.

There was still no sign of Nick. Jemima was puzzled until she went into the kitchen and found him slumped at the table with a half-empty bottle of whisky. Nick raised his head as she approached. As he looked up, she could see that his eyes were glazed. He was clearly having trouble trying to focus.

'You're a selfish bastard,' she hissed. The disregard he had shown for his son was contemptible.

Nick didn't respond but picked up the bottle to pour himself another glass. Infuriated by his attitude, Jemima snatched it from his hand and poured the contents down the sink.

'Wha' you doin'?' he slurred.

'You've had more than enough. You should be ashamed of yourself, getting rat-arsed while your son has to cope with his grief on his own. What sort of a man are you?'

'You can talk. You lef' me to deal with this on m'own,' he complained. 'You' job's a'ways more 'portant than eve'thing else. It's 'bout time you started to pu' us firs'. I needed you today, and you weren't there f'r me.'

'Keep your voice down, or you'll wake James,' hissed Jemima. 'Stay there while I get him off to bed. I'll talk to you later.'

'Wherever,' said Nick, as he folded his arms on the table and rested his head on them.

Jemima eventually returned to the kitchen to find that Nick was no longer there. While she'd seen to James, Nick had made his way into the lounge and was now fast asleep on the sofa, covered by the blanket that she had used to comfort James.

Nick snored loudly. Deep, grating rasps that made Jemima despise him more than she would ever have thought possible. She was livid. Instead of feeling sorry for himself, he should have put his son's needs first. But apparently that had been too much for the selfish, drunken sod.

Jemima had no intention of helping her husband get to bed. Nick could spend the night on the sofa. With a bit of luck he'd wake up with a hangover and have a crick in his neck.

CHAPTER 24

The following morning, Jemima tiptoed into the bedroom to check on James. Finding him still asleep, she was determined not to wake him.

Surprisingly, Nick had already surfaced and was sitting at the kitchen table, looking pale and unhealthy. His hair was greasy, sticking up at all sorts of strange angles, while his eyes were bloodshot and heavy-lidded.

'I'm surprised you're awake, after the amount you put away yesterday.'

'Take it down a notch. My head's banging,' Nick muttered.

'I wonder why?' she said. Her voice dripped with sarcasm. 'You're an absolute disgrace. I've already called my father and he's agreed to take James to school. It wouldn't be safe for you to drive — you'd still be over the limit. Let James sleep for another hour then get him up and make sure he has breakfast. But you have to promise to pick him up after school, Nick. Don't let James down again today.'

'And what about you, Jem? What are you going to do to help James?'

'I'm the one who came home from work yesterday to find him staring blankly at the wall while you were virtually comatose from all the alcohol you'd poured down your neck.

You're his father, Nick. So get a grip. Take a shower before he wakes up. Tidy yourself up. You look and smell like a wino,' snapped Jemima, as she headed for the front door.

'That's it, Jem. Do what you do best. Just walk away from our problems!' yelled Nick.

Jemima had no intention of rising to the bait. She kept walking and refused to turn around.

* * *

Ashton was already at his desk when Jemima arrived at work.

'How're you feeling today?' she asked.

'Fighting fit and raring to go,' he said.

'Word to the wise, Kennedy's gunning for you. He's going to give you a bollocking. If I were you, I'd just take it. Act contrite. Tell him you've learned your lesson, and you'll never do anything like that again. You put us both at risk when you entered that house. Though I've already pointed out to him that if you hadn't gone in, Jason Venter might not be alive. Anyway, it's desk duty for you for the rest of the week.'

'No change there then,' he griped.

'Morning all!' called Peters as he strolled in.

'Hey, mate! I didn't know you were back with us,' said Ashton. He rose to shake Peters' hand.

'Right, let's get to it,' said Jemima, as Broadbent jogged into the room. 'We've got a lot of work to do. So far we haven't been able to get any substantial leads. We've presumed that the killer's primary focus was either Bradley or Sally Rathbone. But after the post-mortem findings, it's by no means certain that's the case.

'Prothero confirmed that the teenagers, Jonathan and Lauren Rathbone, were the first to die. He's based that finding on their core body temperatures. But what surprises me is the level of overkill. Both kids were asphyxiated in their beds and then stabbed repeatedly after their deaths. That suggests three possibilities. Either the killer was completely out of

105

control. Or he felt an excessive amount of rage towards these children. Or he wanted to cause the adults as much emotional distress as possible when they discovered the bodies.

'The other interesting fact is that Lauren had noticeable bruising to her neck. John Prothero seems to think it may have occurred a few days before she died, but whoever grabbed Lauren's throat didn't use enough force to break the hyoid bone, so it couldn't have been the intention to strangle her. She was also stabbed far more times than any of the other victims. I believe it's possible that Lauren may have been the main focus of the attack, but until we have some firm evidence to suggest that that was the case, we need to look at every possibility.

'To that end, we know that some of Bradley's patients were psychopaths. Peters, you've made a start on following up on some of the people from Giles Souter's list and I want you to continue with that today.'

'I'm on it.'

'Ashton, I want you to do some more digging about on Bradley's first wife, Isobel Jones, and her sister Zoe. We interviewed Isobel yesterday. She's got a cast-iron alibi for the time of the murders, but that doesn't mean she couldn't have paid someone to kill the Rathbones. Let's face it, she must have resented Bradley. After their daughter's death he left Isobel high and dry. By all accounts, he didn't make any attempt to visit her in prison and wasted no time in filing for divorce. Isobel is also estranged from her other daughter. As far as I'm aware, Millie's had no contact with her mother since the day of Lydia's death.

'Isobel has always maintained her innocence. Whether or not she was responsible for Lydia's death, she must have felt a tremendous sense of betrayal and abandonment when her husband turned his back on her. There's no suggestion that he ever gave her the benefit of the doubt.

'As things stand, we have a woman who's spent years in prison for a crime, which according to her, she didn't commit. While in prison, she would have had plenty of time to plan her revenge. Bradley and Sally had it all — lucrative careers, a beautiful house and a ready-made family. Isobel must have been livid. They've got everything. She's been left with nothing, apart from a stretch inside. She used to be a pharmacist. Now that she's out she has to adjust to working in a supermarket while relying on her sister's goodwill to provide a roof over her head. It's a hell of a comedown.'

'It's a compelling motive,' said Ashton.

'And who knows what contacts she's made on the inside,' Jemima continued. 'There would have been plenty of opportunities to be put in touch with the sort of people who would kill someone if the price was right. So, we need to look into Isobel's finances, and also those of her sister, Zoe. Those two are close. Zoe's very protective of her sister and is convinced that she went to prison for a crime she didn't commit.

'I want to know more about the Lydia Rathbone case. Were there any holes in the evidence? Does Isobel Jones have any mental health issues? She must have been assessed before her release. Is there any evidence of her having posed a threat to Millie, Bradley or Sally? You know the sort of thing we're looking for. Let's look at Zoe Jones as well. Where was she on the day of the murder? Have any large unexplained withdrawals been made from either or both of their accounts?'

'Sure thing, I'll get on it straight away,' said Ashton.

'In the meantime, Broadbent and I are going to speak to Mariella Derbyshire again.'

* * *

'Are you planning on questioning her about her husband?' Broadbent asked Jemima, as they drove to Mariella Derbyshire's house.

'Amongst other things. I also want to dig a bit deeper into the kids' backgrounds. Get a more rounded picture of Millie and find out if there was anything dodgy about Jonathan and Lauren's parents. After all, those two kids seem to have borne the brunt of the killer's rage. Come to think of it, it might be worth us looking into the speedboat crash that killed them. We're assuming that it was an accident, but maybe it wasn't.'

They arrived at Briarmarsh Close and knocked on the door.

Mariella Derbyshire gave a weary smile as she welcomed them. 'I've got about an hour before I have to head off to the surgery. It's a late start today. Can I get you both a coffee? I've just made a fresh pot. Need the caffeine in my job.'

'I was hoping you'd offer,' said Broadbent. 'I love that smell. It's so much more intense than instant.'

'Erm,' said Jemima, as she cleared her throat and shot Broadbent a disapproving look, 'I thought your husband said that you were all going to stay somewhere else for a while?'

'It's not really practical,' Mariella replied. 'We lead such busy lives and everything we need is here. Have you made any headway on the case, Inspector?'

'We're following up some leads. But I wanted to ask you about Jonathan and Lauren's parents. What do you know about them?' asked Jemima.

'Not a lot. Their names were Connor and Maggie Rathbone. Connor was Bradley's brother. I believe he was a high-flyer in the pharmaceutical industry, though I couldn't tell you which company he worked for. As for Maggie, I don't know if she had a career, but I think perhaps not. I only met her once. She seemed quite ordinary. Came across as a bit mumsy.'

'Pharmaceuticals? That's a cut-throat industry,' said Jemima.

'I've heard that said. Are you asking me whether Connor Rathbone got involved with the wrong people?' asked Mariella.

'I am,' said Jemima.

'I couldn't say. It didn't come up in any conversations I had with Sally. But then again, she may have avoided saying anything controversial about him — to me anyway. After all, if Connor had crossed the line and got caught out sometime in the future, he may have wanted to hire Mark to represent him. If I'd heard of any dodgy dealings and mentioned it to Mark, it could compromise any future chance of legal representation. But I want to make it clear that I'm not trying to keep information from you. I genuinely don't know anything else about Bradley's brother or sister-in-law.'

'I understand that the couple died in a speedboat accident?' pressed Jemima.

'Yes, that's right,' said Mariella.

'Was there any suggestion that the incident was anything other than an accident?'

'None whatsoever,' said Mariella.

'And did you ever get the impression that Jonathan or Lauren was afraid of anyone?'

'No. As I told you the other day, they were quiet and withdrawn when they arrived next door. But that was only to be expected. As time went on, they started to come out of their shells and adjust to their new circumstances. Of course, they were fortunate to have Bradley and Sally, as it provided them with some level of stability when they were most vulnerable.'

'I'm sure that helped,' said Jemima. Her thoughts momentarily turned to James and how he was struggling at the moment.

'What about Bradley and Millie?' asked Broadbent, sensing that Jemima had suddenly lost focus. 'His first wife went to prison for killing her youngest child. How did that affect them?'

'That was an awful tragedy. Mark and I were discussing it last night. I know I said previously that Sally didn't say much about it, but some other details have come back to me,' mused Mariella.

'It occurred a few years before Bradley and Millie moved in with Sally. I know that Bradley was eaten up with guilt. He blamed himself for not realizing that Isobel was suffering from postpartum psychosis. And I can understand why

Bradley felt like that. After all, mental illness was his area of expertise, and he lived with Isobel but didn't spot any of the symptoms.

'As for Millie, I never witnessed it myself, but Sally told me that the girl suffered tremendously until Isobel's trial was over. Bradley told her how Millie was terrified that Isobel would kill her too. Apparently, Bradley had asked Millie if Isobel had ever been violent towards her or threatened her in any way. Millie denied it but said that she'd not witnessed her mother act inappropriately towards Lydia, yet Isobel had still killed her. Sally told me that Millie had doted on her little sister and had been traumatized by what had happened to her. It made her reluctant to trust adults other than her father, and Sally had to work very hard to get Millie to accept her.'

'So would you describe Millie as a damaged child?' asked Jemima.

'Oh no, I wouldn't say that, but she's not a typical teenager. She's a serious girl, quite responsible for her age. She participated in games whenever we got together as families, but she never really seemed to become caught up in the moment. It was as though she didn't really understand the concept of having fun. But that could easily be a residual effect of what happened to her sister all those years ago. Bradley said that they'd had a normal, happy life up until Isobel killed Lydia.'

'Did your husband mention that Sally argued with him recently?' asked Jemima.

'I take it that you're referring to Sally's missing ring, and Mark's crass attempt to comfort her?' asked Mariella.

'That's right,' said Jemima.

'No, Mark didn't mention it. He knows me well enough to know that he wouldn't get any sympathy from me. I would have told him that he deserved the slap. It was Sally who told me. She caught up with me later that day and said she felt dreadful about the whole incident. She said that he'd hugged and kissed her, which is typical Mark. He's such a demonstrative person and a complete sucker for the whole "damsel in distress" thing.

'But then, just like a typical bloke, he had to go and spoil it by telling her that she could always buy herself another ring. He doesn't understand how someone can become emotionally attached to a possession. Of course, it was the last thing Sally wanted to hear. It wasn't the ring itself. It was the fact that it had been her grandmother's. And before she knew it, Sally slapped him across the face.

'The next time Sally saw Mark she was very sheepish. We all had a good laugh about it. She knew that she'd overreacted and didn't want to make things awkward between the four of us. Of course, it didn't. Mark told her that he was going to get her a pair of boxing gloves for her birthday.'

'Did Sally ever find the ring?' asked Broadbent.

'No. Sally was adamant that she'd placed it in the jewellery box, but it never turned up,' said Mariella.

* * *

'What did you make of that?' asked Broadbent once they had left.

'It's thrown up a few discrepancies,' said Jemima. 'For starters, if Bradley felt so guilty about not picking up on any warning signs with Isobel, then why didn't he visit her after her arrest? I can understand him eventually wanting a divorce, but postnatal depression is a recognized mental health issue. Surely he'd want to establish whether or not she was suffering from it? And then there's Mariella's admission that Mark didn't tell her about him kissing Sally, whereas Mark said that he did.'

'And when we spoke to Mark, he said that his wife thought he was emotionally repressed,' said Broadbent. 'Yet Mariella's just told us that he's very demonstrative.'

'Exactly. A few things don't add up.'

'Someone's not telling us the truth,' said Broadbent.

'And if they're prepared to lie about seemingly inconsequential facts, then what else are they prepared to lie about?' said Jemima.

CHAPTER 25

Despite the evidence that pointed at the killer's rage towards Lauren, and to a lesser extent towards Jonathan, it seemed unlikely that inquiries about the teenagers would result in a breakthrough in the case. Nevertheless, Jemima was determined to cover all the bases. That included establishing whether or not any of the teenagers had links to gangs. After all, knife crime had become more prevalent in recent years, and this was usually linked to teenage gang members. Although unlikely, there was a possibility that one of the Rathbone children could have got in with the wrong crowd.

Jemima was convinced Mariella Derbyshire had no real concerns about the Rathbone children. Indeed, Jonathan had developed a close friendship with Thomas and was a regular visitor to the Derbyshire household. It would have been unlikely that the Derbyshires would have been happy for this friendship to blossom had there been any doubts about Jonathan's behaviour.

Mariella had readily agreed that Jemima and Broadbent would return to the Derbyshire house later that day to speak to both Seth and Thomas, as the boys were more likely to know if anything had been worrying Jonathan, but Mariella had been less able to comment on the girls, as she had not spent any significant amount of time with them.

Jemima had already spoken to Stanley Aubrey, the head-master at the children's school. The man had said that he was eager to help in any way he could and suggested that she come to the school at ten o'clock that morning.

When they arrived, the secretary escorted Jemima and Broadbent to the headmaster's office. They entered the room to find that there were two other people present. The three had been mid-discussion and the conversation ended abruptly.

'You must be Inspector Huxley?' said Stanley Aubrey, standing up and offering his hand.

'That's right, and this is Sergeant Broadbent,' Jemima replied.

'I've asked the form teachers for their input in this discussion. This is Lauren and Millie's teacher, Rhian Thomas. And this is Jonathan's teacher, Tyler Black. At this school, form teachers remain with their class through each of the years, as we believe it helps with continuity of care. Rhian, perhaps you'd like to kick things off.' Stanley Aubrey gestured to the tall young woman seated immediately to his right.

'I'm the girls' form teacher,' Rhian said. 'I didn't have any direct responsibility for teaching either of them, but I would see them for a short while each day. I'm sure you'll appreciate that during that time I would have become familiar with the dynamics of that particular group of children.

'To be perfectly honest with you, I'd have to say that Millie is not a typical teenager. She sets herself apart from the others by not getting caught up with usual adolescent concerns. Millie's very self-assured, exceptionally intelligent, far more so than all but one other child in the class. In fact, she's quite possibly one of the most intelligent children I've come across.

'However, I would say that despite excelling academically I've not noticed her form any particularly close friendships, apart from with a girl called Stephanie Newton, though they only seemed to hook up with each other within the last year or so. Stephanie is the other academically gifted child I mentioned. The girls were a natural fit. You see, they're both intellectually so far ahead of their peers that they have little in common with the others. Lauren was also in the same class.'

'Was Lauren placed there to help her settle into the school after her parents died?' asked Jemima.

'No,' Stanley replied. 'Lauren and her brother were already attending this school. Their parents lived in this catchment area.'

'Lauren was entirely different to Millie,' Rhian continued. 'She had slightly above average intelligence, but with a far more rounded, easy-going personality. She had a tough time when her parents died, but she coped reasonably well. Don't get me wrong, Lauren had moments when she was down. Early on there were a couple of occasions when she ran out of the class in floods of tears. We gave her some leeway with her studies for a couple of months, but she eventually settled down. Her friends were a great comfort to her. They were very protective.'

'What about Millie, was she close to her cousin?' asked Jemima.

'They appeared to rub along together, but the girls had very different personalities,' Rhian replied. 'Lauren had a couple of very close friends that I'm aware of. As for Millie, she would join in discussions and was a member of some of the after-school clubs, but apart from Stephanie, I don't recall there being any other person that she was really friendly with. I never saw her whispering or giggling with any of the other girls, or even flirting with the boys. Millie can be charming, engaging, even funny, but I always get the impression she's holding something back. Sometimes she's quite aloof, especially if someone's upset her.'

'Are you implying that Millie has some sort of personality disorder?' asked Jemima.

'No, nothing like that,' said Rhian, shaking her head vigorously. 'I'm just saying that even though I've known her for a few years, I couldn't second-guess what's going on in that head of hers. She's quite inscrutable, but still a perfectly pleasant, well-mannered girl.'

'Tyler, how would you sum up Jonathan?' asked Stanley.

'He was a great kid, always polite and eager to please,' Tyler replied. 'He was a member of the chess club, which I run. He was a pretty smart, tactical player. There was a couple of weeks shortly after he started at the school when there was a bit of bullying from another group of lads, but we sorted that out pretty quickly, and Jonathan went on to flourish. He was very friendly with Thomas Derbyshire. I believe they're next-door neighbours?'

'That's right,' said Jemima.

'Yes, those two were inseparable. I'll have to keep a close eye on Thomas. Jonathan's death will hit him hard,' said Tyler.

'Does the school have any problems with gangs?' asked Jemima.

'Certainly not,' said Stanley, clearly shocked to have been asked the question. 'Tyler's just told you that the bullying incident involving Jonathan was resolved quickly. We have a zero-tolerance policy on anything like that. Any gang trying to operate within these grounds wouldn't last long. If a child starts to misbehave, we immediately call in their parents and make it clear that it will not be tolerated. We're not afraid to expel anyone who doesn't meet acceptable standards of behaviour. The children know it. The parents know it. And it works in our favour.'

'It would be useful if we could talk to some of the children's friends,' said Jemima.

'I can fully understand why you'd like to do that, Inspector,' said Stanley. 'But I'm not at all comfortable about those discussions taking place on these premises. Apart from the fact that it would be exceptionally disruptive having pupils taken out of classes, I feel sure that the parents would wish to be there while you talk to their children so that they can support them. Most of us have only just found out about this dreadful event. It's caused a lot of upset and heartache for everyone at this school, especially those with close ties to Jonathan, Lauren and Millie.'

* * *

Jemima and Broadbent arrived back at the police station to find Ashton and Peters busily working. Broadbent began to contact the parents of the children close to Jonathan, Lauren and Millie to set up appointments to talk to them.

'How's it going, Ashton?' Jemima asked.

'Great timing on your part, guv,' Ashton replied. 'I've just finished speaking to Isobel's parole officer. Her name's Kim Lancet, and for once, luck is on our side. She's had a meeting cancelled, so she's on her way here now. Do you want me to sit in on the interview?'

'It would be useful since you're trying to build up a picture of what Isobel's like,' said Jemima. She turned to Peters. 'Have you been able to make any progress?' she asked.

'Not a lot,' he replied. 'The people on the list you gave me are not easy to track down. I haven't been able to come up with anything yet, but I'll let you know as soon as I have.'

CHAPTER 26

As Kim Lancet entered the interview room, Jemima knew even before a word had been uttered that the woman was stressed. There were dark circles beneath her eyes, and her complexion was pale and blotchy — made worse by the fact that her cosmetics seemed to have been hastily applied and did little to hide a patchwork of broken veins spread across her nose and cheeks.

'Sorry, but I haven't got time for pleasantries,' she said 'You'll have to make this quick. I've got to be back in the office in thirty minutes.'

'You're Isobel Jones's parole officer?' asked Jemima.

'That's right. What's Isobel supposed to have done?' asked Kim, getting straight to the point.

'Nothing that we know of at the moment, but she is a person of interest in a current investigation.'

'Could you elaborate?'

'Isobel's former husband, his current wife, and two other family members were murdered a few days ago. Isobel's daughter is on life support following the incident.'

'That's awful,' said Kim. Her flat tone was at odds with the words.

'You don't sound surprised,' said Ashton.

'Oh, believe me, I am. It's just when you've been in the job as long as I have it takes a lot to shock you. I spend every working day doing my best to help people put their car-crash lives back together. By the time they come out of the prison system, they're at rock bottom. It takes a lot of determination on their part to claw their way back up. As you'll know by the number of repeat offenders that you deal with, the chance of an ex-offender going on to succeed in the real world isn't that great. So, apart from the obvious link to the victims, why is Isobel a person of interest?'

'She was convicted of killing her child, and—'

'Let me stop you there,' Kim interrupted. 'Isobel *was* convicted of killing her infant daughter and was later found to be suffering from postnatal depression, but she has never actually admitted to the crime.'

'I had heard,' said Jemima. She wondered where the woman was going with this.

'Isobel even consented to a course of regression therapy to help her come to terms with what she had done, but the therapist was unable to get her to recall the event,' Kim continued. 'Isobel remembered putting Lydia down for an afternoon nap, and she remembered checking on her later only to find her dead. The therapist said that Isobel was distraught at not being able to remember what she must have done. Of course, it's possible that the actual event was far too traumatic for Isobel to remember. But the therapist said it was also possible that Isobel's memories of that afternoon were in fact true memories, and that she didn't kill her daughter.'

'That's all very well,' said Jemima, 'but I'm far more concerned with how Isobel has been since her release from prison. How often do you see her? And what is your impression of the progress she's making?'

'That's easy,' Kim replied. 'I meet up with Isobel once a fortnight, and she's never missed an appointment. I wish all my clients were like her. She's luckier than most as her sister agreed to take her in. And, as I understand it, there's a strong support network within the local church, which both sisters attend. Fortunately for Isobel, one of the parishioners is the manager of a local supermarket, and he had a job waiting for her when she came out of prison.'

'What does she do?'

'She's part of the online shopping team. She works five days a week, starting at six in the morning and finishing at midday. It's hard physical work. Team members have to do up to six shops at once, and they're timed to ensure that no one is slacking. I keep in touch with her employer and Isobel always turns up for her shift. Some of the more elderly customers have actually taken the time to complete comment cards singling her out as being exceptionally pleasant and helpful.'

'In your opinion, do you think that Isobel would have tried to contact her daughter or ex-husband when she got out of prison?' asked Jemima.

'I wouldn't have thought so. There was no contact between Isobel and her ex from the moment she was arrested. Her husband made no attempt to see her, even when she was on remand. Isobel was so focused on Lydia's death that it all but consumed her. It certainly fuelled her depression. As I understand it, it took a long time for her to recover. She was on suicide watch for quite a while.

'Isobel is well aware of her own fragility. She didn't contest the divorce and accepted that her husband and daughter had moved on with their lives. In all honesty, I can't imagine that she would have wanted to see them again. And she certainly wouldn't have wanted to risk returning to prison for breaking the terms of her licence.'

'Has it ever crossed your mind that she has been playing you?' asked Ashton.

'Of course it crossed my mind,' Kim replied. 'My first reaction with all of my clients is to believe that they committed the crime they were incarcerated for. Most of them are as guilty as hell. And yes, a significant proportion of them try to make me believe that they were wrongly convicted. I've heard it so many times, and quite frankly it bores me. The way some of them bleat on about it, I think they've told the lie so often that they believe it's the truth.

'But Isobel's different. She doesn't play the martyr. I can say without any hesitation that she punishes herself far more than any justice system could. I've not once heard her say that life has dealt her a bad hand or try to blame anyone else for what happened. Her biggest concern is that she cannot remember the moments leading up to Lydia's death. She cannot recall walking into that nursery, picking up that cushion, placing it over her child's face and pressing down so hard that it caused extensive bruising, broke the child's nose and suffocated her. It was an act of excessive force. It wasn't a random act of desperation. And Isobel genuinely can't remember doing it.

'You probably don't know this, but Isobel wears a locket containing a photograph of Lydia. I'd asked her on many occasions if the locket had any special significance, but she'd change the subject so that she could avoid answering. It was only a couple of weeks ago that she showed me the photograph and told me that it was the only way she could keep her daughter close to her heart. You may think it was a corny thing to say. But if you'd seen the pain in that woman's eyes and heard the way her voice cracked as she finally opened up to me, you'd know that she wasn't capable of killing that child.'

* * *

'What did you make of that?' asked Ashton, as they headed back to the incident room.

'Kim Lancet obviously believes that Isobel Jones was wrongly convicted of killing her child, and if that's true it's less likely she would be capable of murdering anyone else,' said Jemima.

'Hey, guv!' said Peters. 'I've finally located Aileen Whittle. I was starting to think I wasn't going to get anywhere, but my persistence paid off.'

'Well done, Gareth,' said Jemima. 'What do you have on her?'

'Aileen's gone and got herself a husband. About four months ago, she bagged herself a rich hubby and became Aileen Schofield.'

'Is that supposed to mean something to me?' asked Jemima.

'Her husband's Harvey Schofield.'

'Harvey Schofield . . . isn't he the property magnate?' asked Jemima.

'Did I hear someone mention Harvey Schofield?' asked Kennedy, as he walked into the room and perched on the edge of the nearest desk.

'You did,' said Peters. 'His wife is on our list of potential murder suspects in the Rathbone case.'

'A word to the wise, lad, you need to tread carefully. Schofield is a powerful and influential man. He's as rich as Croesus and better connected than the national grid. If half of what I've heard about him is true, he's got some high-level politicians in his pocket.

'I'm not telling you to back off on this line of inquiry, but I need to know that if it comes down to it, you have reasonable cause to bring his wife in for questioning. It's not enough that she's a name on a list. You have to establish means, motive and opportunity before you take the next step. Because if you bring her in and it ends up that she had nothing to do with these murders, then we could all be out on our arses. And I for one don't want to lose my pension.

'Schofield's high profile. Loves the limelight. Never shies away from a photo opportunity, and he'd most likely want his new wife on his arm. So put some effort into tracing his movements over the last week. See if you can establish whether Aileen was with him. There are always official photographers at the events people like him attend. At least that way we should be able to determine whether or not Aileen has an alibi for the time of the murders. And don't forget to keep me informed.'

'And there you have it,' muttered Jemima, once Kennedy had left. 'We can't do things the easy way, as Aileen's suddenly become a special case.'

'Constable Riley called around while you were interviewing Isobel Jones's parole officer,' Broadbent told her. 'She said that she's spoken to all of Jason Venter's neighbours, and it seems that he was telling us the truth about being home that day. He gets on well with the people living either side of him and socializes with them whenever he's in Cardiff.

'Frank Cheeseman, who lives three doors away from Jason, said that, at eight o'clock that morning, he and Jason went to the opening of the Better Life Fitness Centre in Llandaff. There's been a lot of hype about it on the local radio. The owner had arranged for a local celebrity to come and cut the ribbon. The first fifty to sign up that morning got a free session with a personal trainer and a complimentary sauna. Jason and Frank were practically the first ones through the doors. He reckons they were there until well past midday.

'On the way home, they called into the Plough and Horses to meet their girlfriends for lunch. Riley said that Cheeseman's story checks out. There was CCTV coverage verifying their time at the gym. The landlord and some of the bar staff confirmed that the four of them were at the pub until about five o'clock. By all accounts, they seem to have made quite an afternoon of it, which makes me wonder why they bothered going to the gym in the first place. One of Venter's next-door neighbours recalls seeing the four of them arrive home about half an hour later, so I'd say Venter's definitely not our guy.'

'I just don't understand why he would agree to attend a charity event in London, and then be a no-show,' said Jemima. 'You'd think he'd be worried about damaging his reputation.'

'Artists are known for being temperamental,' said Ashton.

'I don't know about temperamental,' replied Jemima. 'It seems downright rude to me. A phone call or text message doesn't take much effort. Well, I suppose we can cross Jason Venter off our list of suspects.'

CHAPTER 27

'I've just taken a call from the front desk to say that the Rathbone kids' friends and their parents have started to arrive,' said Peters.

'Who's there at the moment?' asked Jemima.

'Yasmin Brookes and Thea Mantel. Their mothers are with them. They travelled in together.'

'They were Lauren's friends?' asked Jemima.

'That's what it says on the list,' confirmed Peters.

'OK, show the four of them up. I may as well speak to the girls together. They may feel more comfortable that way, and be more ready to open up.'

'Do you need me with you on this, guv?' asked Broadbent.

'No, since Peters is bogged down with Aileen Schofield, I'd like you to look into the speedboat accident which killed Bradley's brother and sister-in-law. It may have nothing to do with these murders, but then again it might just be the missing link.'

* * *

The girls and their mothers were already in the interview room when Jemima arrived.

One of the girls was small, blonde, and almost doll-like in appearance. Her skin was so pale that veins were visible near her eyes and on her neck. She tensed as Jemima approached, and began tearing strips from a tissue she was gripping.

The other was taller, with short, dark hair that emphasized sharp cheekbones. She initially appeared more confident than her friend, sitting straight, her head angled with a defiant tilt, but Jemima quickly realized it was more bravado than confidence, as the girl made no attempt to make eye contact.

Jemima smiled, hoping to put the girls at ease. She was sensitive to the possibility that this was their first experience of death and almost certainly their first encounter with such a violent one. Losing their friend like this would have hit them hard.

'Hello, I'm Detective Inspector Huxley,' she said. 'I'm doing everything I can to find out who did this awful thing to Lauren and her family. Mums, this is just an informal chat with your daughters. They may have information which would be useful to our investigation. And girls, thank you so much for agreeing to come in to talk to me today. You don't need to look so worried. You're not in any trouble. I understand that you were both close friends of Lauren?'

Both girls nodded.

'Well, that's all I want to talk to you about. I need your help to build up a picture of what Lauren was like. Is that OK with you?'

Both girls nodded again, more vigorously this time.

'It's Thea and Yasmin, right? So tell me, who's who?' Jemima asked, looking from one girl to the other.

'I'm Yasmin,' said the dark-haired girl, raising a hand in front of her chest.

'Hi, Yasmin. Hi, Thea.' Jemima hoped her voice sounded reassuring. She needed these girls to open up to her. 'I can see that you're both very upset about what happened to Lauren. I am too. My team and I are doing our very best to find out who did this awful thing and send them to prison for a very long time.

'Lauren can't speak for herself, but I'm sure that she confided in you about things she may not have told anyone else. It's what best friends do. She may have told you something which might not seem important to you, but it could help us find out who attacked her. Are you willing to help me?'

Both girls nodded again.

'Excellent. Let's get started,' said Jemima. 'So how long have you both known Lauren?'

'We've been friends since primary school,' said Yasmin.

'We've always been in the same class as each other,' confirmed Thea. As she spoke, she placed the mound of shredded tissue on the desk in front of her.

'Did the three of you spend time at each other's houses?'

'Yeah,' said Yasmin. 'We've been to both of Lauren's houses. Her parents died just over a year ago, then she and Jonathan went to live with their uncle.'

'And where was her parents' house?' asked Jemima.

'It was in Cyncoed, about a mile from where she lives . . . lived in Lisvane,' said Thea. For those few moments it appeared that she'd forgotten her friend was dead. As reality hit home once again, her shoulders slumped under the strain of what had happened.

'Did you know her mum and dad well?' asked Jemima. She was determined to push on with the questioning.

'We knew her mum,' said Yasmin. 'She was great. Whenever we'd go there, she'd bake us lovely cupcakes.'

'Yeah, they were the best,' said Thea. 'She'd decorate them with loads of fondant icing. She'd put sweets and chocolates on them too. We always wanted to go round there for tea.'

'Those cakes sound amazing,' said Jemima. 'And did you ever have any sleepovers at the house?'

'Yeah, of course we did. We'd all take it in turns,' said Thea.

'So, did you often see Lauren's dad?' asked Jemima.

'Sometimes,' said Yasmin, shrugging her shoulders. 'He was always busy working. Lauren used to say that she wished he'd spend more time at home.'

'And did Lauren say if her parents used to argue much?' asked Jemima.

'No. She said her parents always held hands and kissed each other a lot. To be honest, it sounded a bit gross. They were far too old for that sort of thing,' said Yasmin.

'So Lauren hadn't been worried about her parents at all?' pressed Jemima.

'Definitely not,' said Yasmin, shaking her head emphatically.

'And when Lauren moved in with her uncle, did you have sleepovers over there?'

'Yeah, but not so many,' said Thea. 'It wasn't the same at her uncle's house. He was nice, and Sally was great, but Millie always used to spoil things.'

'In what way?' asked Jemima.

'She didn't like us,' said Yasmin. 'The three of us were into fashion. It was our thing. We like buying loads of things, mixing, matching, upcycling. She used to say we were stupid kids. She'd tell us to stop making so much noise. She'd barge into Lauren's room, and like, spoil things for us. So we stopped going around there so much.'

'What did Lauren think of Millie?' asked Jemima.

'She didn't really like her,' said Yasmin. 'Yeah, she was her cousin, but she said she was a bit of a bully, and was really like sneaky about it. Lauren always said she was a two-faced cow. Millie'd be nice to her and Jonathan when Sally and Bradley were there, but when they weren't she'd be horrible to them. She used to tell them that if they upset her, she'd get her dad to phone social services and have them both put into care. Don't you think that's a horrible thing to say?'

'It is,' nodded Jemima. 'But apart from saying horrible things to Lauren and her brother, did Millie ever do anything horrible to them?'

126

'Like what?' asked Thea.

'I don't know,' said Jemima.

'She didn't like, hit them or anything. But Lauren said that she did see Millie nick a ring from Sally's jewellery box,' said Yasmin.

'That's interesting,' said Jemima. Mariella and Mark Derbyshire had both told them how upset Sally was about losing that ring. The Rathbone children would surely have witnessed her distress, yet Millie had not owned up to stealing it in the first place. If she was afraid of getting into trouble but had experienced a pang of conscience, she could have returned it by leaving it somewhere in plain sight. It would be easy to pretend that Sally had just misplaced it. Yet the girl had been content to let her stepmother suffer.

'Did Lauren confront her about it or tell her aunt or uncle what Millie had done?' asked Jemima.

'No,' said Thea. 'What was the point? Millie's dad wouldn't have believed her anyway. Bradley was nice to Lauren and Jonathan, but Millie was his favourite. And Lauren didn't want to risk her and Jonathan being put into care.'

'Lauren kept a secret diary,' Yasmin added. 'She started it after her parents died. I think it was her Uncle Bradley's idea. She used to write down all sorts of things. She started off writing about how much she missed her parents. She'd write down things she would have told them if they'd still been alive. But recently she said that she'd started writing about the horrible things Millie was doing, as Lauren didn't feel that she could tell her uncle or aunt. But whenever she wrote about Millie she used a secret code. And she hid her diary so that Millie wouldn't find it.'

'And did Lauren ever mention any arguments at her aunt and uncles' house?' asked Jemima.

'No,' said Thea.

'Did she ever mention the adults being afraid or worried about anyone or anything?'

'Nope,' said Yasmin.

'What about any strangers visiting the house?' pressed Jemima.

'Uh-huh,' said Thea, shaking her head.

'Well, that's it, girls. You've been a great help,' said Jemima. 'You're free to go. Thanks for coming in and answering my questions.'

CHAPTER 28

According to Millie's form teacher, Stephanie Newton was the girl's only friend. And after all the bad things the other children had said about Millie, Jemima was keen to hear from someone who must have seen another side of her.

Jemima opened the door to allow Stephanie Newton and her mother to enter the interview room, as Stephanie was in a wheelchair. With the introductions out of the way, Jemima was about to move on with her line of questioning when Stephanie's mother interjected.

'Before you say anything, Inspector, I think you should know that Stephanie is very upset about what's happened to Millie.'

'It's my legs that don't work, Mum, not my mouth. I'm perfectly capable of speaking for myself,' snapped Stephanie. She looked over her shoulder and gave her mother a withering glance.

'I'm sorry, Stevie. It's just that you've been through so much lately.'

'Oh, give it a rest,' muttered Stephanie, shaking her head in despair.

'I understand your concern, Mrs Newton, but this really is just an informal chat, a chance for me to find out a little about Millie. It will be much more effective if you just sit back, relax, and let your daughter speak for herself,' said Jemima.

'Finally! Let's hope she listens to you, 'cos she never listens to me,' said Stephanie.

'So, Stephanie, how long have you and Millie been friends?' asked Jemima. She had immediately warmed to the girl's feisty spirit.

'About a year.'

'And how long have you known each other?'

'We've been in the same class since we started at this school, so about three years.'

'And you weren't friendly before that?'

'We'd talk to each other sometimes, but we only became friends when we partnered up for a school project. Neither of us really had any friends. We're both more intelligent than the rest of those deadheads at school. They like to think of themselves as the so-called "cool kids"' — Stephanie made quotation marks with her fingers — 'but they're really just stupid kids with no ambition or imagination. Dad works at the Central Library, and I love hanging out there. There're so many reference books, and I get to use the computers whenever I want. Dad always makes sure there's one free for me. I'd often see Millie there, but we didn't really talk to each other, even though I always thought she may be a bit like me.'

'What do you mean by that?' asked Jemima.

'I mean that she's more intelligent than most of the bimbos in our year. She's serious about learning and doing things that matter. And I was right. She's exactly like me. She wants to do well at school and have a fantastic career. Not spend her time messing around, trying to attract the boys. The other girls don't get me at all. They think I'm a freak, and it doesn't help that I'm stuck in this metal contraption.'

'I'm sure they don't think—' began her mother.

'Mrs Newton, please let your daughter continue,' said Jemima. She flashed the woman a warning look.

'And it doesn't help, having the world's most over-protective mother who feels that she has to speak for me,' snapped Stephanie.

'You said that you and Millie became friends when you worked together on a school project?' said Jemima.

'That's right. That's when we really got to know each other and found out that we had a lot in common. We both love the library. We used to joke about barricading the doors, locking ourselves inside, and refusing to come out again until we'd read every book in there. I really miss her, you know. Most people don't seem to like her, but I do. She's one of a kind, my BFF. I'll never have another friend like Millie.'

'What sort of books do you both like to read?' asked Jemima.

'Oh, my taste is very eclectic. I'll read pretty much anything. The only thing I avoid is anything gory. But Millie's obsessed with reading science, medical and true-crime books. Until I got to know her, I thought I used to read quickly. But she's something else. We always leave there with a stack of books, but quite often Millie asks if she can take some out on my card. She always seems to want more than her limit allows.'

'She must be a fast reader then,' said Jemima. She recalled the books piled up on Millie's desk at home.

'Is there any chance you can sort through her library books?' asked Stephanie. 'I'm only asking because three of them were taken out on my card, and I don't want to be fined when they become overdue.'

'No problem. So, Stephanie, did Millie ever confide in you about being worried or upset about anything?' asked Jemima.

'No,' said Stephanie. 'We don't talk about personal stuff. We only discuss issues that really matter.'

'What do you mean by that?'

'Duh! It's obvious, isn't it? Things we read in books.'

'Fair enough,' said Jemima. 'But just to be clear, did you get the impression that Millie was afraid of anyone?'

'Of course not! Millie doesn't let anyone or anything get to her.'

'Well, someone did,' muttered Stephanie's mother.

'As the saying goes, Mother, "life's a bitch, and then you die",' snapped Stephanie.

'Don't speak like that, Stephanie. You know I don't approve of vulgarities,' said Mrs Newton.

'I think I'm the one person in this room who's entitled to say that. You see, my legs worked perfectly up until I was three years old. But then, there was the car crash. It killed my birth parents and left me paralysed from the waist down. At that moment in time, my life prospects went down the pan. I was a disabled child facing life in care.

'Being parentless without a seriously restrictive physical disability is hard enough. I doubt there're many people crazy enough to take on a girl like me. But I fell on my feet, excuse the pun, when Owen and Dinah fostered, then ultimately adopted me. I know I'm a pain in the backside most of the time, but I love them to bits. They're the best parents ever,' said Stephanie, as she held out her hand to her mother.

'Oh, Stevie, you're such a wonderful girl,' said Dinah. The woman's face and voice softened as she squeezed her daughter's hand.

'OK, that's enough of the mushy stuff,' said Stephanie. 'I've told Mum and Dad that they have to foster Millie when she gets out of the hospital.'

'Now don't build your hopes up. We don't know that Millie will be well enough to come out of the hospital,' said Dinah.

'You're such a pessimist, Mum. I told you, Millie's a fighter. She'll get through this and be out of there in no time. And when she does, she'll come and live with us. You fostered me when I had no one. I was broken and you put my life back together. Then you adopted me and look how that turned out. You're the best parents ever, and that's what Millie deserves. You have to look after her. After all, she's my only friend. And you both always say that you'll do everything possible to make me happy.'

* * *

Jemima returned to the incident room, frustrated that after two days of giving it their all, they were no further forward with the investigation. They had followed procedure, speaking to those closest to the Rathbones, who in turn had supplied a raft of names of potential suspects. Yet every path they followed led to a dead end. They had put in so much effort yet were no closer to finding the killer. The case was wearing her down and testing her patience. She needed to find the perpetrator before they had a chance to kill again.

As all the victims were members of the same family, it should have been a simple matter of establishing who had a motive, then proving means and opportunity. *Bish-bash-bosh*.

She should be out there doing something. Instead, she'd just wasted a couple of hours talking to teenagers who had no idea why the Rathbone family had been killed. They hadn't supplied any crucial information that would give the police the break they needed. In fact, the only thing they'd convinced her of was that Millie was most likely a deeply unpleasant girl. But surely the girl couldn't have been so vile to someone that they had subsequently gone out and butchered her entire family?

It was a ridiculous thought, and Jemima knew it.

CHAPTER 29

Speaking to the teenagers reminded Jemima that she still hadn't looked at Lauren's diary. Leafing through the ramblings of a teenage girl seemed like a pointless task. Yasmin had already said that Bradley had suggested Lauren keep the journal as a way of trying to come to terms with her parents' death. She had also explained that Lauren had recently developed a code to write about her cousin, as the girls obviously didn't get on particularly well. At best, it might provide an insight into the relationship between two teenagers with their very different personalities and interests. Though it was hardly likely to contain anything of use to the investigation.

Nevertheless, She picked it up and turned to the most recent entries. Straightaway she saw that Lauren was indeed writing in code.

There were three entries, all of which looked like gobbledygook. The first one read:

H'p zuhwhqj hq fngd edfztvd h gnq'w zzqw zqbnqd wn nqnz zkzw h vtvsdfw tqwho h fzq sunyd hw. H'yd ihjtudg ntw vnpdwkhqj zentw Phoohd. Vkd'v z svbfkn! Etw Tqfod Euzgodb gndvq'w vdd hw. H wkhqn Ztqwhd Vzoob nqnzv, etw gndvq'w zzqw wn vzb zqbwkhqj hq fzvd

134

hw tsvdwv Tqfod Euzgodb. Vkd'v qnw Phoohd'v ehuwk
pnwkdu. Zqg Tqfod Euzgodb hv ydub ptfk Wdzp Phoohd.

Z idz pnqwkv edinud Ptp zqg Gzg ghdg, h nydukd-
zug wkdp wzonhqj zentw zkzw kzssdqdg wn Obghz. Vkd
zzv Phoohd'v bntqjdu vhvwdu, zqg zzv nqob z ezeb zkdq
vkd zzv nhoodg. Wkhv zoo kzssdqdg z onqj whpd zjn.
Tqfod Euzgodb'v ihuvw zhid, Ztqwhd Hvnedo, zdqw wn
suhvnq inu nhoohqj kdu, etw Ptp vzhg wkzw vkd ghgq'w
edohdyd wkzw vkd'g gnqd hw. Gzg vzhg wkzw vkd ptvw
kzyd, zv hw zzv wnn zzito wn wkhqn wkzw wkd nqob
nwkdu snvvhehohwb zzv wutd.

H ghgq'w nqnz zkzw wkdb pdzqw. H zzqwdg wn
zvn wkdp, etw h fntogq'w, zv wkdq wkdb'g nqnz wkzw h'g
eddq ohvwdqhqj zkdq h vkntogq'w kzyd. H'yd eddq wkh-
qnhqj z onw zentw wkzw fnqyduvzwhnq. Tqfod Euzgodb
zzv zw znun zkdq Obghz zzv nhoodg. Vn wkzw nqob
odzydv Phoohd.

Zkzw hi Phoohd nhoodg Obghz?

Wkzw ptvw kzyd eddq zkzw Ptp pdzqw. H nqnz
vkd zzv nqob vdydq zw wkd whpd. Etw vkd'v zozzbv eddq
mdzontv ni zqbnqd jdwwhqj pnud zwwdqwhnq wkzq kdu.
Zqg h udzoob edohdyd wkzw vkd fntog kzyd gnqd hw.

Qn nqd wnog pd knz Obghz ghdg, etw h'yd vddq wkh-
qjv nq wkd hqwduqdw vzbhqj wkzw vkd zzv vpnwkdudg
zhwk z ftvkhnq. Wkdb vzhg wkzw hw zntogq'w kzyd wzndq
ptfk diinuw, zqg hw zntog kzyd eddq nydu ydub tthfnob.

Zdoo, Phoohd fntog dzvhob kzyd gnqd wkzw.
H wkhqn Phoohd'v z ptugdudu!!!

Jemima flicked through the two other entries. The code appeared to be the same. It was apparent that the girl had gone to a lot of trouble to keep her thoughts and observations private, and Jemima was keen to know what had troubled Lauren so much that she had found it necessary to take such a precaution, but after a few minutes of failing to decipher the code, Jemima gave up trying.

Spending hours trying to decipher this code was unlikely to help solve the murders. Jemima flicked through the rest

135

of the journal and saw that it was only the final few entries that were written in code. The rest were easy to read. It was more important for Jemima to scan the rest of the journal than try and unscramble the final entries, as she needed to get an overall sense of what life was like inside the Rathbone household.

She quickly flicked through the first few pages and began to read the teenager's private thoughts.

I miss Mum and Dad so much that it hurts. I feel guilty about all the times I played up and gave them a hard time. I feel guilty about the times I refused to hug them and say that I loved them. It was mean. I hope they knew that I loved them, because I really did. But it's too late now.

I missed out on things because I wanted to act all grown up and independent. But now I'm an orphan, I want a time machine to take me back so that I can be a little girl again. I want to have hugs, kisses and cuddles. I want Mum to brush my hair, take me shopping, and make me cringe when she drops me at school, shouting that she loves me, and waving like mad until I'm out of sight.

I'm beginning to forget things about them. Like what it felt like to hold their hands. How pretty Mum was, with her soft, shiny hair, and sparkly blue eyes. Her hair used to smell great. It must have been the shampoo she used. Whenever I go to a supermarket, I open shampoo bottles just to sniff them. But I haven't found the right one. It makes me sad.

Dad used to tell me that he was proud of me. He used to do his best to get home in time to read a bedtime story to me and Jonathan. He was the best at reading stories as he used to do silly voices for the characters. It was great. I used to close my eyes and I could imagine I was in the story. Dad always told me that I was his best girl. It makes me cry whenever I think of it. I'll never be anyone's best girl ever again.

I know we're lucky to be living with Uncle Bradley and Auntie Sally. They're nice people. But it's not the same as it was with Mum and Dad.

Uncle Bradley's great. He looks a lot like Dad, which is weird. He's kind and funny. But Millie's his favourite. She's his best girl. He tries not to show it, but I can see it in his eyes. And Millie's always quick to point out that she's the important one. She'll always come first.

Jemima turned to a later entry.

Millie made Jonathan cry today. I haven't seen him do that since Mum and Dad died.

She's such a bitch. I HATE HER!!!

Millie can't stand anyone else being the centre of attention. Everything has to be about her.

It all kicked off when Jonathan got picked for the school football team, and Uncle Bradley said that he deserved a treat for being so talented. He said that Mum and Dad would have been proud of him.

Jonathan's quite good at footie, but he's not really talented. Let's face it, he's no Gareth Bale or Aaron Ramsey. But he's way better than most of the boys at school. Anyway, Uncle Bradley got tickets for them to both go to a Cardiff City home game. Even I know it's a big deal.

Jonathan was so excited that he kept going on about it as though it was the best thing ever. Jon and Uncle Bradley were planning on making a day of it. They were going to have a pub lunch. And Uncle Bradley said he'd buy them both football shirts and scarves.

Millie asked if she could go. She's never shown any interest in football, and Uncle Bradley saw right through her and told her to stop being so selfish. I think it shocked her. He gave her a right telling off and told her to go to her room.

When Jonathan went upstairs a bit later, she was waiting for him. He told me that she came into his room, shut the door and told him that our mum and dad killed themselves because they didn't want to be around us anymore.

He told her to shut up, but she just kept going on and on. She said that Uncle Bradley didn't really want us there.

He only took us in out of pity, because there was nowhere else for us to go. And she said that we'd better not upset her, because if Uncle Bradley found out that she didn't like us living with them, that he'd contact social services and get us taken into care.

I told Jonathan not to worry. Millie's so full of shit.

Millie's weird. I don't know what she's up to, but she's started making a big thing about being friends with Stephanie Newton. They're always hanging out together in school. We call them the Brainiacs.

Steph's in our class. She's OK, but she's a bit weird too. She's been in a wheelchair since she was little. I don't mean that that makes her weird, because it doesn't. She's weird because she doesn't like the same things as the rest of us. Steph's like mega-super-intelligent. I'd say she's even cleverer than Millie. And even though I hate to say anything good about her, I have to admit that Millie's way cleverer than me.

After school they often take a bus into town and go to the library. I know that because some of the other girls have seen them there. It's not a cool place for kids like us to hang out, but they spend hours there. I mean, what is that all about?

When Millie gets home she's always carrying loads of books. Then she shuts herself in her room so that she doesn't have to spend any time with me and Jonathan. I don't think she realizes that we like it that way. We both hate her. And I think that Aunt Sally doesn't like her very much either. Not that she's said anything to us. She probably hasn't said anything to Uncle Bradley either, as I don't think she'd want to upset him.

It was apparent from these few entries that there was no love lost between the cousins, but apart from Lauren feeling that Millie was a profoundly unpleasant girl, there was nothing to suggest that she, or any other member of the household, was afraid of anyone.

CHAPTER 30

The last task of the day was to speak to the Derbyshire boys, and as they stood outside the Derbyshire house for the second time that day, Jemima and Broadbent could hear music coming from inside.

Jemima pressed the bell. Moments later the door was opened by Seth Derbyshire, the elder of the two siblings. Jemima knew that the lad was only seventeen years of age, but he was already over six feet tall and had the chiselled good looks of his father. It didn't take much imagination to realize that if he wasn't already, Seth Derbyshire was destined to become a heartbreaker.

Before Jemima had a chance to say anything, Mariella appeared and invited them to come inside.

'This is my eldest son, Seth,' she said. 'If you'd like to head into the kitchen I'll get Thomas to join us. He's the one responsible for the awful racket. I'm giving him some leeway at the moment as he's very upset about Jonathan.'

Seth looked and moved like someone who was comfortable in his own skin. He had perfect posture, emphasizing his height, and he had the same black hair as his mother. His complexion was surprisingly flawless, with no sign of teenage acne, the curse of so many lads of his age.

'Hello,' he said, holding out his hand to greet them. Jemima noticed that Seth was unafraid of making eye contact. When he smiled, she also saw that his teeth were perfectly straight and exceptionally white. He seemed much older than his years, exuding a level of confidence in the presence of strangers that would be the envy of many men twice his age.

'You'll probably realize as soon as you meet him that Tom's a bit of a geek. He's exceptionally shy, especially with people he doesn't know,' said Seth.

As the music stopped, the sound of muffled voices and approaching footsteps could be heard.

'This is Thomas,' said Mariella. She was followed into the room by a bespectacled teenager.

Seeing the two boys together, it was difficult to believe they were siblings. Thomas was fifteen yet looked much younger. He was easily six inches shorter than his brother, and it was apparent that he had no interest in his appearance. His lank brown hair lacked shape as it flopped over the top of his glasses. His cheeks were round, ruddy and covered in acne.

As Thomas dragged out a bar stool and hitched himself on to it, he refused to meet their gaze. Jemima's first thought was that she understood how low Thomas's self-esteem must be. She too had grown up in a household where an older sibling had been the one blessed with every physical and intellectual advantage, while she had looked on from the side-lines, frequently feeling inadequate.

At that moment Jemima would have loved to take Thomas to one side and tell him that his life wouldn't always be like this. In a couple of years, Seth would go off to university and Thomas would no longer have to live in his shadow. Things would improve, his confidence would grow, and he'd find his own way to shine. But now wasn't the time or the place to impart that wisdom.

'Thank you both for agreeing to speak to us,' began Jemima. 'As your parents may have told you, we don't yet know who killed the Rathbones, so we have to consider every possibility. We've already spoken to your parents as they were friends of Bradley and Sally's. Now we need to speak to both of you because, as unthinkable as it may seem, it's possible that whoever did this had a grudge against one or all of the teenagers. If that turns out to be the case, they may have told you something which could help us find the person responsible.'

'They wouldn't have said anything to me,' said Seth. He snorted loudly as though it was a ridiculous suggestion. 'I wouldn't hang out with those losers.'

'Seth! Apologize now!' ordered his mother.

'Why? I'm only telling it as it is.'

'You'll have to forgive my son. Seth has an image he likes to maintain. It's a very unattractive trait. I'm afraid that for the last few years he sees himself as far too mature and sophisticated to socialize with teenagers who are not part of his select group of friends.'

'Even though you didn't socialize with the Rathbone children in recent times, presumably you would have seen them from time to time, around here, or at school?' pressed Jemima.

'Yes, but I didn't know what was going on with any of them. I saw Jonathan when he came around to spend time with Tom, but we'd only say hello and goodbye. We didn't have any actual conversations. He was just a kid. I didn't have anything in common with him.'

'He was only two years younger than you,' said Broadbent.

'Two years is a lifetime,' said Seth.

'What about the girls? asked Jemima.

'They're even younger than Tom,' replied Seth. His tone suggested that the question was ridiculous.

'Well lads of your age sometimes go out with younger girls,' said Broadbent.

'I don't,' said Seth. 'I had nothing in common with Millie or Lauren. And Millie's definitely not the sort of girl I'd hang out with. I'd see her in the school library sometimes.

But we didn't talk to each other. She was a bit of a loner. Only ever seemed to talk to some girl in a wheelchair. Always had her head stuck in a book. A boy in my year asked her out, but she knocked him back. He reckoned she's a lesbian.'

'That's enough, Seth!' snapped his mother.

'What about Lauren?' asked Jemima.

'Now, she definitely wasn't a lesbian,' said Seth. As he spoke, he flashed his mother a defiant smile.

'You know that's not what I meant,' said Jemima.

'Oh, he's well aware of that, Inspector,' said Mariella. 'Seth, while you live in this house, you'll treat people with respect. Or you can leave now and make your own way in this world. Our friends have been murdered, and we have to help the police in any way we can so that we can bring their killer to justice. You've known Sally all of your life. She was like a sister to me, and she was exceptionally kind to you and your brother.'

'OK, I'm sorry. I just don't like to think about what happened next door. It totally freaks me out,' said Seth. 'Lauren was a nice enough girl. She was too young for me to hang around with, but she always tried to flirt with me whenever we saw each other. I told her to back off a couple of times. It got a bit embarrassing. But I didn't really know much about her, other than the fact that she came to live here when her parents died.'

'What about you, Thomas? Jonathan was your best friend, wasn't he?' asked Broadbent.

'Yeah,' he replied. The boy stared at his hands as he picked at the skin around his fingernails.

'Was Jonathan worried about anything or scared of anyone?' pressed Jemima.

'Not really.'

'What does that mean, Thomas?'

'Well, he wasn't scared of anyone, but he didn't like Millie. He told me that he'd sometimes get upset because he missed his mum and dad. Millie used to laugh at him and told him that no one loved him anymore.'

'But Bradley and Sally loved him and so did Lauren,' said Mariella. She sounded shocked by what her youngest son had just said.

'I know. I told Jonathan that,' said Thomas. 'But Millie said they had no right living there. Bradley was her dad, not theirs. She used to tell them that if they upset her, Bradley would contact social services and they'd have to go and live with foster parents. He said that Millie was a bitch, and that's why she didn't have any friends apart from that Stephanie girl.'

'What about Lauren, did you have much to do with her?'

'Not really. She seemed nice enough. Jonathan told me that she didn't like Millie either. You should ask her friends. They'd probably know more than me.'

As they left the Derbyshire's house, Jemima felt even more dispirited. 'We're getting nowhere. Let's call it a night,' she told Broadbent.

CHAPTER 31

As she made her way home that evening, Jemima's thoughts turned to James, and how, yet again, she hadn't rung Nick to find out how things were back at home. Jemima felt her cheeks glow with shame. She owed James some attention. He needed her now, more than ever, but she had just spent another exceptionally long day at work.

On a personal level, the Rathbone case couldn't have come at a worse time. Jemima knew that with everything going on at home she had to compartmentalize things more effectively. James needed her, and it was evident that Nick wasn't coping. But the Rathbone case was so awful. It had got under her skin like an itch she was compelled to scratch.

With Wendy out of the picture, Jemima appreciated that she was no longer in the privileged position of playing at being a mother during the good times. The time had come to step up and be a real parent to her stepson. She had to be there for him, to ensure that he knew without any doubt that he was loved, safe and valued.

Jemima arrived home to find the house in darkness. She opened the door and crept inside, kicking her shoes off so as not to make a noise on the tiled floor. The entrance to the lounge was closed, so she opened it, felt for the light switch, and flicked it on.

She jumped and caught her breath as she noticed an unexpected movement in the room. It was Nick.

'Why are you sitting in the dark?' she asked.

'Because,' he said.

'That's no answer.'

'It's the only one you'll get,' he slurred.

Jemima noticed that he was holding another bottle of whisky. 'Oh, not again, Nick!'

'Yes, *again*, Jemima!' he growled.

'Think of James. It's not good for him to see you like this.'

'I told the little bastard to go to bed.'

'Nick! Don't talk about James like that! Whatever's going on in that messed up head of yours, James is still your son, and—'

'No, he isn't!' Nick hurled the bottle at the wall.

As the bottle shattered, splinters of glass flew out in all directions. Jemima stood there, open-mouthed, watching the golden liquid splash on the carpet and run down the walls. As the smell of alcohol hit her nostrils, it brought her back to her senses, and she suddenly realized what Nick had said. It made no sense at all.

'What did you just say?' she asked. Jemima looked directly at Nick for the first time since she'd entered the room.

'Nothing. I said nothing!' he shouted.

'Shhh. Keep your voice down or you'll wake James.'

'Oh, we mustn't disturb *James*. Let's all tiptoe around playing happy bloody families, shall we?'

'What's got into you, Nick?' She walked towards the sofa.

'Nothing's got into me, Jemima! I'm just a man trying to do the best he can for my ex-wife's son. I'm putting a brave face on it, but I'm doing my best.'

'But James is your son too.'

'Ah, that's where you're wrong. Call yourself a detective? You're not very good at picking up on the clues, are you my love? He's not my boy. I'm not his father. I will never be anyone's father!'

'Of course he's your son.'

'My name may be on his birth certificate, but I'm not his father. That fucking bitch lied to me. I was there at the birth. I even cut the umbilical cord. I've doted on that boy since the moment I laid eyes on him. He was everything to me. But yesterday . . . well, yesterday I found out it was all a lie. I was a soft touch. But that's me all over, far too easy-going. And what a surprise, she took advantage. It was just a way for that cunt to bleed me dry.'

Jemima's legs suddenly felt too weak to support her weight. She lurched towards the nearest chair and slumped back against the cushions. She couldn't believe what she'd just been told. She felt like she'd been punched in the gut. No matter how abhorrent Nick's behaviour had been over the last twenty-four hours, this put a different slant on things. Jemima suddenly appreciated that Nick must be going through hell at the moment. It was no wonder he was so messed up.

'Nick, tell me you haven't told James that you're not his father?'

'What do you take me for? Of course I haven't. How could you even think that?'

'That's good,' said Jemima. She breathed a sigh of relief. 'Stay there and we'll talk this through. I just have to check on James first. I need to make sure that he hasn't woken up. The last thing he needs right now is to hear about any of this.'

Jemima headed upstairs as quietly as she could. There was no sound coming from James's room. The bedroom door was closed and creaked loudly as she opened it. It had been that way for a couple of weeks, and she cursed herself for not oiling the hinges. It was one of the tasks on an ever-increasing domestic to-do list.

James stirred, kicking the duvet off as he turned over in bed. The astringent smell of urine hit her as she tiptoed towards him. His mother's death was taking its toll. He had wet the bed. It was something he hadn't done for at least six years.

Jemima got out the rubber sheet they had kept from James's younger days and made the bed up in the guest room. It seemed the best option for that night. James was still asleep when she returned to his bedroom. She rummaged around in the chest of drawers until she found a clean pair of pants and pyjamas, then shook him gently until he roused.

'Come on, little man, let's get you to the bathroom,' she said. She helped him out of bed and spoke in what she hoped was a soothing voice.

James looked confused as he tried his best to focus on her face. He was so exhausted that he didn't understand what was happening. Seeing him like this, so young and vulnerable, made Jemima feel helpless. Without warning, she felt the hot sting of tears on her cheeks. She turned her head and quickly wiped them away with the back of her hand. The last thing she wanted was for James to think that he had upset her.

'Wh-wha's tha' matter?' he asked, stifling a yawn.

'Nothing, darling.' Jemima stroked his head reassuringly. 'Your bed's a bit wet. I need you to go to the toilet. After that I'll get you changed into something dry. You can sleep in the other room tonight. Is that OK with you?'

James nodded slowly as he padded across the floor, rubbing his eyes as he went. Jemima kept a guiding hand on his shoulder, steering him gently so that he didn't bump into anything. When James was clean, dry and had a fresh set of clothes, she sat on the bed and stroked his cheek. She watched his eyes grow heavy until he eventually fell asleep again.

Seeing to James had taken far longer than Jemima had anticipated. She hoped that Nick hadn't fallen asleep, as they really needed to talk about this devastating turn of events. But first, Jemima returned to James's room, stripped the bed and carried the soiled linen to the washing machine. As she walked into the room she saw that Nick had made it out of the lounge and was standing at the kitchen sink with blood dripping from a cut on one of his fingers.

'You took your time,' he said antagonistically.

'James wet the bed. But never mind that, what have you done?'

'Cut myself trying to clear up that bottle, as if things aren't bad enough already.'

'Let's take a look at it,' she said. 'Stay where you are. I'll stick this wash on, then grab the first-aid kit and get you sorted out.'

'Thanks,' he muttered.

As she met his gaze, Jemima could see that he was crying too.

With the wound cleaned and dressed, Nick sat at the kitchen table.

'I'm going to make you a pot of strong coffee because you need to sober up so we can talk,' Jemima said.

'Why do you think that James isn't your son?' she asked, once she had handed Nick his mug.

'I had a message from the health centre. They had my test results and asked me to go in to discuss them.'

Jemima felt an instant pang of guilt. The test results Nick was referring to were the ones she had insisted upon having. They were the first step towards establishing the reason for her failure to become pregnant.

'What did the doctor tell you?' she asked. As she reached out to touch his arm, Nick batted her hand away. It was the moment she realized that he blamed her for this unwanted knowledge.

'She told me I'm infertile.'

'Well, that doesn't mean you're not James's father. There's any number of reasons why you could have subsequently become infertile.'

'No,' he said. 'No, I was born this way. I have Klinefelter syndrome.'

'What does that mean?' she asked.

'You understand basic genetics?' he asked.

Jemima nodded.

'Well, most men are born with an X and a Y chromosome. But I have XXY. They printed off some leaflets. Take a look at those. It supposedly affects one in every 660 males. So it's not exactly a rare condition. There are some possible symptoms, none of which apply to me, apart from the main one — infertility.'

'OK, so you're not James's biological father. But that's just DNA, Nick. You're his father in every way that counts. You were there when he was born. You've brought him up. You've been there for every key stage of his life. That makes you his father.'

'If someone else were going through this I'd be saying the same thing. But it's all empty words. You can't possibly know how messed up my head is at the moment. I feel let down, betrayed. The most fundamental truth in my life has turned out to be a lie,' said Nick.

'But Wendy's responsible for that, not James. James is still the same boy he's always been. He loves you unconditionally, and he needs you now more than ever,' pleaded Jemima.

'I know that. But I don't feel the same way about him.'

'Stop being so stupid and selfish, Nick. You can't turn your back on James. Look at me, I didn't give birth to him, but I love him as though he were my own.'

'Well, what can I say? I'm not a saint like you, Jemima. It's different for you. When you came into our lives, you accepted James for who he was. You weren't duped into believing he was your own flesh and blood. Do you realize that I used to look at him and think that he looked like a mini-me? How stupid was I?'

'You need to snap out of this, Nick. Put your anger aside and do the right thing. You're James's dad in every way that counts. He can't work through this without you. You have to rise above it and be his father!'

'Oh just fuck off, Jemima. Fuck off and leave me alone!' yelled Nick.

CHAPTER 32

The following morning, Jemima walked into the incident room to find the mood just as sombre and depressing as it was at home. They needed to identify the killer and get him locked up as soon as possible, but there was little hope of that if they didn't even understand the motive behind the attack. There were still a few people of interest to follow up on, but at the moment there were no solid leads.

'What have you got so far on Aileen Whittle?' Jemima asked Gareth Peters.

'Not a lot,' he replied. 'As far as I can tell she keeps a low profile. Schofield owns a house just outside Cowbridge. Whittle is listed on the electoral register as living there too. As it's not part of Cardiff, the only way she'd be able to get to Lisvane without a lot of hassle and wasted time would be by road. If she drove, it would take at least three-quarters of an hour to get there. I haven't got definitive proof that she was in Lisvane on Saturday, but I also haven't been able to rule her out of being in the area at the time of the murders.'

'That's no good,' said Jemima. 'We have to have some-thing concrete in order to bring Whittle in. You heard Kennedy. We need evidence to suggest that she was in north Cardiff on the day of the murders.'

'I know for a fact that Harvey Schofield spent the weekend away. He hired a private plane for a corporate jolly. They were stag hunting. There're photographs of them on the website.'

'Did Aileen go with them?' Jemima asked.

'Not as far as I know, but I still need to check a few things out. I've spoken to the person in charge of the bookings, and Aileen definitely didn't join them for the hunt, but that doesn't mean she didn't go on the trip. They chose not to stay at one of the hunting lodges, so I'm working my way through a list of local hotels to see if I can verify the names of everyone in the group. There's also the possibility that one of the hunting party owns property in that area, in which case, we'll be no further along.'

'Surely there must be a regulation for the company operating the private flight to keep some sort of passenger list?' asked Jemima.

'I hadn't thought of that,' said Peters. His cheeks reddened with embarrassment.

'Well, you should have. Look into it immediately. It'll probably be a quicker way of establishing whether she went on the trip. Anyone else got any updates on Whittle?'

'I've managed to get the registration number of Aileen's car,' said Ashton. 'It's a black Range Rover, and I'm working my way through CCTV tapes for the day of the murder to see if her vehicle was anywhere in the area. But so far I've drawn a blank.'

'OK people, keep on it. She's a person of interest until we can prove otherwise. She's linked to one of the victims, and Giles Souter believes that Aileen's more than capable of murder.'

* * *

The morning passed slowly, as for once, the team all remained at their desks and continued with various lines of investigation. Despite having been told that Cameron Short

151

was unlikely to have killed the Rathbones, Jemima was determined to question him. After all, there was no disputing the fact that Short had attacked Bradley. That certainly made him a person of interest in this investigation.

* * *

A few hours later, Peters broke the silence. 'Well, guv,' he said. 'I've finally got to the bottom of what Aileen Whittle was doing when the Rathbones were killed. You're not going to believe what she was up to.'

'Does it put her in the frame for the murders?' asked Jemima. She could feel her heart racing at the thought of a breakthrough in the case.

'Hardly, she's another one with a rock-solid alibi.'

'What was she doing?' asked Jemima.

'She was giving a lecture to a few hundred people at one of the university buildings in Cardiff.'

'You what?' said Broadbent.

'It seems that Aileen's somewhat of an expert on Ancient Egypt. Over the weekend the university hosted a convention which was open to anyone for fifty pounds a pop. Aileen Whittle was one of the guest speakers. She's a well-respected authority on many aspects of Egyptology. Last weekend she lectured for an hour on Egyptian temples, followed by a thirty-minute question-and-answer session.'

'But that's only ninety minutes of the day accounted for,' said Broadbent.

'No, it isn't,' Peters replied. 'Due to the number of people attending the event, each lecture and Q-and-A session occurred four times that day — twice in the morning, twice in the afternoon. Which means there's no way that Aileen could have committed those murders. It would have been impossible.'

'Are you sure that she didn't back out of any of her sessions?' asked Jemima.

'Absolutely sure. Each guest lecturer was assigned an assistant for the event. In every case, it was an undergraduate student from the Archaeology and Ancient History department. I've just spoken to Osian Meredith. He's a third-year student who spent the entire day, apart from a few brief comfort breaks, with Aileen. He confirmed that she arrived at the event shortly before eight in the morning, as they needed to set everything up in advance of the lectures, and she didn't leave until almost six o'clock that evening. He even said that she barely had time to eat her lunch as there were so many people keen to ask additional questions.'

'Good work, Gareth,' said Jemima. 'That makes our life easier, especially with her husband's connections. Cross Aileen off the list and move on to the next person.'

CHAPTER 33

Shortly after the update on Aileen Whittle, Jemima's phone rang. It turned out to be the information she needed and resulted in her making a few more phone calls.

'Listen up everyone, we're going to interview Cameron Short,' she told the team. 'He was released from hospital a few weeks ago. I've managed to get his address. He's prone to psychotic episodes, so I've asked Giles Souter to arrange for someone from his team to accompany the officers when they pick him up. At least that way Short can be evaluated as soon as we get him back to the station and we can be certain that he's compos mentis when we speak to him.'

'You're not going to believe this,' said Broadbent, a few moments later. 'An incident was reported at Short's address less than ten minutes ago. Officers are in attendance.'

'Shit! What's going on there?' demanded Jemima.

'Neighbours reported a disturbance. He lives on the fourth floor of a high-rise. And there's no suggestion that the attending officers know that he's likely to be delusional.'

'Ashton, get a message to the officers at the scene. Peters, contact Giles Souter's team and tell them that whoever's going to Short's address needs to get there pronto. Broadbent, you're with me.' Jemima grabbed her coat and ran out of the door.

They were both out of breath as they reached the car. Jemima threw herself into the driver's seat and started the engine before Broadbent had time to shut his door.

'Steady on, guv, a few seconds either way isn't going to make much difference,' he said.

'You're wrong. With someone like Short, every second counts,' said Jemima, as she forced the gearstick into position.

Broadbent called out directions as Jemima drove at speed. They weaved through lanes of traffic, lights flashing and siren blaring.

After what seemed an eternity, the car skidded to a halt outside a run-down block of flats, leaving traces of rubber on the asphalt. Two police vehicles were already there.

Even before she'd had a chance to get out of the car, Jemima knew which apartment belonged to Cameron Short. Her eyes were drawn to a balcony on the fourth floor where an altercation was taking place. Down at ground level, a crowd had gathered, and a couple of officers were doing their best to get everyone to move back. But no one was listening. Some people had their phones out and were filming the incident.

'Leave him the fuck alone!' yelled a deep, menacing voice from somewhere in the crowd.

'I'm going up!' Jemima shouted. 'See if anyone's got some sheets or a mattress to try to break his fall if he jumps. Tell Ashton and Peters to get that shrink to hurry up. The last thing we need is for Short to get his brains splattered all over the pavement.' She sprinted towards the entrance of the apartment block.

Giles Souter had already explained to her how unstable Cameron Short could become during one of his psychotic episodes and from the little she'd seen and heard since their arrival at the scene, Jemima knew that there was a genuine possibility that things could end badly for the man.

She jabbed the button to summon the lift but noticed that it had stopped on the sixteenth floor. There was no time to waste. She had to take the stairs.

It was on occasions such as this that Jemima wished she'd taken her personal fitness regime more seriously. She took the steps two at a time. Even before she'd reached the third floor, her thighs burned with the effort. Jemima gritted her teeth and pushed on. There was no time to lose. A man's life was at stake, and the people with him didn't realize it.

By the time she reached the fourth floor landing, her breath was coming hard and fast. Her ears buzzed and Jemima felt like retching. She winced as her weight came down on her left leg and realized that she must have pulled a muscle. But there was no time to slow down, so she set off along the corridor, towards the sound of raised voices.

There was a small group of people gathered outside the entrance to Cameron Short's flat. The door was ajar, but not fully open. The fact that two police officers were already inside appeared to have been enough to stop bystanders from taking a closer look.

'Get out of here before I'm forced to arrest you,' demanded Jemima. She flashed her warrant card, sensing that there would be no point asking them nicely. There were a few grumbles and the odd insult thrown her way, but surprisingly enough, everyone complied and headed back along the corridor.

It was at the forefront of Jemima's mind that she must do everything possible to calm the situation as quickly as she could. She wanted to get inside the flat to assess the situation for herself but knew that she had to take things slowly. The last thing she wanted to do was spook Cameron further, or surprise the two officers already there, who undoubtedly would have no idea who she was.

Jemima slowly pushed the door and tentatively stepped over the threshold. As the door swung inwards, the hinges creaked, announcing her arrival. She grimaced. With her first breath she became aware of an overwhelming smell of excrement, and as her eyes focused on the walls, Jemima realized that they were smeared with it. Her stomach flipped, but she fought the urge to gag and headed inside, determined not to touch anything.

In the distance, she could hear Cameron wailing and muttering a collection of jumbled words that made no sense. As she turned a corner, Jemima could see him standing on top of a flimsy wooden chair near the edge of the balcony. His only item of clothing was a pair of soiled underpants. His entire body was smeared with faeces. His limbs were painfully thin, his ribs visible for all to see. His eyes darted about, and his arms flailed as he swatted invisible foes.

Jemima's breath caught in her throat at the thought that this man had been left to cope alone when he was undoubtedly a danger to himself.

'Cameron, Dr Souter's asked me to tell you that he's sending someone to help you,' she said. But Cameron was too far gone to know she was there.

'You shouldn't be here. This is a police matter,' said the nearest officer.

'I'm DI Huxley,' she said. She kept her voice low and even as she held out her warrant card. 'You both need to back away from him. Cameron's suffering a psychotic episode. You're not helping matters by trying to get him to come inside. He's supposed to have medication to stabilize him, but by the look of it, he's stopped taking it. At the moment he's hallucinating, terrified, and likely to harm himself. He'll probably believe you're a threat. You both need to back off right now before this ends badly.'

'So he's not just having a bad trip?' whispered the closest officer.

'No. This man's a psychiatric patient in desperate need of help,' said Jemima.

'Move back,' said the officer, touching his partner on the shoulder.

'Uh?' said his colleague rather too loudly. He jerked wildly as he felt his colleague's touch. He had been so focused on Cameron that he was oblivious to the conversation that had just taken place behind him.

The unexpected noise and movement momentarily attracted Cameron's attention. It immediately ratcheted up the man's level of distress.

'G'way! Leave me 'lone!' yelled Cameron. He shifted his stance precariously close to the edge of the chair, which became even more unsteady. 'Won't let you! Gerr out of my head! No, no, no, no, no!'

All of a sudden, even above Cameron's rants, there was a noticeable commotion from somewhere outside. There was an exceptionally loud hiss as a firework launched upwards in the vicinity of the balcony.

All three officers were caught off guard by the unexpected noise and the sight of the rocket, but whatever shock they had felt was nothing in comparison to the effect it had on Cameron. The man screamed hysterically and launched himself over the edge of the balcony.

There was nothing any of them could do to save him. One second he was there, the next he was gone.

There were screams and gasps of horror from below. Jemima rushed to the balcony and looked down to find out what had happened to Cameron.

'He's alive!' yelled Broadbent. 'We managed to break his fall.'

Jemima breathed a sigh of relief. It had been a close call.

'Fucking nutter,' said the officer standing next to her.

'You're out of order,' snapped Jemima. She was disgusted by the lack of empathy. She turned to leave but took it slowly as she headed down the stairs. By the time she reached ground level, Cameron Short was being loaded into an ambulance.

'He's lucky to be alive,' said Broadbent. 'A few of the residents brought out blankets and sheets. We layered them to increase their strength. Thankfully they didn't break when he fell. He'll probably have some nasty bruises, but at least we prevented a full impact.'

'Still no sign of the shrink?' asked Jemima.

'No. Fat lot of use they've turned out to be. The paramedics sedated Cameron. They said he'll most likely have to be sectioned.'

'It's the best thing for him,' said Jemima. 'As for our investigation, I don't think he's a likely suspect. If you'd seen the state of his flat, it's pretty clear that he's been off his meds and delusional for a while. There's no way he could have travelled across the city, attacked the Rathbones and made it out of there without anyone seeing him. It would have been impossible. What happened with that rocket?'

'Some teenage numpty set it off. One of the lads is giving him a good talking to at the moment,' replied Broadbent, as they headed back to the car.

After the stress of the last hour, Jemima and Broadbent were both relieved to be heading back to the station.

'You can drive,' said Jemima, tossing him the keys.

They were just approaching the castle when Jemima's phone rang. 'Thanks for letting me know. We'll be right there,' she said.

'What now?' groaned Broadbent, taking his eyes off the road.

'You're not going to believe this. Millie Rathbone is awake and talking.'

'That's one hell of a recovery,' said Broadbent.

'I know. I can't believe it either.'

'I take it we're heading to the hospital?' asked Broadbent.

'Yes,' said Jemima. 'Millie's the one person who could crack this investigation wide open. She may have seen the killer and be able to identify him. This is our best shot at closing the case. There's no time to waste. We have to speak with her now.'

'Somehow I knew you were going to say that,' said Broadbent.

CHAPTER 34

Jemima and Broadbent arrived on the ward to find Millie asleep. The girl's facial injuries were more apparent today, as the swelling had reduced. What had initially been hideous purple mounds were flattening and fading as they took on a greenish hue.

Jemima spotted one of the nurses and was about to ask her where the police constable charged with watching over Millie was, when the woman spoke first.

'This little darling's taken everyone by surprise, beating the odds like that. She's booked in for various tests over the next few days so that we can thoroughly assess the damage, and we'll continue to monitor her closely while she's with us. When we're satisfied with her progress, she'll be transferred to one of the regular wards until she's fit enough to leave.'

'We had a call to say she was awake and talking,' said Jemima.

'She was,' the nurse replied. 'But it'll be a while before she regains enough strength to stay awake for any length of time. Her mind and body need time to recover. We expect her to sleep a lot over the next few days.'

'Great,' muttered Broadbent. 'What a waste of time.'

'Where have you been?' asked Jemima, as the police constable standing guard walked back into the room.

'Comfort break, ma'am,' he said, refusing to meet her gaze.

'Did she say much when she woke up?' asked Jemima.

'Not a lot, ma'am. She asked where she was, so I told her. But then the medical team asked me to stand outside while they checked her over. By the time they allowed me to return, she was fast asleep again.'

'Let us know when she's awake again. But don't tell her what happened,' said Jemima.

'No problem.'

Jemima and Broadbent had barely had a chance to make it to the door when the constable called to them. Millie was waking up again.

They stood at the girl's bedside for what seemed like an exceptionally long time, but which in reality was probably no more than a few minutes. During that time, Jemima's mind raced with thoughts of how best to play this. There were so many questions that needed answers, though she knew that it would be best to rein in her initial enthusiasm. The girl was weak. There was no way that Jemima could avoid telling her what had happened to the rest of her family, and there was no predicting how that would affect the teenager.

As Millie's eyes flickered, then opened, Jemima's heart skipped a beat. This was it. She moved closer.

'Hi, Millie,' said Jemima. She moved into the girl's line of sight and gave what she hoped was a reassuring smile. 'You're in the hospital. How are you feeling?'

'Like I've been hit by a truck,' croaked the girl.

'I'm Detective Inspector Huxley, and I'd like to ask you a few questions.'

'Where's my father?' croaked Millie. Her eyes flitted from side to side until they came to rest upon Jemima's face.

'Millie, do you remember what happened to you?' pressed Jemima.

'There was a man . . . in the house. Blood. I saw blood. Where's my father? I want my father,' she sobbed.

'Shh, shh now. You're safe,' said Jemima. 'Did you know this man? Had you seen him before?'

'N-no, he was a stranger. He was holding something shiny. What was it? What did he do? There was blood. There was lots of blood. Why was there blood? Where's my father? Daddy! Daddy! Daaaddeee!' she wailed, looking around wildly as she tried to shield her face with her arms.

Millie's sudden movements caused a few of the sensors attached to her body to lose contact with her skin. Suddenly alarms sounded on various pieces of equipment that were monitoring her vital signs.

'That's enough,' ordered the nurse as she came running across from the other side of the room.

'But . . .' protested Jemima.

'I said that's enough!' The nurse grabbed Jemima's arm and pulled her away from the bedside. 'Leave now! Can't you see the poor girl's distressed? It's not good for her. I'll have to give her something to calm her down.'

'Well done, guv. Nicely played,' said Broadbent, shaking his head in despair.

'Oh, fuck off, Dan!' snapped Jemima, as she marched ahead. She didn't need him to point out that she'd messed up by pushing the girl too hard.

Neither of them spoke as they travelled back to the police station. They sat stiff and still, like a couple on the verge of divorce.

'I'm getting some lunch,' said Broadbent as they arrived at the car park. He was out of the car and trotting towards the building before Jemima had time to shut the passenger door.

Jemima hated it whenever they fell out. Not that it happened very often. But this time she knew that it was her fault. She shouldn't have snapped at Broadbent like that.

CHAPTER 35

When Jemima arrived in the incident room, Ashton and Peters were busy at their desks.

'Was Millie Rathbone able to tell you anything useful?' asked Ashton.

'Only that there was an unidentified male inside the house. She didn't give us a description. I should have handled it better. I was too eager to find out what she knew, and I pushed too hard,' sighed Jemima.

'You did what you needed to do. Don't beat yourself up about it, guv.'

'Thanks, Ashton. Have you got any updates for me?' She was grateful for his supportive words.

'I've completed a background check on Zoe Jones,' said Ashton. 'The woman's never so much as had a parking ticket. She's a deputy head at a local primary, been there for fifteen years. She's an active member of the PTA. Gets involved with all of their fundraising activities, makes costumes for the kids, whenever they have school concerts. She appears to be a devout Christian. Regularly attends church and sings in the choir.

'In fact, that's where she was when the Rathbones were killed. There was a wedding of two parishioners at two o'clock that day. Zoe and three other women had been at the church from nine o'clock that morning to spruce it up and arrange the flowers. The choir had a rehearsal at eleven o'clock. It lasted an hour. Then the entire choir and the vicar had lunch in the church hall and returned to the church at one o'clock to get ready for the ceremony. After the wedding, everyone attended the reception.

'Zoe Jones has an alibi for the entire time. I've spoken to at least five different people who confirmed her whereabouts. There are also photographs and videos of her on social media.'

'So she didn't do it herself, but did she pay someone else to do it for her?' asked Jemima.

'At the moment, I'm not sure about that. I've accessed Zoe's financial records, and there's a lot of activity. Firstly, there're the usual standing orders and direct debits. The biggest payment is for the mortgage, but there've been a few occasions when she's failed to make those payments. When you take her salary into account, she shouldn't have a problem making the repayments.'

'Where's the money going?' asked Jemima.

'Bear with me, guv, I'm getting to that,' said Ashton. 'I've noticed money going out to five accounts. Not huge amounts, we're talking fifty to a hundred quid a time. But the payments are frequent, though not on set days. As far as I can see, it's been going on for the last six months, though she's been making payments to one of the accounts for almost a year.'

'Have you been able to establish who these accounts belong to?' asked Jemima.

'Not yet. I've put in a request, but I'm still waiting on it.'

'How frequent are these transactions?'

'They've increased over the last four months. There's one account in particular where Zoe's been making payments on almost a daily basis.'

'How much money are we talking about?' asked Jemima.

'In total, I'd say a rough estimate of between twenty-five to thirty-thousand pounds.'

'People have killed for less,' said Jemima. 'Though, I can't imagine any hitman offering a payment plan. The idea's bizarre. But who knows? Until we've established who these accounts belong to or ensure that they're not shell companies linking back to some dodgy individual, we have to look into it. What about Isobel? Is there anything to suggest that she's making payments to any or all of those five accounts?'

'No. Isobel only has the one bank account, and there's hardly any activity on it. Her wages get paid in. She has a monthly standing order to her sister, which you'd expect since she lives with her. Apart from that, there are no large payments.'

'Do either of them have credit cards or other loans?' asked Jemima.

'Isobel doesn't have anything. But Zoe's a different matter. She's got three credit cards, two of which are maxed out, and she's getting pretty close to the limit on the third.'

'Any bank loans?'

'Five thousand taken out about six months ago.'

'Bring her in for questioning. Chances are there'll be a legitimate explanation. But at this moment in time, we're clutching at straws. Go to her school. Take a uniformed officer with you. I'll interview her with you when you get back.'

Jemima walked over to Peters, who was engrossed in his latest task. The list of psychopathic patients that Giles Souter had given them was open on his desk. Jemima pointed at the next name. 'Have you managed to make any headway with Ophelia Charles?' she asked him.

'Still trying, guv. She may very well be one of the psychopaths that Bradley Rathbone treated, but the woman doesn't appear to have a criminal record. It would have been so much easier for me if she did. But I think I've managed to track her down.'

'Excellent work. So, what have you got?'

'Have you heard of the term "rinsing"?' asked Peters.

'No,' said Jemima with a shake of the head.

'Then sit back and prepare to be educated. A rinser is a woman who cultivates friendships with rich men online so that they'll buy her expensive gifts or fund an extravagant lifestyle. It's a modern twist on the age-old lifestyle of what used to be referred to as a gold-digger. The big difference is that in the past, a young woman met face to face with her so-called sugar daddy. More often than not she would have had a physical relationship with him. Occasionally some of them took things further and married the guy.'

'That still goes on today, with rich older men and their trophy wives,' said Jemima.

'It sure does,' agreed Peters. 'But rinsers are different. They don't meet up with the men. Everything is done over the internet with webcams.'

'So they con them out of money. That's obviously a crime,' said Jemima.

'You're misunderstanding what I'm saying. There is no crime. These men are willing participants. They know upfront that the rinser only wants their money, and they're happy to play along. These women are determined to have extravagant lifestyles. They want the bling, the penthouse, the Ferrari, the luxury holidays. But they've no means of paying for it. They post wish lists on social media. Men send them friendship requests. There's lots of charm, flirting and massaging of egos. The rinsers often get what they want and more.'

'I don't understand,' said Jemima. 'I can see why the women would do it. But what's in it for the men? Why would anyone be stupid enough to buy things, especially expensive things, for someone who has no intention of ever meeting you?'

'Everyone's different, guv. Think of it this way — you're in a straight relationship, I'm in a gay one. We're both comfortable with that. It's the way we are. Some people just want to shag around. They're satisfied with a casual hook-up and don't want a commitment of any kind. As long as they make that clear when they get together with someone, then nobody gets hurt. It's the same with rinsers. As long as they're upfront with the men, and the men are willing participants, then what's the harm?'

'It's morally wrong,' said Jemima.

'In your opinion, but with respect, your opinion doesn't matter. The rinsers are happy. The men are happy. They may very well spend ridiculous amounts of money on these women, but in return, it might give them a feeling of satisfaction that they've been able to do it. It's like a macho thing where you get a kick out of knowing that you're able to spend the money and not miss it.'

'I suppose we could say Ophelia Charles is a financial dominatrix and has found a rich man who's stupid enough to spend a lot of money on her.'

'Not just one rich guy. She's got at least seven of them on the go,' said Peters.

'Really? Seven men? Bloody hell! I guess that as a psychopath this helps satisfy her need to control and humiliate people. I suppose that it's a good way to channel her energy. She gets what she wants and no one suffers. But I bet you anything that if one of those men tried to redress the balance further down the line, and attempted to change the dynamic of the relationship, Ophelia could turn nasty.'

'Not our problem, guv,' said Peters.

'How does your fact-finding mission help us with the investigation?' asked Jemima.

'I'm not sure that it will, but Ophelia posts a high volume of messages on social media. There's a lot of banter going back and forth. I've given it some thought, and I'm going to ask Ashton if he can hack into her accounts for Saturday. It's his area of expertise, and I'm sure he'll relish the challenge. Perhaps that way we can establish where she was over the time frame we're looking at.'

'I'll pretend I didn't hear that. But I suppose Ashton's smart enough not to get caught, and it would help us rule Ophelia in or out of the investigation. Just don't mention it in front of Kennedy.'

* * *

Jemima headed to the canteen to get something to eat. As she scanned the room for somewhere to sit, she noticed

Broadbent, alone at a table in the far corner of the room. He had finished his main course and was about to begin eating a jam roly-poly and custard. She walked up to him and placed her tray on the table. It was time to build bridges.

'I'm sorry,' she said. 'I shouldn't have spoken to you like that.'

'No, you shouldn't have. You wouldn't put up with it if I told you to fuck off, so why did you think it was acceptable to say that to me?'

'You're right. I wish I hadn't said it. But I did, and I regret it. Is it OK for me to sit here?'

'It's up to you.'

'Don't be like that. I'd like to put the incident behind us. It was a mistake. I was annoyed with myself, and I took it out on you.'

'Yeah, well . . .'

'It's no excuse, but everything's going pear-shaped at home.'

'What do you mean?' he asked. As he held the spoon midway between the bowl and his mouth, a dollop of custard dropped on to the table in front of him.

'Well, you know that James is living with us on a permanent basis now, but it's coincided with Nick finding out that he's got Klinefelter syndrome.'

'What does that mean?' asked Broadbent, as he replaced the spoon in the bowl.

'In a nutshell, it's a rare genetic condition, which means that he's always been infertile.'

'Shit!' hissed Broadbent. 'So he's not James's father? How's he dealing with that?'

'Badly. Nick's having a meltdown. Drinking too much, and resenting James, just when James needs him the most.'

'Do you want me to have a word with him?' asked Broadbent.

'Thanks for the offer, but I don't think it would do any good. I tried to talk some sense into him last night, but Nick just doesn't want to hear it. And I'm sure it would just add to his resentment if he realized that I'd spoken to you about it. Nick's in a vile mood at the moment, just as James is trying to come to terms with what's happened to his mother.'

'Poor kid. Does he know Nick's not his father?'

'I hope not. I've told Nick that he shouldn't say anything to him. But as I've said, he's drinking far too much, so who knows what he'll say. He's hurting, and he's lashing out. The only thing I know for sure is that it'd break James if he found out about it. I couldn't forgive Nick if he blurted it out.

'They both need me at home. But because of this case, I can't afford to take any time off. At least James is at school during the week, which takes a bit of the pressure off. My father helps out when he can, but I don't want to tell him about this latest development with Nick as it'll only make things worse. I'm just hoping he'll pull himself together and accept that biology isn't important. Right now, James needs his dad and Nick has to look after him when I'm not there.'

'And I just added to your stress levels by having a hissy fit,' said Broadbent.

'Forget it. You had every right.'

CHAPTER 36

When Jemima returned to her desk, Ashton was waiting for her.

'I've just taken Zoe Jones into the interview room. Are you ready to make a start?' he asked.

'You've done all the work, so you can take the lead on this,' said Jemima.

'Really?' Ashton stopped abruptly and almost dropped his folder of paperwork related to Zoe Jones's financial records.

'Steady on there,' Jemima said. 'Why do you look so surprised?'

'Because you rarely ask me to interview anyone with you and this is the first time you've asked me to take the lead.'

'Yeah, well, that's down to me. It's no reflection on you. You've worked hard, done all the research, and compiled the records. It's only fair that I allow you to see it through. Anyway, it'll be good experience for you. Come on, we can't stand around here all day.'

'Thanks, guv. I appreciate it.'

'You're welcome. I heard on the grapevine that you've got your sergeant's exam coming up soon?'

'That's right,' he replied. 'I suppose I should have said something.'

'It would have been nice, but I don't blame you for keeping it to yourself. It's no one else's business, and you don't need people winding you up.'

'It's not that, guv. I just thought you wouldn't be interested.'

'Seriously?' It was Jemima's turn to stop dead in her tracks. She was shocked by what he'd just said. 'Why wouldn't I be interested? You're part of my team. I asked DCI Kennedy to offer you a permanent posting. Of course I'm interested in you.'

'Sorry, guv. I didn't realize,' said Ashton. 'It's just that since I've arrived, I've been under the impression that you've been sidelining me. Whenever you go anywhere, you take Broadbent with you. You've never once asked me to accompany you anywhere.'

'And you haven't figured out why?' asked Jemima.

'I thought it was because you didn't value my input.'

'Well, you've got that wrong for a start. The reason I don't ask you to come with me is that I see you as the brains of this team. I can trust you to work independently. There are not many officers I could say that about. Finlay, you're by far the smartest person I know. No one knows their way around a computer as well as you. Your skills are like gold dust. You can do in a matter of minutes what it would take most of us at least a day to achieve. As far as I'm concerned, you're wasted as a DC. You'll walk the sergeant's exam and wow them at the interview.'

'Thanks, guv. That means a lot,' said Ashton.

'What I'm about to tell you is in the strictest confidence. DCI Kennedy's had funding agreed to fill an additional sergeant's post. As far as I'm concerned, if everything goes well for you, the job will be yours if you want it.'

Jemima and Ashton entered the interview room to find Zoe Jones hunched in her chair. The woman's elbows were on the table and her forehead rested heavily on the palms of her hands.

Sharing a quick look of surprise, they both took a seat opposite her. As they made themselves comfortable, Zoe sat up and shuffled backwards as though she was doing her best to disappear into the backrest.

Jemima was immediately struck by the fact that the woman's demeanour was so different from the way she'd acted during their previous encounter. She was dressed more formally, which was to be expected as Ashton had collected her from her place of work. Yet for a woman who held a position of authority, Zoe appeared haunted to the point of distraction. In fact, Jemima had seen many victims look in better shape than Zoe did at that moment.

'Are you feeling all right?' asked Jemima.

'I'm not ill, if that's what you're implying. I'm angry and I'm stressed,' said Zoe. Her voice was unnaturally high-pitched. It quivered like a string that was about to snap.

'Why is that?' inquired Ashton.

'Because I can't believe that you came to my workplace and insisted that I accompany you to the station. I'm a dep-uty head teacher at a primary school. People look up to me and trust me with their children. Any hint of wrongdoing on my part could be catastrophic for my career.'

'No one's suggesting that you've done anything wrong, Miss Jones,' said Ashton. 'As you know, we're investigat-ing a multiple murder. And given your sister's link with the victims, and the fact that she could have had a motive for murdering those people, we are obliged to look into every aspect of her life.'

'I'm sure that Constable Ashton would have informed you at the time that you're not being charged with anything. We just need you to help us with our inquiries,' said Jemima.

'I did,' Ashton confirmed. 'When I arrived at the school, I explicitly said that you were not under arrest, but that we needed you to accompany us to the station to answer some questions. You were formerly cautioned, asked whether or not you wanted to have a solicitor present, and you declined.'

'Is it still the case that you do not wish to have a solicitor present?' asked Jemima.

'I don't need one. I haven't done anything wrong,' said Zoe. 'I just don't understand why you're dragging me into this. You've already ruled Isobel out of the investigation. You told me so yourself.' She shot Jemima a look that could have withered a vine.

'I told you we were content that Isobel did not carry out the murders herself,' said Jemima. She kept her voice low and even, so as not to inflame the situation further.

'What are you implying? You can't seriously be suggesting that I killed Bradley and the others? You're crazy! What evidence could you possibly have to make you think that I would be capable of doing such a thing?'

'As Inspector Huxley has already said, our investigation has thrown up a few questions which we need answered,' said Ashton. He spoke slowly, in a matter-of-fact tone, trying to dial down the rising tension.

'Like what?' asked Zoe.

'We've been looking at your finances, and there is a lot of unusual activity on your—'

Ashton was mid-sentence when Zoe Jones's expression crumpled, and she began to sob loudly and inconsolably.

As Jemima stared at the woman, her mind raced through various scenarios as she tried to figure out what was going on. It was then that she noticed the marks on one of Zoe's wrists. Suddenly, in one of those light-bulb moments, it came to her. Everything made sense.

'Get some tissues and a glass of water,' ordered Jemima.

Ashton looked bewildered but did as she asked.

'Look at me, Zoe. Look at me. It's all right,' said Jemima. In the space of a few seconds her tone had changed from professionally detached to compassionate. 'I've just noticed the bruises on your wrist. Do you owe money to a loan shark? Is that the man who was at your house the other day? Is he after you for money? Has he threatened you?'

Zoe was too upset to speak but nodded almost imperceptibly.

'Did he hurt you, Zoe? Did he make those bruises on your wrist?'

Zoe nodded again, just as Ashton re-entered the room carrying a box of tissues and a plastic cup containing water.

'Take a moment,' said Jemima.

Zoe reached for a handful of tissues. It took a while for her to stop crying. As her sobs subsided, Ashton opened his mouth to speak, but Jemima kicked his ankle to tell him to shut up and let her take the lead. He yelped, shot her a look of contempt, and shuffled his feet away.

'I don't understand why you're so desperate for money that you had to borrow from a loan shark,' began Jemima. 'You've got a well-paid job. Surely your mortgage payments can't be that high? What's happened?'

'O-o-on-line g-g-gambling,' whispered Zoe. The woman was so ashamed that she could barely raise her chin from where it rested on her chest. 'I-I-I'm a-a-addicted to it.'

'Zoe, tell us the man's name. We can do something about him. Lending money without authorization from the Financial Conduct Agency is a criminal offence. We have an Illegal Money Lending Unit who will look into it. You won't be the only person he's loaned money to. He won't have an official set of accounts, but there will be some sort of paper or electronic trail the unit can follow.

'But apart from that, we can arrest this lowlife straight-away for causing you actual bodily harm. I've seen him at your house. He won't be able to deny being there. Trust me on this. You won't do yourself any favours by keeping quiet. Things will only get worse if you don't make a stand.'

'Kenneth Shanklin,' she whispered.

'Repeat the name, but louder, for the tape,' said Jemima.

'His name's Kenneth Shanklin. I think he lives in Cardiff.'

'Ashton, get someone on it immediately,' said Jemima.

'Yes, guv,' said Ashton, as he pushed his chair back and headed for the door.

'Look, I know it's easy for me to say, but you don't have to continue like this,' said Jemima. She reached for Zoe's hands in a gesture of support. 'Take back control. You can fight your addiction. I won't pretend it's easy, because it's not. There's going to be temptation everywhere you go. But there's support out there to help you quit, and I can put you in touch with some organizations that can help. The question is, are you ready to give it a go?'

'Yes,' sighed Zoe. 'I've got to stop doing this before I lose everything. Izzy needs me. If I lose the house, I don't know what will happen to either of us.'

'Before you leave, I'll give you some leaflets and set up an appointment for you with a support group. But first, I want to know if there's anything you, or your sister aren't telling us about the Rathbones?'

'No. We've told you the truth. Neither of us has had any contact with Bradley or Millie for years. I despised Bradley for the way he abandoned Izzy after Lydia's death. He refused to give her the benefit of the doubt and willingly bought into the idea that she was guilty because it suited him. My sister needed his support. She was grieving the death of her child. Yet she was wrongly labelled a child-killer. And by doing that he's allowed a murderer to go free.'

'It doesn't make sense. Why would he do that?' asked Jemima.

'Bradley's abhorrent treatment of Izzy was all about him trying to bury his own guilt.'

'You think Bradley killed Lydia?'

'No, of course not. But neither did Izzy. She's incapable of hurting anyone. My sister's the sweetest person I know. Doesn't have a bad bone in her body. She loved Lydia, but she was struggling back then.

'I know for a fact that she'd tried to tell Bradley that she was depressed, exhausted and needed his support. But he ignored her, as it didn't fit with his idea of domestic life. He expected her to be the perfect wife and mother.

'Bradley was always happy to go the extra mile to help his patients, because that care and dedication raised his professional profile. But that generosity didn't extend to his wife. If only he'd taken Izzy's concerns seriously and done something to help . . .'

'It still doesn't mean that your sister didn't kill Lydia,' said Jemima.

'I'm telling you she didn't do it. She couldn't have, but I've got no proof. What I'm trying to say is that Bradley turning his back on her was about him trying to justify his own shortcomings as a husband and a father. By abandoning Izzy, he immediately became the righteous bereaved parent. Yes, he'd lost a child, but he was able to start over again and there was no blame placed at his door.'

Jemima realized that they weren't getting anywhere with this conversation. Lydia Rathbone's death was an undeniable tragedy, but it was not relevant to the current investigation. If Zoe truly believed what she was saying, then the woman should try to get the case re-opened. But that really was none of Jemima's concern.

CHAPTER 37

By the time Jemima arrived home that evening her head was banging. They had spent the day ruling out possible suspects. The only problem was there was no one left in the frame, and the stress of getting nowhere was taking its toll. What's more, Jemima knew that there would be no respite at home. No matter how hard she tried she knew that she was coming up short in every aspect of her life.

It was at times like this that it would be good just to be able to take off and leave everyone to it, but realistically, that wasn't ever going to be an option. On odd occasions throughout the last few days, Jemima had found her thoughts turning to the packet of razor blades she had hidden inside the bath panel. Over the last few years, cutting herself had become an addiction, one that she had recently fought to control. But whenever she felt trapped, inadequate or low, the deliciously painful sensation of slicing through her skin held such an enormous appeal.

As she opened the front door, James jumped up from the step he had been sitting on and rushed into her arms. He hugged her so hard that it began to hurt, and she immediately felt guilty about not being there to support him throughout the day. She returned the boy's embrace and bent down to kiss the top of his head.

'Where's your dad?' she asked.

'In the kitchen. He's drunk.'

'Have you had anything to eat?' she asked.

'Only a slice of toast. I'm starving,' replied James.

'Well, let's leave your father to it, and go for a burger.'

* * *

The next few days were more of the same, with no progress being made on the case, and Nick drinking himself into a stupor at home.

Jemima's father helped out as much as he could with the school runs, and James had been booked into some after-school activities. All of which allowed the boy to spend less time with Nick.

Jemima told herself that she had to remain strong. It was more important than ever for her to control her demons. As things stood, she was the only parent that James could rely upon.

Having suggested that Nick talk to someone about his problems, she was shocked when he laughed in her face and told her that it was none of her business. For a couple who had once been close, there was now a chasm between them, and it was widening by the second. Their marriage was in tatters. Yet there was nothing she could do about it.

Worst still, it was obvious that James knew something was wrong. But the boy was too scared to ask. And Jemima didn't have a clue what to tell him, as she knew it would break his heart. She desperately wanted Nick to come to his senses before their son became aware of what was really going on.

She had a better understanding than most of how easy it was for things to spiral out of control, and she had first-hand experience of how you could self-destruct as a result of it. She also knew that in order for Nick to get his life back on track, he needed to accept that he had a problem and want to make changes for the better. No one could do that for him. It was a step he had to take for himself.

A few weeks passed with no new developments on the case. Millie Rathbone had made significant progress and was placed on a low-dependency ward in the children's unit. They had spoken to her on a few occasions, but the girl was unable to remember anything other than the vaguest of details about the day of the attack.

Even Giles Souter had taken it upon himself to speak to her. He had insisted, given his connection to Bradley, that he be the one to break the news of what had happened to the rest of the family. Millie had initially fallen apart, though over the course of a few days she appeared to regain her composure. Giles had also attempted to find out what she remembered. He eventually concluded that her mind was most likely blocking out the memories, as they were too traumatic for her to cope with.

At work, it was getting to the stage where they were going to have to shelve the case, but before that happened, Jemima was determined to have one last shot at trying to make sense of everything.

When she arrived at work, Jemima grabbed a coffee and sat down to review the case notes. She was determined to be as thorough as possible. She felt she owed it to Millie to find the person who had wiped out most of her family and left her for dead. Especially as the girl had been left for dead during the attack.

Before she started to read through the notes, Jemima decided to ring the hospital to find out how Millie was doing. It was a call she made every few days, as it saddened her to think that the teenager had no one looking out for her.

'What do you mean she was discharged two days ago? Where did she go?' Jemima couldn't believe what she was hearing. When she eventually hung up the phone, she pushed back her chair and marched into Kennedy's office. 'Why did Millie Rathbone not have one of our officers guarding her?' she demanded.

'Usual story, lack of resources and competing priorities. Has something happened to her?' he asked, with a concerned expression.

'Did you know that the hospital has discharged her?' she asked.

'No, I hadn't been made aware of it. Where's she gone?'

'Stephanie Newton's parents have taken her in.'

'Well, that's good, isn't it?' asked Kennedy.

'Good for Millie, but I don't know whether it's in the Newtons' best interests. We still have no idea of the motive for the attack. The Newtons could be putting their lives on the line.'

'That's a bit dramatic, Huxley.'

'Once I've gone over the case files again, I'm going to go and see the Newtons. Make sure they understand what they could have let themselves in for. I'll check out their security while I'm there. They should at least have panic buttons linked directly to the station,' said Jemima.

'I think you're making a mountain out of a molehill, but I suppose there's no harm in demonstrating that we're taking their safety seriously. It'll look good on the report.'

Jemima turned on her heel and marched out of the room without uttering another word. She didn't trust herself to keep a civil tongue in her head.

CHAPTER 38

Jemima had given up ringing Dinah Newton's mobile. Each time she dialled, it went straight through to voicemail, and she had already left three messages asking the woman to return the call. Jemima decided that if she hadn't heard back from her by midday, she'd drive up to the house to check things out.

'Did anyone make sure that the relevant books in Millie's room were returned to the library?' she asked.

'Yeah, Owen Newton collected them last week,' said Broadbent.

'I don't suppose anyone listed the titles and authors?'

'Didn't seem any point,' said Broadbent.

Jemima tried the library, only to be informed that Owen Newton was overseeing an event in one of their conference rooms. Despite not being able to speak to him, it put her mind at rest, as if Owen was at work, there couldn't be any problems at home. She left a message for him to ring her back, as she wanted to know which books Millie had borrowed, and also which ones she had taken out on Stephanie's card.

After a few hours of poring over the case notes, Jemima's hair was sticking up in all sorts of strange directions, as she had a habit of playing with it whenever she concentrated on something. She was grateful that everyone had meticulously documented their findings. It made it easy to follow the various strands of the investigation, and Jemima was satisfied that the team had been thorough in their approach.

Ashton had hacked into Ophelia Charles's social media account and had been able to rule her out of the investigation.

Broadbent had even followed up on Connor and Maggie Rathbone's deaths in case there was the slightest possibility that they had not been accidental. But in the end, there was nothing to suggest that there had been any foul play. It had just been a tragic accident.

However, something niggled away at the back of Jemima's mind. She sensed that there was something important that had been overlooked, but try as she might she couldn't identify what it was.

'Huxley, make a note in your diary that there's a meeting we both need to attend,' said Kennedy, as he walked into the room.

Of course. Lauren's diary! She hadn't deciphered the coded entry. Jemima opened the middle drawer of her pedestal, and there it was, hidden beneath a pile of papers.

'Did you hear what I said?' asked Kennedy, looming over her desk.

'Yes, I did. What date was it?' she asked in a distracted manner. She was already flicking through the pages of the book.

'It's a week today. Ten o'clock start. What have you got there?'

'Lauren Rathbone's journal. I'd looked at a few of the entries but didn't read all of it. The latest one was written in a code that I couldn't decipher. Chances are it's not going to be relevant to the case. But I thought I'd better try to decipher it, just to be sure.'

'You should have passed it on to Ashton. He's into that sort of thing. What if it contains something pertinent to the investigation? We could have wasted valuable time here,' said

Kennedy. 'I realize you've had a lot going on in your personal life, but you've dropped the ball on this one. Let's just hope for your sake that this girl's journal doesn't contain some vital piece of evidence. Otherwise, it'll be hard for you to explain the delay away.'

'I'll sort it,' said Jemima, feeling sick with guilt. She was about to head over to Ashton's desk when her phone rang.

'It's Owen Newton. You asked me to return your call.'

'That's right. Thanks for getting back to me,' said Jemima.

'What's it about? Is there a problem?'

'Not really, I'm just trying to tie up a few loose ends. Your daughter told me that Millie was a big reader, so much so that she used to take out some library books on Stephanie's card. I was just wondering if you'd be able to give me a list of all the books that Millie took out under her own name, and also a list of those she took out under your daughter's name?'

'Of course I can do that, but is it really relevant to your investigation?'

'I honestly don't know. Like I said, I'm just tying up some loose ends.' Even to her own ears, Jemima sounded unconvincing and desperate.

'Give me your email address and I'll send you over the list from Millie's account within the hour. You can have all of those on Stephanie's account too, but until I've spoken to the girls, I won't be able to identify which of the books were for Millie. If I spot anything surprising on Stephanie's list, I'll highlight it as a possibility.'

'That would be helpful. Thanks for your cooperation,' said Jemima. 'Before you go, how are things at home now that Millie's moved in with you?'

'I can't say that I have much to do with her. That's more Dinah's department. The girl only moved in two nights ago. Stephanie's obviously happy to have her friend there, but it's Dinah's routine that will be impacted the most. Millie hasn't returned to school yet, so the burden of looking after her will fall on Dinah's shoulders. I have noticed she's quite withdrawn, but I suppose that's only to be expected. Give her a few months and that might change. Hopefully it'll do her good spending time with Steph. She's such an optimistic kid. Remarkably resilient. Just the sort of attitude that young Millie will need to see her through this terrible time.'

'Would I be able to call around this evening?' asked Jemima.

'I don't see why not.'

'Perhaps I could take a look at your security measures at the same time?'

'Are you suggesting we're in danger?' asked Owen.

'No. It's just that we haven't been able to identify the person responsible for killing the Rathbones. If he knows that Millie's alive, she could still be a target, as there's a possibility that if those memories surface she could identify him.'

'No one mentioned that to us when we took her in,' he said. 'Stephanie more or less railroaded us into looking after the girl, but she can't stay with us now. I'm not having my family put in danger like that. She'll have to go. Can you arrange for her to be placed in witness protection?'

'It might not be that easy, Mr Newton, but I'll do my best to find out what options are available to you.'

'I'd appreciate it if you could do that sooner rather than later. Thank you, Inspector.'

'Is there any reason your wife has been unable to answer my calls this morning?' asked Jemima.

'She's taken Millie for a hospital appointment. I believe they're doing some more tests to determine the most efficient course of rehabilitation therapy. As far as I know, it's supposed to take most of the day.'

CHAPTER 39

Jemima opened Lauren's journal to the final entry and sighed. It was such a daunting task trying to crack the code, as it just looked like line after line of gobbledygook. She thought she had quite a broad range of skills. Yet faced with something like this she just didn't know where to start. Kennedy was right. Ashton was the ideal person to try to decipher it.

'Ashton, take a look at this,' she called.

'What is it?' He stared at the text with a quizzical expression on his face.

'It's Lauren Rathbone's journal. The last three entries are written in code. We need to find out what they say, and I wouldn't have a clue how to set about it.'

'Want me to have a go at it?' he asked.

'I was hoping you'd say that,' she said.

'It shouldn't be too sophisticated. Lauren was only a kid, and from what we know about her the code is likely to be fairly straightforward.'

'If you say so, but how will you start?'

'Well, there're a few single-letter words, so they will most likely represent the letters A and I. See here,' he said, pointing at the letters Z and H. 'At first glance I can see that there're also some repeated words which begin with a capital letter.'

'So they're likely to be names?' asked Jemima.

'Exactly,' said Ashton.

'Lauren's friends said that she switched to writing in code because she didn't want Millie to be able to read the journal. It's safe to assume that a lot of what's written is about Millie.'

'And that makes it even easier, as Millie is a six-letter word, which will begin with a capital letter, have either a Z or an H in the second and fifth position, and also have a repeated letter in the third and fourth position.'

'You're a genius,' said Jemima.

'Not really, it's just the way my brain works. There, you see?' he said, pointing at a word. '*Phoohd*. It's repeated a few times throughout the text, and I'd put money on it that *Phoohd* represents Millie. I can use those letters to help decipher the remainder of the text, and as the only other single-letter word is likely to be A, I'd say that it's represented by the letter Z.'

'Believe me, Ashton, you are a genius,' said Jemima.

'OK, believe that if you like, but just go away and let me get on with it. I can honestly say that this will be the most fun I've had in ages.'

'How long do you think it will take?'

'Give me a couple of hours,' said Ashton.

Jemima was at a loose end until either Ashton deciphered Lauren's journal entry or Owen Newton emailed through the list of books that Millie had been so eager to read.

Grabbing the case file, she opened it and began to peruse the paperwork. She soon came across lists of the victim's personal effects. There were few items for the dead teenagers, which was unsurprising as they had both lost their lives while in bed. The adults were a different matter. Sally's wedding and engagement rings were recorded, together with a pendant and her watch. Bradley's wedding ring was on the list too, but there was no watch.

Jemima did a double take. She scanned the list of his personal effects once more, dragging her finger down each item to ensure that she hadn't overlooked it. It was the first moment on this case that Jemima felt a frisson of excitement.

'Dan, dig out the footage of the Rathbones at the super-market car park,' said Jemima.

'What's up? Have you found something?' he asked, as he looked up from what he was doing.

'Bradley Rathbone's watch isn't listed as part of his personal effects.'

'He was definitely wearing one. I remember saying at the time that it was a Rolex, and you all laughed at me.'

'Yeah, I remember. As it's not listed here, it suggests the killer's taken it. But as to where it is . . . well, that's another matter. We need a decent image of that watch. Drop whatever you've been doing and treat this as a priority.'

As she waited for Broadbent and Ashton to make headway on their tasks, Jemima started to feel jittery. She still had a niggling feeling that the Newton family could be in danger as long as Millie remained in their care. And it was alarming that Owen Newton and his wife hadn't been warned of this, or even considered it as a possibility.

Millie could be in immediate danger too. If the killer found out that she was alive, he would know that there was the possibility that she could identify him. Even if the girl didn't know who he was, she might be able to help the police construct a photofit. And when that image was released into the public domain, there was an increased chance that someone somewhere would recognize him.

Jemima didn't want to risk anyone else being killed by this psychopath and thought that it would be better for all concerned that Millie be placed into protective custody. So she picked up the phone to make some calls.

She was part way through dialling when her computer pinged to announce the arrival of an email. Jemima jumped at the sound. She was uptight, even though she didn't want to acknowledge it. She replaced the handset, toggled to the relevant screen and saw that the message was from Owen Newton. Two files were attached. She was about to open the first one when her phone rang.

'Have you read it yet?' asked Owen Newton. He spoke rapidly, and his voice crackled with fear.

'I was just about to open the attachments. I've only just received the message. Is everything all right?' she asked.

'No, it's not. Look at the list of books. I know my daughter. Stephanie's interests are eclectic but benign. She's a gentle girl who reads about the history of art, classical music, astronomy, mathematics and physics. Stephanie has an aversion to the sight of blood. Presumably, it's as a result of the car crash which claimed the lives of her birth parents and resulted in her becoming a paraplegic. Seeing even a small amount of blood causes her to vomit, and in extreme cases, pass out. It's well-documented on her medical files. But look at the list of books. Look at the list!'

'Calm down, Mr Newton. I'm opening the file now,' said Jemima, as she clicked on the relevant document.

'I've marked on there when Stephanie became friendly with Millie. I've also highlighted books I can categorically say that Stephanie would have no interest in reading. Do you see what I'm getting at?' pressed Owen. His voice was becoming higher and increasingly agitated with every word. 'That girl's not going to spend another night under my roof. I want her out now. You'll have to find her some emergency accommodation straight away. No excuses. I've already spoken to Dinah and told her to leave the child at the hospital. Millie Rathbone's not our problem.'

'Has your wife told Millie she's no longer welcome at your home?' asked Jemima.

'No. The girl was having a scan when I spoke to Dinah. I told her not to say anything, just to leave, head home and lock herself in. I'm going there now. We'll pack a few bags, pick Stephanie up from school and head off for a couple of weeks until everything's sorted. Stephanie's not going to be happy about it, but I'll put her straight. We've got to look after ourselves.'

'I'll send an officer to pick up Millie at the hospital, and keep you updated,' said Jemima.

'I've cracked it, and it makes interesting reading,' said Ashton, just as Jemima ended the call.

'Let me take a look,' said Jemima. She rushed towards his desk in her eagerness to see what he'd found.

CHAPTER 40

'I underestimated Lauren,' said Ashton. 'It wasn't a simple code after all. Each consonant was plus three letters. The vowels were minus one. It caused a bit of confusion as there were no Ls, Rs or Xs used in the code. Zs were used to represent both A and W, and Ts to represent both Q and U.'

'Well done, but I really don't need to know the details. I just want to know what Lauren wrote,' said Jemima.

Ashton held out the decoded transcript and Jemima began to read through the first extract.

I'm writing in code because I don't want anyone to know what I suspect until I can prove it. I've figured out something about Millie. She's a psycho! But Uncle Bradley doesn't see it. I think Auntie Sally knows, but doesn't want to say anything in case it upsets Uncle Bradley. She's not Millie's birth mother. And Uncle Bradley is very much Team Millie.

A few months before Mum and Dad died, I overheard them talking about what happened to Lydia. She was Millie's younger sister, and was only a baby when she was killed. This all happened a long time ago. Uncle Bradley's first wife, Auntie Isobel, went to prison for killing her, but Mum said that she didn't believe that she'd done it. Dad said that she must have, as it was too awful to think that the only other possibility was true.

I didn't know what they meant. I wanted to ask them, but I couldn't, as then they'd know that I'd been listening when I shouldn't have. I've been thinking a lot about that conversation. Uncle Bradley was at work when Lydia was killed. So that only leaves Millie.

What if Millie killed Lydia?

That must have been what Mum meant. I know she was only seven at the time. But she's always been jealous of anyone getting more attention than her. And I really believe that she could have done it.

No one told me how Lydia died, but I've seen things on the internet saying that she was smothered with a cushion. They said that it wouldn't have taken much effort, and it would have been over very quickly.

Well, Millie could easily have done that.

I think Millie's a murderer!!!

Jemima's blood ran cold. She turned to the second extract.

Earlier today I was home alone so I decided to go into Millie's bedroom to try and find some proof of what she'd done to Lydia. Millie doesn't like anyone going into her room, not even Uncle Bradley or Auntie Sally. But the rules don't apply to her as I've caught her snooping around in other people's things.

I had to be careful to leave things the way I found them, as I'm sure she'd notice if anything was out of place. But it turned out to be a big waste of time.

I looked through her stuff and didn't find anything.

But Millie is weird. There were a few library books she hadn't returned. They were about forensics, just like CSI. She loves that programme. She's told Uncle Bradley and Auntie Sally she wants to be a forensic scientist.

Now that's creepy and weird!

Her mind racing, Jemima quickly read over the third and final extract.

Millie was in a right strop earlier on. We were eating dinner when she accused Uncle Bradley and Auntie Sally of going in her bedroom. Of course they both denied it, because they hadn't. Millie glared at me and Jonathan. I tried not to go red, because then she'd know it had been me, but I don't think it worked.

Later on, Uncle Bradley and Auntie Sally went to the pub with our next-door neighbours. I was doing my homework when I heard a noise coming from my aunt and uncle's bedroom. I went to take a look and there was Millie, with Auntie Sally's jewellery box. That's when I saw her take a ring.

Millie saw me and realized that I'd caught her out. Suddenly she was on me. She's way stronger than she looks. She pinned me against the wall, grabbed my neck and squeezed really hard. It hurt so much. I couldn't breathe! She said the ring was payback for Auntie Sally snooping around her bedroom. Millie said she'd kill me if I blabbed about what she'd done. She said she'd get away with it, as she knew all about destroying evidence at crime scenes.

I thought I was going to die right there.

She didn't let go of me until I swore not to say anything.

It hurt to swallow after that. I've got ugly bruises on my neck. I'll have to cover them with make-up.

SHE'S EVIL!!!!

I'm sure she killed Lydia. She'll probably wait until I'm asleep in bed then kill me too.

Jemima's mind went into overdrive as the pieces of the jigsaw began to slot together. It seemed almost unthinkable that Millie Rathbone could be the person responsible for the murders. She was only fourteen years old and had looked so weak and broken when they'd seen her after the attack. But Jemima acknowledged that that initial impression had clouded her judgement and reinforced the belief that the girl was a victim.

They'd followed up leads, checked people's alibis and had come up with nothing. It had been easy to think that because Bradley had been a psychiatrist who had dealings with psychopaths, one of his patients must have been the murderer. But their investigation had proved that none of the people on Giles Souter's list could have done it.

The more Jemima thought about psychopathic traits, the more convinced she became that Millie could actually be a psychopath. The girl had no friends, apart from Stephanie. And from what Jemima had just seen on the list of books that Owen Newton had forwarded to her, it seemed that Millie hadn't forged a friendship with Stephanie for friendship's sake.

If anything, Millie had used Stephanie to enable her to take out books from the library to study true crime and understand forensic techniques. If Millie were genuinely interested in having a career as a forensic scientist, then there would have been no reason for her computer history and her library history not to be full of searches on these subjects. But they'd examined the family's computers, and the search history on each of the machines was benign.

Millie had covered her tracks at the library, as her personal record was full of books with no link to forensics. Another factor that pointed to the premeditated nature of the murders was that none of the library books that they had removed from her bedroom had been linked to forensics or murder. Most likely because the teenager realized that books of that subject matter would set up a red flag and lead the police to suspect her.

Every way you looked at it, Millie had the means, motive and opportunity to carry out the murders. It explained why there was no sign of a break-in at the house, and also why the weapon used was one of the knives from the kitchen.

Millie would have been at home with her cousins while her father and stepmother had gone shopping. There were independent accounts from both Lauren's and Jonathan's friends that Millie didn't like her cousins and was vile to them whenever possible. Then there was Lauren's journal.

John Prothero's post-mortem findings had revealed that the teenagers had been the first to die. After death, the level of overkill on Lauren's corpse had been shocking, as the girl had been stabbed far more times than any of the other victims. It bore out the fact that there was animosity between the girls, as she had been the focus of Millie's rage.

It was conceivable that Millie hadn't intended to kill her father or stepmother. She could have planned to stage her cousins' murders in such a way to make it look as though she was a fortunate survivor of a random home invasion. But if Bradley and Sally had returned earlier than Millie had anticipated, it would have changed everything. If Millie hadn't had the opportunity to stage the scene to make it look like she was a victim too, then the adults would suspect that she may have had something to do with it.

Even more disturbing was the entry in Lauren's journal that stated that Millie may have killed her baby sister when she was only seven years old. It would have been unthinkable at the time to suspect a young child of such a heinous act. But on reflection, it bore out Isobel's continued assertion that she had no recollection of killing her baby, despite having undergone regression therapy in an attempt to help her remember committing the act.

Now that the idea was out there, Jemima wouldn't be surprised if Zoe Jones confirmed that she believed that Millie was responsible for Lydia's death. Despite the fact that the woman had not once voiced that particular concern.

CHAPTER 41

Jemima picked up the phone and hurriedly called the duty sergeant. 'Do you have a team at or near the UHW?' she asked.

'Yes,' he confirmed.

'There's a teenage girl who's got an outpatient appointment for a scan. It's Millie Rathbone, the kid whose family was murdered. I need you to get the officers to locate and apprehend her. They're not to let her out of their sight. I'm on my way there now to arrest her.'

'Will do,' he said.

'Ashton, Peters, head over to the Rathbone house. We need to find Sally Rathbone's ring and Bradley Rathbone's watch. If I'm right, they'll be hidden somewhere in Millie's bedroom. Dismantle the furniture, take up the floorboards. Do whatever you have to but find them,' said Jemima. 'Broadbent, you're with me. Hurry up. We're off to the hospital to arrest Millie Rathbone.'

'What?' he asked. There was a look of bewilderment on his face. 'Are you going to tell me what's going on?'

'I'll tell you on the way but get a move on. You're driving.' She tossed him the set of keys. 'We need to get there as soon as possible, so get the blues and twos going. I've got a call to make.' She sprinted out of the room.

The ringtone sounded four times before Owen Newton picked up.

'Inspector?' he said.

'Where are you?' she asked.

'I'm at home with Dinah. We're about to head over to the school to collect Stephanie.'

'Listen carefully. I've just come across some new evidence that suggests that Millie might have murdered her family. I'm on my way to the hospital to arrest her. I suggest that you and your family stay well away from your house until I confirm that we have her in custody. Ring the school and tell them to keep Stephanie there. Ask them to confiscate her phone, as we don't want the girls communicating with each other. They mustn't let Stephanie leave the premises until you arrive to collect her.'

'Will do, Inspector, we're on our way now,' said Owen.

Broadbent had barely skidded to a halt outside the hospital when Jemima unfastened her seatbelt and legged it out of the car. She was already familiar with the location of the Radiology Department where Millie's scan would have taken place, and raced up the stairs and along the corridor, much to the consternation of people ambling along at a more leisurely place.

'What do you mean you haven't been able to locate her?' demanded Jemima, when she came face to face with the officers at the hospital.

'We've looked everywhere. The staff confirmed that Millie attended her appointments, but she must've left the building before we arrived.'

'Shit!' growled Jemima, as she kicked a vacant seat, sending it toppling to the floor.

'What do you want us to do?' asked the officer.

'Use your bloody initiative. Get out and look for her. She can't be too hard to find. The girl's on crutches. That should make her stand out in a crowd and slow her down. I want every available officer on this. Millie Rathbone's suspected of killing four people. She knows something's up, even if she doesn't realize that we're on to her. If she feels cornered, she'll do whatever it takes to survive, even if that means killing anyone who gets in her way. Don't under-estimate her, and whatever you do, don't be fooled by her appearance. She looks weak and vulnerable. But she's a psy-chopath, and we need to find her.'

Broadbent appeared at her side, breathing heavily.

Jemima was about to call the station when her phone sounded. 'Ring Kennedy and tell him to get all available officers on to this,' she said to Broadbent, before answering her phone.

'Inspector, its Owen Newton here. Stephanie's not at the school. No one knows where she is. Someone saw her in the study area at lunchtime, but she had a phone call and left the building. Have you arrested Millie?'

'No, she'd already left the hospital, so we must assume that the girls are meeting up,' said Jemima.

'You have to find them. I'm not having her hurt our girl,' said Owen.

'I'm getting every officer on to it, Mr Newton. Do the girls have access to money?'

'Stephanie doesn't. She'll have a few pounds on her just in case of an emergency, but that's all. I can't answer for Millie.'

'I think it's safe to assume they'll stay within the city, and Stephanie being in a wheelchair plays to our advantage. People will notice her, so we should be able to locate her quite easily. Do you have any idea where they would go?'

'Not really. As far as I know, the library's the only place they used to visit,' said Owen.

'In that case, we'll head over there now,' said Jemima.

'We'll keep driving round to see if we can find Stephanie,' said Owen. 'She wouldn't be able to afford a taxi, so she must've got on a bus.'

'There're a limited number of buses on that particular route into the city centre. I'll get someone to alert Cardiff Bus drivers to keep an eye out for her. If she's on one of their buses, we'll know about it and hopefully be able to get officers to her before she meets up with Millie. If you come across Millie yourselves, don't approach her. Either call me direct or dial 999.'

As she turned to face Broadbent, she noticed that the colour had drained from his face.

'We need to get to the Central Library,' he said. 'Kennedy said that reports are coming in of some sort of major disturbance. A large group of people have taken over the building. There are no other details at the moment, but it's one hell of a coincidence since we're trying to locate Millie, and the library's the one place she knows well.'

CHAPTER 42

Jemima and Broadbent had no option but to abandon their car long before they reached the city centre. Traffic was at a standstill, and some roads had already been closed. Horns blasted in frustration as drivers became impatient and angry.

Pavements were crowded with groups of people heading towards the centre on foot. Many of them looked as though they were ready for a fight. Jemima was glad that neither she nor Broadbent wore a uniform, as they would have instantly become targets for those looking for trouble. It didn't take a genius to realize that things were about to kick off big time.

The area was under siege. Emergency vehicles manoeuvred slowly through the crowds, often taking to the pavements to enable them to keep moving forwards. A major incident had been declared, and there was already a heavy police presence on the streets, with officers wearing riot gear.

As they neared the library, Jemima spotted some film crews setting up to broadcast the scene.

It was as though a mass brainwashing had occurred. People screamed, shouted, and chanted. At first, it was virtually impossible to understand their message. But as she began to make sense of the words, Jemima's blood ran cold.

'*Millie's innocent! We'll protect her! Millie's innocent! We'll protect her!*'

Jemima grabbed Broadbent's arm to get his attention. 'Millie's outplayed us!' she yelled.

'What do you mean?' he asked.

'She must've got wind of the fact that we suspect her. She's changed the narrative. Somehow Millie's managed to rouse this mob to support her. Look at them. They're not going to accept that she's the manipulative little bitch who slaughtered her family in cold blood. Listen to what they're shouting. Somehow she's convinced them that she's a defenceless child and we're about to stitch her up.'

'You're right. It's all over social media,' said Broadbent, staring at his phone. 'The girl's a genius.'

'More like a high-functioning psychopath,' growled Jemima.

'It says here that everyone's converging on the Central Library to protect her. They're talking about police stitch-ups and corruption. Some people are even calling us the enemy of the state.'

'Anyone in a police uniform who enters that building is going to become a target for those thugs,' said Jemima. 'It's obvious that these people don't care whether Millie Rathbone's innocent or guilty. They're not interested in facts or evidence. They just want the buzz of being part of a cause, regardless of whether it's justified. Truth and justice are irrelevant to this lot.

'We've got to regain control of the area before they smash up the city centre, or someone loses their life. These streets need to be locked down. The Chief Constable has to get hold of the First Minister because this is too big for us to handle. They've got to call in the army. Someone in authority has to get the Royal Welsh Regiment down here if we're to have any chance of restoring law and order. I'm going to contact Kennedy. They need to know what's going on and realize just how serious this situation is.'

As Jemima spoke to Ray Kennedy, she had to shout to make herself heard. She was mid-sentence when Broadbent grabbed hold of her arm and dragged her away from where she was standing.

A crowd had gathered around a nearby police van. They were rocking the vehicle from side to side. Suddenly a petrol bomb flew through the air and shattered on the pavement yards from a group of tourists who were busy filming the scene on their phones. Their excitement at being caught up in the rapidly evolving situation soon turned to fear as they realized that it was only through sheer luck that they had escaped severe harm. At first, they stood rooted to the spot, until one of them spotted a potential escape route. They all set off in that direction. One of the younger females continued to film as she ran.

Moments later there was an almighty crash as a shop-front window was smashed to smithereens. Jemima turned to see a group of eight young men making their way along the street. They were each wielding a baseball bat. Things had turned ugly very quickly. There was no doubt in Jemima's mind that people were going to get hurt or possibly even die.

The usually peaceful pedestrianized area of the Hayes looked and sounded like a war zone. People screamed and shouted. Parents scooped children into their arms before running for cover. Innocent bystanders, terrified and bewildered by the rapidly changing events, tried to make their way out of danger.

Up ahead, Jemima noticed an elderly couple frozen to the spot. The man held his wife close, doing his best to protect her. Unfortunately for them, an opportunistic lowlife had identified them as an easy target and wasted no time in heading straight for them. The lad was well known by the police, and Jemima knew precisely what his intentions were.

'We've got to stop him,' she said, as she made a beeline for the pensioners.

Jemima surprised herself by how fast she moved, reaching the lad when he was about ten paces from his intended target. Her forward momentum caught him off balance, and she crashed to the floor on top of him.

'Gerroff me, you mad cow!' he yelled, as he struggled to break free.

'I know what you were about to do. Now fuck off!' ordered Jemima as she scrambled to her feet. 'Go on, get out of here, right now before I change my mind!'

The lad stood up and shuffled away, head down, holding an injured arm as he went.

'We're police officers,' said Broadbent, as he took charge of the pensioners. 'Come on, let's get you to safety.'

Progress was slow as they made their way out of the danger zone. They had both hoped to leave their charges at a shop or café along the way, but word had spread, and everywhere was shut. Retailers with metal shutters had closed them for their own protection while they waited it out inside.

'We'll take you to the police station. You'll be safe there until everything's calmed down,' said Broadbent.

But as they emerged from the underpass, they realized that would not be possible. The station was under siege too. As they looked on in horror, a face appeared at a window in the nearby Crown Court building. It was Mark Derbyshire. He mimed at Jemima to answer her phone. As she did, he told her to make her way around to the back of the building and take cover inside.

CHAPTER 43

With the city centre at a standstill, roads were shut to all but military and emergency vehicles. There was no public transport of any kind, and the only way out of the area was on foot. The University Hospital of Wales had activated their major incident plan. A message was issued to television and radio stations asking them to advise the public that they were not accepting patients, as they were anticipating exceptionally high numbers of casualties from the riot.

The level of violence escalated rapidly. The local police were overwhelmed and insufficiently resourced. Soon the army was drafted in, along with reinforcements from neighbouring police forces.

It took almost eight hours to regain control of the streets, by which time millions of pounds worth of damage had been done to businesses throughout the city centre. Hundreds of people had been injured, and some of the supporters remained barricaded inside the library where they live-streamed their support for Millie, achieving millions of hits worldwide.

Cardiff was centre stage as the world watched closely, eager for it all to play out. In this gripping real-time drama, South Wales Police was cast as the villains. Millie Rathbone was the vulnerable child — the fragile sole survivor of a heinous crime who, unless the public intervened, was destined to become a patsy to cover up police failures.

The incident was the ultimate display of people power. It was one of those rare occasions where right-minded people across the world had the opportunity to influence an outcome. They were policing the police, shining a spotlight on an injustice occurring in a country that had the audacity to hold itself up as a beacon of light for morality and human rights. An innocent girl's life was hanging in the balance, and she needed to be saved.

The standoff at the library continued throughout the night. All forms of negotiation failed to resolve the situation, as it suited their purpose to make the police look bad. Millie refused to speak to anyone in authority but broadcast regular podcasts where she claimed to be terrified for her future.

The teenage psychopath had the world in the palm of her hand. The authorities couldn't allow it to continue. It was time for law enforcement to take control and end the farce once and for all. They fully appreciated that public opinion was against them, and any tactic employed to end the standoff would be broadcast and scrutinized as it happened, so they held a meeting to agree on a way forward.

As the sun's rays appeared on the eastern horizon, they stormed the building in a joint police and military operation. Tear-gas canisters forced the protesters to evacuate the library. Once outside, they were treated for the effects of the gas, then arrested.

Millie was taken into custody.

Stephanie was being treated at the scene when she asked to speak to Jemima.

'How're you doing, Stephanie?' asked Jemima.

'That's not important. You need to prioritize taking my statement.'

'The paramedics need to check you over and make sure that you're fit. You've just been through a terrible ordeal,' Jemima told her.

'Correct, Inspector! *I've* been through it. Not you. And you must listen to me because I want to make a statement. Millie Rathbone played me and I'm not going to let her get away with it.'

'It's not that simple—' began Jemima.

'It never is,' said Stephanie.

'If you'd only let me finish, I was about to say that in order for you to make a statement you'd have to have an appropriate adult with you. We've already called your parents to let them know that you're safe, and they're on their way. Once you've been checked over and we know that you're fit to leave, I'll have an officer give you a lift to the police station and I'll take your statement there — as long as your parents are happy with us doing that.'

'It doesn't matter if they're happy or not. I'll tell them what I've just told you — I'm not going home until I've given you a statement. I'll see you at the station, Inspector. You'll want to hear what I have to say.'

* * *

As things calmed down, it was clear to see that the police station had taken a battering, though the structure of the building remained fundamentally sound. Throughout the siege, they had managed to barricade it against the rioters, even as it was fire-bombed and battered with numerous makeshift missiles.

Ashton and Peters had missed much of the action. They had been at the Rathbone house when everything kicked off, and due to the rapid escalation of events, had been unable to return to the city centre before the station was locked down. They had eventually managed to locate Sally Rathbone's ring and Bradley's watch, hidden inside a decorative tin placed beneath a loose floorboard in Millie's bedroom. The tin was placed inside an evidence bag and brought back for testing in the hope that Millie's fingerprints would prove that she had been the one to put it there.

Jemima wasted no time setting the interview room up to enable Stephanie Newton to make her statement. She was eager to hear what the girl had to say.

With the formalities out of the way, Stephanie began her account.

'I feel incredibly stupid, Inspector. I allowed Millie Rathbone to make a fool of me. I was excited when Millie and I became close. Even yesterday, I would have called her a friend, but now I appreciate that we never really were. Millie duped me, and I allowed her to do it because I was so desperate to find someone who truly understood me.'

'Don't be so hard on yourself,' said Jemima. 'From conversations I've had with a number of people, it appears that Millie's been doing that for most of her life. Even her family didn't realize what she was capable of.'

'Yes, but I should have,' said Stephanie. 'Family is everything to me, and yet I railroaded my parents into giving that psycho a home. I was devastated when I heard that Millie was on life support. It didn't enter my head that she had murdered her family. I immediately thought of her as a victim — someone who had lost absolutely everything.

'She rang me at school yesterday and asked me to meet her at the library. In retrospect, I know that it was a final roll of the dice. She couldn't do a runner because of her leg, and she was desperate. She realized that something was up when my mother abandoned her at the hospital. She knew Dinah well enough to realize that she wouldn't do that without having a very good reason. And the only reason she could think of was that you must have figured out that she was the one who had killed her entire family.

'She had to do something to draw attention to herself. Only the other day, she commented on the bad press you lot were getting when that poor man jumped off his balcony. She said it was trending on Twitter. That incident must have inspired her to send out those Tweets and get those moronic thugs on her side. She whipped them up to do her bidding.

The truth didn't matter. It was all about being part of a cause and fighting the establishment.

'When I arrived at the library, Millie was busy typing something on her phone. She barely acknowledged me. I asked her who she was messaging but she didn't answer. When she pocketed her phone she said that she'd needed some space as everything was starting to get to her.

'We went upstairs to our usual spot, and Millie said that she loved the building and couldn't imagine what it would be like not to be able to spend time there again. I asked her why she said that, and she said that life doesn't always go to plan — which I thought was a bit strange.

'I went off to choose a reference book. When I looked over, Millie had logged on to one of the terminals and was typing away as though her fingers were on fire. I wheeled myself back over and saw that she was on Twitter. The next thing I knew, there were raised voices in the reception area. Moments later, crowds of people were coming up the escalators and they were all shouting Millie's name.

'I knew something bad was about to happen, so I filmed some of it on my phone. I got away with it because I'm stuck in this wheelchair. For once, it worked to my advantage because they didn't see me as a threat, and Millie was so focused on the others that she didn't see me at all.

'One moment Millie was her usual self, the next it was as though she was a different person. She started crying and telling everyone how the police were out to frame her for murdering her family. She kept talking about police incompetence, police corruption. She whipped them into a frenzy, insisting she was an injured, defenceless child who had lost everything. No one stopped to think whether she was telling the truth. They were too busy lapping it up. She begged them to protect her by taking action against the police.

'I had to say something, but first I hid my phone under my jumper. When I tried to tell them that she was lying, I got shouted down. The next thing I knew, someone grabbed my wheelchair and locked me in the disabled toilet. Millie saw what was happening and did nothing to help. She caused those riots. She'll deny it but she orchestrated the whole thing. The proof is on this phone and I'm prepared to testify against her.'

'Can we see the footage?' asked Jemima.

They sat there in silence as they watched the recording of the events inside the library. Stephanie Newton's evidence was a vital help in the case against Millie Rathbone.

CHAPTER 44

'I'm sitting in on the interview,' said a bleary-eyed Ray Kennedy as he stifled a yawn. He was unshaven and looked the worse for wear, having spent more than twenty-four hours at the station. 'That little bitch has turned this whole sorry mess into a global circus, and I want to be there when we send her down.'

'Why not take the opportunity to get your head down for a couple of hours?' said Jemima. 'Before we interview Millie, I want to speak to Isobel and Zoe Jones. It's possible this isn't the first time that Millie's killed someone. I think she might have murdered her baby sister.'

'Seriously? The girl would have only been seven years old!'

'I know it sounds ridiculous. Believe me, until Ashton decoded Lauren's journal entries, the thought hadn't occurred to me. But Lauren said she overheard her parents talking, and her mother was convinced that Millie had done it. It could explain why Isobel still maintains that she's innocent. Perhaps she was telling the truth.'

'Was she was covering for Millie?' asked Kennedy.

'I don't think so. Isobel's parole officer told me that after it happened, Isobel was suicidal. Apparently, she was so desperate to remember the events leading up to Lydia's death that she undertook regression therapy, but she was still unable to recall killing her daughter. According to the investigating officers, there was never any suggestion that anyone else had entered the house. The only other person it could have been was Millie. Let's face it, no one would suspect a seven-year-old child of murder.'

'You're not wrong there,' said Kennedy.

'My theory is going to come as a shock to Isobel. But it's something she needs to hear. I'll ensure that Zoe's there with her and be as gentle as possible.'

* * *

There was no mistaking Isobel Jones's trepidation as she walked into the interview room with her sister.

'It looks like a war zone out there,' said Zoe, as she pulled out a seat and sat down.

'It's been a rough twenty-four hours,' said Jemima.

'All courtesy of Millie, as I understand it,' said Zoe.

'You don't seem surprised.'

'I'm not,' said Zoe.

Isobel had remained silent throughout this short conversation. As Jemima stole a glance at her, she was surprised to see that the woman was crying.

'You don't need to be worried, Isobel. I've had you both brought in for an informal chat, nothing more. It's my intention to gather some background information on Millie before we interview her later today. We believe she's responsible for the recent murders, as well as inciting yesterday's riots.'

'See, Izz, it's not just me,' said Zoe, squeezing her sister's hand.

Isobel didn't react.

'What do you mean by that?' asked Jemima.

'You need to understand that you're not dealing with a run-of-the-mill teenager,' Zoe replied. 'Millie's extremely intelligent, manipulative and dangerous. She likes to get her own way, and when she doesn't, you'd better watch out. Did you know that when she was five years old she killed Izzy's dog?'

'No, that was just a horrible accident,' whispered Isobel.

'It's time you faced the truth, Izz. Gustav's death was no accident. You insisted that I was lying, but I saw it with my own eyes.'

'What happened?' asked Jemima.

'Gustav was a chow chow,' Zoe said. 'He looked like a cross between a lion and a fluffy teddy bear. Bradley bought him as a surprise for Izzy's birthday, about a year before Lydia was born. Wherever Isobel went, Gustav went too. He was devoted to her. He used to follow her around the house, lay next to her on the sofa, and even sleep in the bedroom with her.

'Everyone loved Gustav. He was a cutie with the sweetest temperament. Millie soon became jealous of the attention he was getting. Until Gustav came on the scene, Millie had had Izzy's undivided attention. Suddenly she had to share her mother and that didn't go down well. Even at that age, she was clever enough not to let Izzy see how mean she could be. But I spotted her kick Gustav on a couple of occasions when the poor thing was fast asleep, and it wasn't an accident. She deliberately went over to him and kicked him on purpose, though Izzy insisted that I was exaggerating.

'A few weeks before Gustav died, a road-safety officer visited Millie's school to explain how difficult it was for drivers to see pedestrians, especially in bad weather or when it was dark. It's a standard approach. They visit all schools. The children learn about the importance of wearing reflective clothing in order to stay safe, and they participate in exercises designed to teach them how to cross roads safely.

'I was at Izzy's house the afternoon that Gustav died. Izz had an appointment, so I'd agreed to look after Millie for a few hours. It was the first week of the school summer holiday, warm enough to spend time in the garden. I was sat on a garden lounger, reading a book, sipping a glass of chilled orange juice. Gustav had been pining for Izzy but eventually stopped whining and was asleep in the sun. Millie was playing on the swing.

'I was about to take another sip of my drink when I sensed movement and realized that there was a wasp on the glass. It was so close to my mouth that I panicked and jerked my arm, spilling the juice down myself. As Izzy and I are the same size, I told Millie that I would pop up to her parents' bedroom and find something to change into. I said I wouldn't be long and told her to stay on the swing.

'I was about to go downstairs when I heard a faint sound coming from the front garden. I glanced out of the window just as Millie opened the gate. Before I had a chance to shout, she threw a ball on to the road, and Gustav chased after it. That poor driver had no chance of stopping. And Gustav . . . well that was it. He died playing his favourite game.

'Millie wasn't allowed in the front garden, and there was no reason for her to open that gate other than to let Gustav run into the road. She did it on purpose. She meant to kill him. I felt sick when I realized what I'd seen, and it took me a second or two to get moving. But when I did, I ran downstairs only to find Millie sitting on the swing. I asked her why she'd done it, but she denied everything. She wasn't even upset that Gustav had died.

'It caused a rift between me and Izz. We didn't speak to each other for a few months after that. But I learned that day that Millie wasn't to be trusted. I've worked with thousands of children in my school and some of them can be very challenging, but throughout my entire career I've never come across a child so cold, calculating and manipulative. If you ask me, that girl doesn't have a conscience. She's capable of anything, and we should all be afraid of her.'

'If you truly believe that, why didn't you speak up earlier?' asked Jemima.

'Because she's Izzy's daughter and my sister has been through so much. She's my top priority.'

Jemima was determined to move the conversation forward to the day of Lydia Rathbone's death. And in order to do that she had to get Isobel to open up.

'You've had a rough time, Isobel,' Jemima said. 'Your whole world was turned upside down. I can't begin to imagine how awful it must have been to find Lydia dead, and then not to be believed. Being sent to prison for something you didn't do. Tell me about Lydia. What was she like, Isobel?'

'She was a beautiful little girl,' said Isobel, with a faraway look in her eyes. 'I think about her all the time. I loved Lydia from the moment I knew she was inside me. I was excited to become a mother again but hadn't anticipated the overwhelming feeling of exhaustion that hit me after she was born. Between Lydia and Millie, I was on the go all the time, which would have been manageable if Bradley had helped out a bit more. But he didn't. I was the one who was expected to do everything, including getting up three or four times a night, every night. Looking back on that time, I realize now that I was suffering from postnatal depression. But at the time, well . . .'

'Was Millie pleased to have a little sister?' asked Jemima.

Zoe snorted contemptuously, and Jemima shot her a warning look.

'She seemed to be at first,' said Isobel, 'but after a few weeks of getting less attention, Millie regressed. Lydia took up so much of my time. I did my best to include Millie in things, make her feel as though she was helping, but she soon got bored with that and started to behave badly. In retrospect, I think she played up and did things to upset Lydia.'

'Such as?' asked Jemima.

'Slamming doors and yelling for no apparent reason other than to wake Lydia up or make her cry. But I suppose older siblings are like that. They have to make a huge adjustment as they've had their parents all to themselves and suddenly they're no longer the centre of attention. It's a huge thing to come to terms with.'

'Why didn't Bradley help out more?' asked Jemima.

'He said it was my job. I gave up my career as a pharmacist when Millie came along. It was my choice. But Bradley said that as he was the only one earning the money, it was my responsibility to run the home and see to the kids. If he'd given me a break every now and then so that I could catch up on some sleep, I would have found everything so much easier. But I was running on empty. Lydia was teething. Millie was playing up. And Bradley just kept complaining that I wasn't keeping on top of things.'

'You must have felt so low,' said Jemima.

'I did. I'd try my best, but even simple things like getting Millie to the collection point for the school 'walking bus' became a nightmare.'

'What's a walking bus?' asked Jemima.

'It was something the school organized. Led by a woman named Delyth Pierce. Children were collected and dropped off at agreed points along the way to school. It's a safe way for the little ones to walk. Gives them a feeling of independence. It's reassuring for the parents too, as the leader and helpers are familiar people who have been doing it for years and have been CRB checked.'

'That's good to know,' said Jemima. Not having heard of this before, she decided to look into it to see if James's school offered such a service.

'Some mornings I'd had so little sleep that I felt like death warmed up. I had to see to Lydia, then Millie would have a strop about me brushing her hair. She insisted on having it long but hated the fact that I had to get the tangles out of it. Every morning she'd scream and shout, until it made Lydia cry. I couldn't understand it. Millie never used to be that badly behaved.

'I'd do my best to make sure that Lydia was asleep when I'd go to collect Millie after school. If we could make it back home without Lyds waking up, it meant that I could spend some quality time with Millie — help with her homework or play a game. But it didn't happen often.

'I'd got to the stage where I felt that I was letting everyone down. My confidence was at an all-time low. It was such a monumental task to set foot outside the house. I was convinced that some of the other mothers were ridiculing me. I used to be capable, competent, energetic and up for any challenge life threw at me. I prided myself on being a go-to sort of person. Yet there I was — dressed like a bag lady and acting like a zombie with cotton wool for brains.'

'Did you tell your husband that you were struggling?' asked Jemima.

'Of course I did, but he never took my concerns seriously. His response shocked me. He loved to boast about how he helped society's most vulnerable people, but when it came to me, he was an absolute shit. He'd smile sympathetically and spout empty platitudes, trying to reassure me that what I was feeling was perfectly normal. It reached the stage where I had virtually given up trying to communicate with him. He either refused to believe me or just didn't care about what I was going through.'

'Would you mind talking me through your last few days with Lydia?' asked Jemima.

'They weren't good. As usual I was exhausted, not coping. Lydia was fractious. I didn't realize until later that she was teething. On the Friday night before it happened, it was particularly bad. Lydia and I were awake for most of the night. Bradley had responded as usual by clamping a pillow over his ears, and when it didn't block out the sound, he complained about the noise Lydia was making. There was no offer of help. He could see how exhausted I was, but his own wellbeing was always uppermost in his mind. So I ended up taking Lydia downstairs.

'I remember it was an endurance test, pacing back and forth as I rocked, cooed and sang ditties with made-up, nonsensical words. By that stage anything would have done. I applied a small amount of gel to her gums and encouraged her to chew on a teething ring. But nothing seemed to work, and the crying had continued. My arms were aching from holding her, so I finally sat on the sofa, with her on my chest. I must have dropped off because I remember jerking awake. I almost cried out with relief when I realized that I hadn't let go of Lyds. I watched the sun come up that morning. I remember being relieved that it was Saturday. The mornings were always more relaxed on weekends and school holidays, as I didn't have to face a mad rush to get myself and the children ready to leave the house.

'I shuffled off the sofa, taking care not to disturb Lydia, and carried her up the stairs. I was hoping to lay her in the cot without waking her, so that I could go back to bed and get some sleep. For once, she didn't stir as I put her down. I'd almost made it to my bedroom door when I sensed a movement and saw Millie standing there. I whispered to her to go back to bed as it was far too early to get up. But Millie was having none of it. She wanted me to read her a story. I told her that she needed to go back to sleep and that I'd read her a story after breakfast. That's when Millie had a full-blown temper tantrum.

'In the space of a few seconds, the house was filled with noise. Lydia woke up and started crying. Millie was yelling, and to top it all, Bradley came stomping out of the bedroom. He was telling us to keep the noise down as he was trying to get some sleep. That was the tipping point. I pushed past him, grabbed a pillow from the bed and headed for the en-suite bathroom. I locked the door behind me, pulled a bath sheet off the rail, stuck some cotton balls in my ears and made myself comfortable on the floor. I stayed there until the evening. It wasn't the most comfortable of experiences, but at least I got some sleep.

'Of course, Bradley didn't make it easy for me. His initial annoyance turned to cajoling as he tried his best to coax me out of the bathroom. But I refused and told him that I was taking the day off to catch up on some much-needed rest. It was his turn to look after the kids. He finally stopped hassling me when I told him that if he didn't leave me alone, I would pack my things and walk out on all of them.

'When I woke up, I was stiff and sore, so I treated myself to a bath. The water had started to cool when I heard a tentative knock on the door. It was Bradley. He told me that Millie was about to go to bed and wanted me to read her a bedtime story. I told him that he could do it as it would make a nice change.

'When I eventually went downstairs, Bradley was on the sofa, with Lydia sprawled against his stomach and chest. He was angry that I left him on his own to look after the kids. He said it was my fault the kids had had a miserable day and that I'd better shape up, as he'd promised Millie that we'd all go to Techniquest on the following day. I told him that I was going back to bed as I didn't feel well.

'Even though I'd slept through much of the day, I fell asleep as soon as my head hit the pillow. At some stage I heard Lydia cry. The sound became louder until Bradley nudged me and told me to go and see to her. I was angry that he thought we could just carry on as usual, so I lied and told him that I felt sick. I ran to the bathroom before he could reply. After all, Bradley owed me.

'I don't think he believed me because I heard his footsteps heading towards the en suite, so I dropped to my knees and stuck my fingers down my throat. When he heard me retching, he told me that he'd see to Lydia and that when I was able to, I should get myself back to bed.

'I stayed in the bathroom until I was certain that Bradley had taken Lydia downstairs. Next thing I knew, the sun was streaming through the window. Bradley was up, dressed and didn't look any the worse for wear, despite having been forced to see to Lydia during the night. He even seemed concerned about me. It was as though the old Bradley had returned. The man who loved and cared for me.

'Millie jumped on the bed and told me to get ready for the trip to Techniquest. I told her that I didn't feel up to it, so Bradley asked if I could look after Lydia instead. By this time Millie was practically begging, but unfortunately, I really did feel sick, and only just made it to the bathroom. Millie was in a full-blown rage. It was clear that she had set her heart upon this trip. There was no reasoning with her. Bradley eventually managed to calm her down. As she walked past the en suite, she shot me a look of pure hatred.

'I spent much of that day in bed, and throughout the night, Bradley saw to Lydia without complaint, despite the fact that he had to get up early for work. But I knew I would have to see to Lydia and get Millie off to school in the morning.'

'And that was Lydia's last morning?' asked Jemima.

'Yes,' replied Isobel, stifling a sob.

'Shall we take a short break?' asked Jemima.

Isobel nodded.

CHAPTER 45

'Are you able to continue?' asked Jemima, once Isobel was more composed. She was aware that she needed to interview Millie as soon as possible, but she was determined to go into the interview armed with as much information as possible to try to get the teenager to drop her guard.

'Yes. I'd like to get on with it,' said Isobel. 'That morning, Bradley had already left the house by the time I got out of bed. It was early, and as the girls hadn't woken up, I took the opportunity to have a quick shower. After I got dressed, I looked in on each of them. They were both still asleep, so I headed down to the kitchen to prepare breakfast. I wanted to get organized as there were so many things needed sorting within the next hour.

'Millie's timetable was pinned to the noticeboard, and I realized that later that morning she had a violin lesson. After the previous lesson, the teacher had handed Millie a note asking us to spend time helping her to learn a particular piece of music, as a group of pupils were due to perform it during a school assembly. What with Lydia taking up so much of my time I had forgotten all about the violin practice.

'To make matters worse, there was a PE session sched-uled for the afternoon. Usually, it would have been fine, but

Millie had complained that her trainers were too small for her, and I hadn't got around to buying her a bigger size. It was yet another way I'd let her down.

'When I went upstairs Millie had already made it out of bed. I told Millie that she should go downstairs and have her breakfast while I got Lydia ready. When I went into the nursery Lydia smiled, gurgled and kicked her legs in delight. As she stared at my face, she reached out to grab my nose. It was a special moment and I laughed, and blew a raspberry on her tummy. I loved her so much and our interaction seemed far more relaxed that morning, which I attributed to the fact that I wasn't suffering from the effects of sleep deprivation.

'After the girls had eaten, I told Millie that it was time for me to brush her hair. That's when all hell broke loose. Millie was still angry with me and said that she hated me. She jumped out of her seat, causing it to topple over and crash on to the tiled floor. Millie stormed upstairs, and I shouted up, telling her to hurry as she was going to be late for school. There was the inevitable screaming and stamping of feet as I brushed and plaited her hair. Then she picked up her school bags and waited by the front door for us.

'That morning she refused to interact with us as we headed towards the collection point. Millie took her place in line without a backwards glance and refused to wave good-bye. To be honest, it was a relief to see her go.

'When we returned home, I selected some music, swept Lydia into my arms and danced around the room with her, twirling, dipping, whooping and singing. Lydia loved it. I didn't care that there were so many chores to be done. I decided that everything could wait, as it was about time we had some fun together. I sensed it was a turning point, a fresh start where I could begin to enjoy motherhood again. I made a decision to sit down with Bradley that evening and insist upon him doing his fair share through the night. He had to accept that I needed to get a reasonable amount of sleep to enable me to be a good wife and mother.

'It was approaching midday when Lydia's energy levels dropped, and her eyes began to close. I carried her upstairs, placed her in the cot and switched on the baby monitor. She was fast asleep when I left her. I gathered up some soiled clothes and headed downstairs to the utility room. I was confident that the washing cycle would finish well before we needed to go and collect Millie.

'That's when everything started to go wrong. I made the mistake of thinking that as Lydia was asleep, it was the ideal opportunity to sit down and relax for a while. You see, there was almost two hours before we needed to leave the house. I thought I'd watch a film, as it was something I rarely had the opportunity to do. I selected a romcom and settled down on the sofa. In no time at all, I was fast asleep.

'The next thing I knew, my heart was thumping. It took a few seconds to realize that I must have been asleep. I had no idea what time it was, but the film had already finished. I heard Lydia's snuffles coming from the monitor. It made me think that I couldn't have slept for long, otherwise she would have woken up.

'I swung my feet on to the floor just as the doorbell sounded and someone hammered on the door. I realized that it was that sound which must have woken me. I opened the door to be confronted by Delyth Pierce. She was in charge of the walking bus, and she was livid. Before I had a chance to say anything she launched into an angry tirade telling me that I was an unfit mother as I should have collected Millie fifteen minutes earlier. She ordered Millie to get in the house.

'I tried to apologize to the woman. I told her it was an honest mistake as I'd fallen asleep, but she told me that tiredness was no excuse. I was too shocked to reply. When I eventually found the strength to shut the door and turn around, I saw that Millie was standing there, arms crossed. She demanded to know why I hadn't collected her. I tried to explain and apologize, but Millie was having none of it. She kept telling me that I was a liar and that I didn't care about her. I told her it wasn't true, that I'd made a mistake and I was ashamed of myself. I reached out to hug her, but she turned away and headed upstairs.'

'So it's safe to say that Millie was angry with you?' asked Jemima.

'Definitely, but with good reason, as I'd let her down again,' said Isobel. 'I asked her to let me give her a hug, but she just kept on walking. I knew I'd messed up and was desperate to make things right. I told her we'd do something special at the weekend. That's when she said that she didn't want to do anything with me. She said that since Lydia came along, I never had any time for her, so she didn't want to do anything with me. She said she hated me.'

'You never told me about this,' said Zoe.

'It didn't seem important after Lydia died,' said Isobel.

'Of course it's important. It shows that Millie was angry with you and Lydia. She was the only other person in the house. Don't you get it, Izz? Millie must've killed Lydia!'

'No!' shouted Isobel, shaking her head in despair. 'It's unthinkable.'

'Which is why she managed to get away with it,' said Zoe.

'We don't know that for certain, and after all this time we may not be able to prove it,' said Jemima. 'Talk me through what happened next, Isobel.'

'I wanted to spend time with Millie. Give her some attention. Make her realize that I loved her. So I suggested that we get her sequin art kit out—'

'The one I got her for her birthday?' asked Zoe.

'That's right. We hadn't had a chance to open it, and Millie wanted to do that for a while. She said that she just wanted it to be the two of us, and I told her that as long as Lydia didn't wake up, we could make a start on it. I stuck my head into the nursery and saw that Lydia was still fast asleep. I told Millie that I was going to quickly hang the washing out, and asked her to listen out for Lydia, and then we would start the sequin art.

'When I came back inside, Millie was already down-stairs. She was sat at the kitchen table and looked happier than she had when that awful woman dropped her off. She asked if we could make a start on the sequin art. I told her that I'd quickly check on Lydia first.

'I headed upstairs as quietly as possible so as not to disturb Lydia. I couldn't hear any sound coming from the nursery, but I could hear Millie moving about in one of the downstairs rooms. She was singing, which was strange, as Millie wasn't a child who liked to sing, but I thought no more of it. I opened the nursery door and went inside.

'Lydia was on her back. From a distance, I thought she was asleep. I tiptoed towards the cot and as I got closer I noticed that the covers had been kicked off. It was only as I reached in to readjust them that I saw that Lydia's eyes were open and her face bruised.

'I felt as though I was drowning. I knew that something was seriously wrong but couldn't figure out what it was. I've since learned that my mind was subconsciously trying to protect me from the truth. I'd never known Lydia to be so still. I bent down to close the gap between us and whispered her name. When Lydia didn't move, I tickled her tummy. She didn't react. That was the moment when I knew . . . I think I screamed. I snatched her out of the cot, laid her on the floor and began to give mouth-to-mouth resuscitation.

'Millie came in at some point, though I don't remember when. I just remember looking up at some stage and she was staring at us, with a strange expression on her face as though she was doing her best not to laugh. She could see that something was wrong, yet she asked me when we were going to start on the sequin art. It seemed to be the only thing that mattered to her. I shouted at her to get out, and she yelled at me. She said I'd broken my promise, because Lydia was asleep so there was no reason for us not to do the sequin art . . .'

Isobel trailed off and the three women looked at each other.

'I think it's pretty clear Millie killed Lydia, don't you think, Inspector?' asked Zoe.

'It certainly looks that way,' said Jemima. 'But as for proving it . . .'

CHAPTER 46

'How'd it go with the sisters?' asked Kennedy. He looked more refreshed than when Jemima had last seen him.

'Looks as though Millie killed the family pet when she was five years old, and then went on to murder her own sister,' Jemima told him. 'Isobel opened up about the days leading up to Lydia's death. A lot of what she said in there was news to her sister. I honestly believe that Isobel had closed her mind off to the facts because acknowledging what Millie had done was such an awful prospect for any parent to come to terms with. Has the duty solicitor arrived?'

'Apparently, she doesn't need one. After yesterday's publicity, some high-profile lawyer has offered to represent her pro bono,' muttered Kennedy.

'Any idea who?'

'Not a clue, but they'll be here within the hour.'

When an officer rang to say that Millie's lawyer had arrived, everyone's hearts sank.

'Prudence Dwight? You've got to be joking!' yelled Kennedy. At the mention of her name, his face turned an unhealthy shade of purple.

'She's the bitch from hell,' said Broadbent.

On this occasion, Prudence Dwight was already settled on a seat next to Millie Rathbone. The woman's bulk made Millie appear small and fragile. It was legal theatre at its finest.

Millie began to sob. Everyone in the room knew it was staged, to give Prudence Dwight the perfect opportunity to go on the attack.

'You can see that my client is in no fit state to answer your questions. Look at her, she's exhausted,' she said.

'Since her arrival at this station, your client has been examined by a doctor, who has confirmed that she is fit to be questioned,' said Kennedy. 'Millie has been offered refreshments and allowed to rest until your arrival. Now stop playing games and let's get on with the interview, Ms Dwight.'

'Why did you steal your stepmother's ring?' asked Jemima.

'No comment,' said Millie.

As the question was put to her, Kennedy and Jemima both noticed a flicker of surprise in her eyes and an almost imperceptible tightening of the muscles around her mouth.

'Very well, what about your father's watch?' pressed Jemima.

'No comment.' Millie's voice wavered, as she uttered the words.

'You may as well talk to us, Millie. You see we have you bang to rights. Both items were found hidden inside a tin which was placed beneath a loose floorboard in your bedroom,' said Jemima.

'That in itself is not proof of anything,' said Prudence Dwight.

'I agree, but we have CCTV footage of Bradley Rathbone in the supermarket car park shortly before he was murdered. This is an image taken from that footage,' said Jemima, as she removed the photograph from the file in front of her and pushed it across the desk for Millie and her lawyer to see.

'Take note of your father's wrist,' she continued, using a pen to point to it. 'You'll see that he's wearing the watch.

It's the same watch that we found covered with bloodied fingerprints, which we have matched to you. You took that watch off your father's wrist after you stabbed him. There can be no other possible explanation. And we'll soon have confirmation that the blood is your father's.

'We also have Lauren's journal,' said Jemima, as she extracted a copy of the translated excerpt. 'It took a while for us to translate this as Lauren was so scared of you that she wrote this in code. As you can see,' she said, placing it on the table as she read aloud:

> '*I was doing my homework when I heard a noise coming from my aunt and uncle's bedroom. I went to take a look and there was Millie, with Auntie Sally's jewellery box. That's when I saw her take the ring.*
>
> *Millie saw me and realized that I'd caught her out. Suddenly she was on me. She's way stronger than she looks. She pinned me against the wall, grabbed my neck and squeezed really hard. It hurt so much. I couldn't breathe! She said the ring was payback for Auntie Sally snooping around her bedroom. Millie said she'd killed me if I blabbed about what she'd done. She said she'd get away with it, as she knew all about destroying evidence at crime scenes.*'

'Anyone can claim anything. It doesn't make it true,' said Prudence Dwight.

'We also have evidence that Millie borrowed numerous books from the library, under her friend's name, to enable her to study the subject,' said Jemima, as she presented them with the list supplied by Owen Newton.

'This merely shows that Stephanie Newton borrowed these books,' said Prudence Dwight. 'I'm afraid it'll be her word against my client's. You're clutching at straws here. You have no real case.'

'Let's move on to yesterday's events inside the library. What happened there, Millie?' asked Jemima, determined to ignore Prudence Dwight's intervention.

'I had nothing to do with that,' said Millie.

Both Jemima and Kennedy noticed Prudence Dwight give her client a warning look, but the girl continued to speak.

'I don't know why those people acted like that. I'm not responsible for what they did. I admit sending a few Tweets. But I only did that because I was frightened. You people have given up looking for whoever murdered my family and almost killed me. I didn't know what else to do. I was just trying to get you to do your job. After all, I'm just a kid. I'm the victim here. I'm the one who's lost everything.'

'You incited people to commit acts of violence,' said Jemima.

'You're clutching at straws. You have no proof to back up what you're saying,' countered Prudence Dwight.

'That's where you're wrong,' said Jemima. 'You may very well think you're clever, Millie. But you're nowhere near as clever as you think you are. Luckily for us there was someone at the library yesterday who is even cleverer than you.'

'Like who?' asked Millie, rising to the bait.

'Stephanie Newton.'

'Stephanie's not more intelligent than me. She was oblivious to the fact that I was playing her and her sappy parents. She couldn't have done what I did. No one could.'

Jemima and Kennedy sat back and listened in silence as Millie admitted to the murders. Prudence Dwight initially tried to stop her from talking, but it appeared that Millie craved admiration more than she valued her freedom.

'I've outwitted people since I was five years old,' said Millie, as she went on to boast about how she killed her mother's dog. 'Everything would have been all right if my parents had valued me. Lydia ruined my life from the moment she was born. I didn't ask for much, I just wanted their attention. But Lydia's needs always had to come first.

'It was easy killing her. I went into the nursery and picked up a cushion which said, "L is for Lydia". As I walked towards her, I remember thinking it was so unfair that I didn't have a cushion which said, "M is for Millie". It was another way in which they favoured her over me. Lydia looked up and smiled at me as I bent over her. It was over quickly. She didn't suffer.' Millie shrugged her shoulders dismissively.

'Didn't it bother you that your mother went to prison for a crime she didn't commit?' asked Jemima. She knew that Millie was a psychopath but was still shocked at the matter-of-fact description of how she killed her sister along with her obvious lack of remorse.

'Why would it bother me? She deserved it. She treated me badly.'

'And what about your father, Sally and your cousins? What did they do wrong?' asked Jemima.

'My father and Sally should never have taken Jonathan and Lauren in. No one asked my permission. I accepted Sally into our lives and we were getting on nicely until my cousins turned up. If they'd just shut up and got on with life, things would have been different. But there was always some sort of drama with them. Jonathan was a wimp, and Dad felt sorry for him. It wasn't as if I got to spend much time with my dad anyway, as he worked long hours, but when he came home he was spending more and more time with Jonathan. That had to stop.'

'What did Lauren do wrong?' pressed Jemima.

'Sally liked her more than me,' said Millie. '*I* was Sally's stepdaughter, not Lauren. She should have put me first. That's why I took her stupid ring. It was payback. It was never my intention to kill my father or Sally. I just wanted things to go back to the way they used to be. But I don't regret killing Jonathan and Lauren. They both got what they deserved. I did it when my father and Sally were shopping, but for some reason they came home earlier than usually. If they'd stayed out longer, they wouldn't have had to die.

'I was staging the scene to make it look like a home invasion and was still stabbing Lauren when they arrived home. I was so focused on what I was doing that I didn't hear Sally until it was too late. The only option was to hide behind the door and attack her as soon as she walked into the room.

'I was exhausted. It's surprising how much energy you use up when you stab someone, but I still had to kill my father, and that's when I slipped up. I needed to act quickly to make sure that everyone thought that I'd had a lucky escape. I removed my clothes and put them in the washing machine, along with a selection from everyone else. I showered, and once I'd dressed again I gave myself a few superficial slashes then placed the knife in the dishwasher. I was going to tell everyone that I'd hidden when the others were killed, and made a run for it when my father was being attacked. That the killer saw me and lashed out but had to make sure my father was dead. Which was why he couldn't come after me.

'I went back upstairs to take a final look around. I was satisfied with the way I'd staged things. Everything was pretty much perfect. But when I came out on to the landing, I saw that my father had dragged himself out there. I panicked at first, thinking I'd have to stab him again. I bent down to take a closer look, tried to see if he was breathing. As far as I could tell there was no sign of life. I was convinced he was dead. His arm was outstretched and I kicked his hand to make sure that I was right. I wasn't expecting him to react. It took me by surprise when he grabbed my ankle and pulled. I ended up falling down the stairs.'

'Millie Rathbone, I am charging you with five counts of murder, inciting violence, encouraging civil disorder, and theft of property,' said Jemima. It was a relief to know that they had finally got the killer. There was no doubt in Jemima's mind that Millie would kill again if someone got in her way.

Jemima gulped as she forced herself to suppress her emotions. This case had compelled her to confront the unthinkable. She knew that evil came in all shapes and sizes. Yet Millie Rathbone had duped everyone into believing that she was a victim. The girl had committed the most heinous acts of violence and showed no remorse for the lives she had taken.

'This interview is over. Return the prisoner to the cell,' said Kennedy. As they headed down the corridor, Kennedy patted Jemima on the back. 'Well done, Huxley. You played a blinder in there.'

CHAPTER 47

The time had come for Jemima to sort out her own family's problems. James needed her support, and she wanted to be there for him.

These days, Jemima felt nothing but contempt for Nick. She barely recognized him anymore. He hadn't shaved or washed in days and seemed content to wallow in self-pity instead of doing what was best for his son.

'At last! The great detective has deigned to grace us with her presence,' slurred Nick, when she walked through the door.

Jemima didn't even bother to respond. There was no talking to Nick when he was like this. He was so drunk that he probably wouldn't even recall the conversation when he eventually sobered up.

Hearing the sound of the TV, Jemima opened the door to the lounge to find James huddled on the sofa. The sight of the boy took her by surprise as he was supposed to be having a sleepover at a friend's house.

'I thought you were going to Dominic's?'

'I was, but his brother got chicken pox, so I couldn't.'

The boy looked and sounded miserable.

'Who picked you up from school?'

'Grandad. He took me to the park and then brought me back here. He said that he couldn't stay any longer, he had a doctor's appointment. But he'll ring you later.'

Jemima wrapped her arms around the lad.

'I'm hungry,' he said.

'Hasn't your father made you anything to eat?' she asked.

'There's nothing here, and he doesn't want to talk to me. He's horrible.'

'How about we go to the chip shop? I don't know about you, but I fancy some pie and chips.'

'Sausage, chips and curry sauce,' said James.

'Excellent! Get your shoes on. You can come with me. I know it's impossible for you to believe this at the moment, but things will get better. No matter what happens with your father, I'll never leave you, James. I love you, and I promise that I'll do my best to look after you. I'll probably make a lot of mistakes along the way, but we can help each other out, can't we?'

'Yeah,' replied James, as he stretched up to kiss her on the cheek. 'I love you too, Jem.'

They returned home from the chip shop, only to find that Nick had gone out. He hadn't left a note and must have walked or got a taxi as his car was still on the drive. Jemima was glad that he'd gone and relieved that he hadn't been foolish enough to drive. The last thing James needed was to have another parent involved in a car crash.

Jemima did her best to ensure that James had as good an evening as possible. She forced herself to stay awake and, after dinner, they played some computer games. Jemima was pleased to find that James hadn't lost his competitive streak. It was good to see him being a typical child for a while.

Nick arrived home shortly before two in the morning. Jemima was asleep on the sofa when she was woken by the sound of him struggling to get the key in the lock. Before she had a chance to reach the hallway, Nick started hammering on the door.

'Open up, you bitch! You can' lock me ou' of my own house!' he shouted.

As she opened the door, Nick stumbled over the threshold reeking of alcohol and ready for a fight. His eyes were glassy, and he could barely stand upright. His mouth was stained with lipstick.

'Wha' th' fuck you doin', lockin' me ou' like tha'?' he snarled.

'I didn't lock you out. You were too pissed to open the door. And keep the noise down. James is asleep.'

'Don't tell me wha' to do!' he bellowed. He lunged at Jemima, grabbing her shoulders as he pushed her up against the wall. 'No bitch is gonna take me f'r a ride again.'

Nick's face was inches from hers. His breath was rancid. It was the final straw. Jemima knew she had to get him out of the house immediately, or else she wouldn't be responsible for her actions.

'Back off, Nick,' she ordered.

'Make me,' he sneered, leaning in to lick her cheek.

If it hadn't been for the fact that she was backed up against the wall, Jemima would have recoiled in disgust. As it was, there was nowhere for her to go, and Nick had the advantage of size and strength. So Jemima did the only thing she could think off and brought her knee up as hard and as quickly as she could. Nick howled and released his grip on her as he doubled over in pain.

Jemima had dealt with plenty of ugly drunks in her time, but had never imagined she'd be faced with one in her own home. She had run out of patience and compassion. At the moment, Nick was not someone she wanted to spend time with. And it certainly wasn't in James's best interests to have him living under the same roof as them. So without further hesitation, Jemima grabbed one of Nick's arms, twisted it behind his back, and frogmarched him to the door. On the way she noticed that his key had fallen to the floor, which made the whole process far more manageable.

As she pushed him outside, Nick stumbled and fell. Jemima didn't even bother to ask if he was all right. Instead, she slammed the door and engaged the deadbolt.

Jemima hoped that would be the end of it. But no such luck. Nick was down but not out. It took a few moments for him to struggle to his feet. When he finally made it upright, he staggered back towards the door and began to kick it, shouting obscenities at the top of his voice.

It was usually a peaceful residential area, which made the altercation more noticeable. As Nick made a racket, lights went on in neighbouring properties, curtains twitched, and someone nearby opened an upstairs window and shouted at Nick to pipe down. But Nick was having none of it.

'Mind ya own fuckin' business, you stuck up bastard!' he yelled.

Jemima knew that the situation had escalated to a point where she had to take decisive action. Nick was out of control and someone could get hurt. As much as she hated doing it, she rang the station and asked for assistance, knowing that they would treat it as an emergency.

'Wot's 'appenin'?' asked James, yawning as he staggered to the top of the stairs.

'Nothing for you to worry about,' she replied. Jemima was aware that the reassurance sounded unconvincing.

'Is Dad making that noise?' asked James.

Before Jemima had a chance to answer, there was a loud crash as the lounge window shattered.

'Shit,' she muttered to herself.

'What was that?' asked James, as he began to run down the stairs. His voice was almost an octave higher than usual.

'Go back upstairs! Shut your bedroom door and stay there!' ordered Jemima. Her police training had taken over. 'Don't come out until I tell you too. It'll be fine. Now go!'

There was the sound of raised voices from somewhere nearby. Jemima opened the lounge door to find glass strewn over the floor. Nick was half-in-half-out of the window, and two of the neighbours were struggling to drag him out.

'We've got this, don't worry,' puffed one of the men, seconds before Nick elbowed him in the face.

From the corner of her eye, Jemima spotted flashing blue lights and breathed a sigh of relief. There was no fear of the embarrassment of becoming the talk of the station. She'd made the right call. Nick could sleep it off in a cell and face charges in the morning when he was sober. He'd reached a point where he needed something to shock him back to his senses.

It was only then that Jemima noticed that James hadn't gone back upstairs. The boy was standing a few feet away, watching his father act like a thug.

'Oh James, you shouldn't have seen this,' said Jemima, as she rushed to his side.

James said nothing but clung to Jemima as though his life depended upon it.

* * *

The day after Nick's arrest, Broadbent called around to inform Jemima that Nick had been charged with being drunk and disorderly and also with common assault. He had been bailed to appear at the local magistrates' court. On the morning of his hearing, Jemima took James to her sister's house, before heading to the court, where she paced the corridor waiting for Nick to arrive. She wasn't ready to give up on her husband and wanted him to know that even though he had behaved appallingly, she was prepared to give him a second chance.

The hearing was scheduled for ten o'clock. As time went on, Jemima became more agitated. She knew how important it was for Nick to be on time, as the legal system came down hard on anyone who refused to take it seriously.

As the minutes ticked by, Jemima called Nick eight times. On each occasion, it went through to voicemail. She left messages. The first one sounded conciliatory, the second calm and polite. By the fifth one, Nick would have easily recognized the concern in her voice. The court usher called his name just as Jemima was ringing Nick for the sixth time.

Jemima begged the woman to give Nick some leeway and tried ringing him again.

Ten minutes later the usher informed Jemima that Nick had been found in contempt of court, and a warrant had been issued for his arrest. The final voice message that she left was not her finest moment. It ended up being a full-blown rant.

Despite everything that had happened, Jemima had expected Nick to show up, even if it was right at the last moment.

When she returned home, Jemima had a feeling that Nick had been there. She didn't know why. It wasn't as if anything was out of place. Jemima didn't want to say anything, as she didn't want to upset James, so she waited until he had gone to bed before she started to look around. Her suspicions were soon confirmed. Nick's passport was gone, as was the emergency cash they kept in the small safe box under the stairs.

EPILOGUE

A few months later, Jemima elbowed her way through the crowd to reach the bar. Gareth Peters was close behind, sticking to her like glue. There was little point in being polite if you chose to come to a city pub on a match day, as the area was a wall of sound, sweaty bodies and slopping pints. Social niceties wouldn't get you anywhere, but generally, most people were good-humoured, mellowed by camaraderie, booze and the anticipation of watching an exciting game with their mates. Jemima had never seen the place so crowded. But then again, she usually avoided the city centre like the plague whenever there was a match on. It was these occasions that kept the hospitality trade afloat. And rugby enthusiasts tended to be better behaved than the average football crowd.

Throughout the country, any pub that televised an international would be guaranteed to pull in the punters. But in St Mary's Street, a stone's throw from Wales's hallowed ground of the Principality Stadium, there was barely room to breathe. Rugby union was held in high esteem in Wales, especially in the capital where international matches were hosted. In the build-up to the game, traders had been out on the streets selling scarves, hats and other rugby paraphernalia.

236

Children and some of the more extroverted adults had their faces painted to resemble the Welsh dragon.

The game was due to get underway in a matter of minutes, and for the last hour the stadium crowd had belted out renditions of Sosban Fach, hymns and arias, and Cwm Rhondda. It was a typically Welsh occasion — songs and poetry were part of the national psyche.

Jemima placed her elbows on the bar, smiled and waved a twenty at the barman. He must have taken pity on her as he came straight over to take her order. She took a few mouthfuls to minimize the risk of spilling her own drink, picked up one of the remaining four, and headed away from the bar, towards the area where the rest of the team had gathered. Peters skilfully carried the remaining three drinks.

'There you go,' she said, as she handed Ashton a glass.

They didn't usually venture into town but had a few things to celebrate. Given her age, Millie Rathbone had been detained in secure children's home, awaiting trial. The CPS was confident of getting a conviction for four counts of murder, inciting violence and encouraging public disorder. However, as she had been under the age of ten when she killed Lydia, it was uncertain whether she would stand trial.

Ashton had been promoted to sergeant and had agreed to remain on the team. And Gareth Peters had also accepted a permanent posting as their latest detective constable.

'Any news on Nick?' asked Broadbent.

'No, he's long gone,' said Jemima, 'and we're better off without him. James and I are getting on just fine. Of course, I couldn't manage without my dad. He's been a godsend, always picking up the slack when it comes to James.'

Broadbent was about to say something when he was interrupted.

'Here's to my dream team,' said Kennedy, raising his glass. 'I know I'm often a difficult bugger to work for, but I want you all to know that I appreciate your efforts.'

Jemima joined the others in raising a glass and smiled as she looked around at the four men. Kennedy was right

— they were a great team, and Jemima felt privileged to be part of it. It had been a tough case, and an emotional roller-coaster at home, but she was feeling better than she had in a long time.

THE END

Thank you for reading this book.

If you enjoyed it please leave feedback on Amazon or Goodreads, and if there is anything we missed or you have a question about, then please get in touch. We appreciate you choosing our book.

Founded in 2014 in Shoreditch, London, we at Joffe Books pride ourselves on our history of innovative publishing. We were thrilled to be shortlisted for Independent Publisher of the Year at the British Book Awards.

www.joffebooks.com

We're very grateful to eagle-eyed readers who take the time to contact us. Please send any errors you find to corrections@joffebooks.com. We'll get them fixed ASAP.

Lightning Source UK Ltd.
Milton Keynes UK
UKHW040738030323
417983UK00004B/299